Born and brought up in Cardiff, Jane Cable now lives on the Sussex Hampshire border with her husband. In 2007 they almost moved to Great Fencote in Yorkshire, and New Cottage is the home they never had. *The Cheesemaker's House* is Jane's first published novel and won the Suspense & Crime category of The Alan Titchmarsh Show's People's Novelist competition in 2011.

# The Cheesemaker's House

Jane Cable

Matador
9 Priory Business Park,
Wistow Road, Kibworth Beauchamp,
Leicestershire. LE8 0RX
Tel: (+44) 116 279 2299
Fax: (+44) 116 279 2277
Email: books@troubador.co.uk
Web: www.troubador.co.uk/matador

ISBN 978 1783061 242

British Library Cataloguing in Publication Data.
A catalogue record for this book is available from the British Library.

Typeset in 12pt Bembo by Troubador Publishing Ltd, Leicester, UK
Printed and bound in Great Britain by Clays Ltd, St Ives plc

**Matador** is an imprint of Troubador Publishing Ltd

*For my mother, with grateful thanks*
*for her constant encouragement.*

*And for Jim, for his patience and his love.*

With thanks to...

Brett, Carole, Caroline, Clare, Coral, Cynthia, Debra, Faisal, Gill, Jason, Kerrie, Lisa, Paula, Roger, Stella and Tanya.

And Mark and Victoria, who loved New Cottage as much as I do.

*Charmers work largely with non-herbal cures for complaints. Secrecy surrounds their work, which must not be done for gain, and while men or women may be charmers, the gift must be passed contra-sexually, man to woman or woman to man; charmers often receive their powers and word-charms from old persons anxious to pass their skills to a worthy successor.*

# Chapter One

It is the sort of day when the roads melt. So William and I don't take them. Instead I clamber over the garden fence and pull some of the chickenwire away so that he can squeeze under the lowest bar. I must remember to put it back securely later; I'd never forgive myself if he disappeared over the fields towards the Moors.

The grass ripples around my feet and ankles, filled with the buzz of summer. William's lead tightens around my hand and his nose quivers with excitement. We pick our way through the thistles, eager to reach the shade on the other side of the pasture.

Close up I can see that the trees mark the bank of a beck. I resist the temptation to dip my toes into it so we wander along the path towards the River Swale. The stream bends sharply and there are alders on either side, their boughs arching together into a tunnel of dark green.

As we approach the river I hear splashing; not panic, nor playful exuberance, but a rhythmic, solitary sound. I tie William's lead to a tree and creep forward.

My view is restricted by the undergrowth but I catch sight of a man swimming in the river. His buttocks are taut and white as he ploughs through the water, droplets flying from his arms where they break the surface. He moves out of my field of vision and the splashing stops. I hold my breath.

When he reappears he is floating with the current, arms akimbo and eyes shut beneath the fair hair plastered across his forehead. His upturned nose and firm chin jut from the water. They don't seem to fit together and are separated, rather than joined, by a pair of generous lips curved into the merest trace of a smile. Then he is gone, and I am left staring at the rippling water.

I am about to move away when I hear splashing again and the pattern repeats itself. I feel guilty invading the swimmer's privacy but there is no reason to drag myself away until William whimpers. I turn to see what is wrong, but my top catches on a dog rose. I ease it away from the thorns, one by one.

There is an enormous crash of water followed by silence. My T-shirt rips as I yank myself free and run up the bank to get a clearer view of the river. It takes me seconds, but the surface of the water is completely undisturbed. The Swale flows freely, calm and clear.

I cast around me to see where the swimmer might be. I am on a grassy knoll three or four feet above the water; the only break in the undergrowth which lines the banks. A couple of hundred yards to my left is an old stone bridge which spans the river in three arches. On the bank opposite willows dip their branches.

It is too long now for the swimmer to have held his breath. A cloud passes over the sun as I scan the water, but the only sign of life is a heron feeding close to the bridge. I am suddenly cold, inside and out, and I hug my arms around me. My fingers meet the stickiness of blood where the thorns ripped into my flesh.

# Chapter Two

The beaten up Land Rover pulls out in front of me onto the High Street but it's my lucky day and the parking space is mine. I ease the gearstick into reverse and look over my shoulder, edging backwards until I am perfectly aligned with the kerb. I didn't screw it up, either – I must be feeling more relaxed.

It surprises me how small things make the difference when everything around you is new; the sheer relief of not having to hunt for the pay & display when you don't know your way around town, the simple pleasure of parallel parking well. I pat the bonnet of my car and set off in search of a newsagent.

The pavement on this side of the road is narrow and although you wouldn't call it crowded if it were Reading, an elderly lady with a shopping trolley jockeying for position with a double buggy probably passes for rush hour in Northallerton. Age triumphs over beauty when a man in a suit holds open the door of Barkers Department Store; as the pushchair stops in front of me I glimpse a blonde toddler chewing a banana with a baby sleeping beside her.

The glass front of the newsagent jars with the elegant Georgian structure it has been rammed into, but looking around I find this is typical of the town. I push the door open; the place reeks of newsprint and spilt milk – I try to hold my nose but it makes my breath come in funny little gulps so I grab a copy of the Yorkshire

Post, all but throw my money on the counter and escape into the fresh air.

I need a coffee. Badly. I spy Costa's opposite but from an opening to my left comes a wondrous waft of baking mixed with roasting beans. I skipped breakfast and I didn't even know I was hungry.

It takes a moment for my eyes to adjust to the shade of the alleyway. I grope my way down the side of a haberdashery and past a florist before the paving opens out onto the edge of the supermarket car park. It isn't a promising location, but the door of the café is clean and newly painted so I go in.

The coffee shop is completely devoid of customers and at first there seems to be no-one serving, but then a fresh faced guy of about thirty pops up from behind the counter. I stare at him, open mouthed, because he is the man I watched swim in the river yesterday. Same fair hair falling forwards over his oval face; same generous lips; same jutting chin.

"Can I help you?" He looks at me curiously as I continue to gape. "Err…do I have a smudge of coffee on my nose or something?"

I manage to recover myself. He is so beautifully turned out, perfectly shaven and wearing a crisply ironed linen shirt, that he would be the last person in the world to have a smudge on his nose. "I'm sorry. It's just I thought I recognised you from somewhere, that's all."

He smiles politely. "Strange how that sometimes happens, isn't it? Now, what can I get you?"

"A skinny latte and..." I scan the display of cakes, temptingly mouth-watering in their glass cabinet. "Oh my God – are they all homemade?"

"My business partner, Adam, bakes them. He's very gifted in the kitchen department." He leans forward. "I'd go for a caramel shortbread if I were you; it's still warm and gooey from the oven."

I hope he will not notice that my hands are shaking as I pick up my tray and take it to a table by the big picture window. I spread my newspaper in front of me. But I'm not looking at it – I'm not even looking at the shoppers walking past; I'm wondering how the hell he got out of the river without me seeing him.

Don't get me wrong, I'm really pleased that he did. He disappeared so suddenly and so completely I've been worrying all night and fretting over whether I should have raised the alarm. And when I did sleep of course I dreamt about him; that we were standing on the riverbank together and he kissed me so gently, reverently, almost. The brush of his lips on my cheek lingered long after I woke.

It's quite a while since I've been kissed like that, if at all. Neil was my first boyfriend – we met when I was nineteen – and we were never much into demonstrations of affection. We were comfortable with each other though, happily married – or so I thought – and probably best friends. It was just a shame he never told me that being friends wasn't enough. Instead he acted like every bloody stereotypical businessman and had an affair with his secretary – a clinging, doe-eyed blonde – the exact opposite of me.

I am so average it must have been really hard for him to find my opposite. I'm not that tall – but she was tiny; I'm not that thin – but she was all curves. But my hair is dark, so I suppose hers was something different. As was her down-with-the-kids dress sense and text-speak vocabulary. It made dreary old Neil seem like her father.

And made me wonder if, at the tender age of thirty-five, I'd become my mother. It does make you think when your man runs off with someone else. I mean, I can't be that awful – I did used to get quite a few wolf whistles from the mechanics at work. Even so, when I moved up here I had a serious wardrobe clear out and although my tops are now much lower and my jeans much tighter, I do still prefer to speak in proper sentences.

Ridiculous as it sounds, I could have probably coped with the affair, but the secretary fell pregnant and Neil said he had to do the right thing. Despite the fact the bastard never wanted children. But what about the right thing by me? He was shocked when I yelled and cried and screamed; he said he'd never imagined I'd felt so strongly about him, that if he had, the affair would never have happened, but now it was too late to do anything about it.

All I wanted to do was run away. My friends told me I was nuts to cut myself off from them and hide at the other end of the country, but to be honest I was frightened I might need them too much. They have their own lives; they don't really want a bad tempered divorcee hanging around their necks, however much they protested otherwise.

The escape route was ready. Three years earlier Neil had inherited some money and we'd bought New Cottage; we were such smug marrieds we'd bought our retirement home in our early thirties, but in the great property carve up that comes with the end of a relationship I told him I wanted the cottage and he could keep the house in Reading. I think he was surprised but he was in so much of a hurry to have everything sorted out before the baby arrived he would have agreed to anything.

Maybe it was guilt too; but whatever it was I pressed home my advantage and walked away with most of our savings. Not just for the hell of it; I have to eat, after all. Plus the house needs a small fortune spending on it. That's my plan: do it up – including the barn, which would make a fab holiday let, and if I don't like living in Yorkshire then I can sell it and move on.

I rouse myself and shake the newspaper – that's why I bought it, after all – to look for a builder. As I flick to the small ads I sink my teeth into the caramel slice. It is still a little warm and the shortbread crumbles deliciously over my tongue, sweet but somehow not over sickly; it has bite to it. I could get fat as a mole if I keep coming here and I'm not going to let that happen – the best bit of divorcing is the weight dropping off and now I'm an ever-so-slightly top heavy size 10 I have every intention of staying that way.

The guy from behind the counter pulls out the chair opposite me and sits down. At close quarters I am treated to a studied gaze from the darkest blue eyes I have ever seen and goosebumps tingle on the back of my arms. I'm glad I bothered to put on a bit of make-up.

"More coffee?" he asks.

"Have I outstayed my welcome on just one cup?"

"No, not at all." He indicates the empty café. "We don't exactly need the table."

"You should be packed, with those wonderful cakes."

"Oh, we are some of the time, but then we haven't long opened," he says, pushing his hair back from his face and running his long fingers over the top of his head. "Look, what I really came over to say is that we have seen each other before, I've worked it out."

I am about to die of embarrassment when he continues "It was in church last Sunday – St Andrew's at Great Fencote." I sink back into my chair. He is right, I did go to church, but I've tried to blank the visit from my mind.

"I noticed you when I was reading the lesson – we don't often get new people. But didn't you leave before the end?"

"Err, yes. I…I had a frog in my throat and I didn't want to cough all through the sermon."

The truth of the matter is that the second hymn had been one we'd sung at my wedding and I'd started to well up. My intention had been to go outside, take a walk around the church to control myself then go back to the service. But in the far corner of the graveyard was a young woman kneeling by a freshly covered grave and that had upset me even more so I just went home.

"That was nice and considerate of you." He reaches his hand across the table to shake mine. "I'm Owen Maltby, by the way."

"Alice Hart. I've just moved into New Cottage."

For a fraction of a second it feels as though he is going to drop my outstretched hand but I must have imagined it because he continues smoothly: "Nice property."

"It needs a bit of work doing to it though."

"Is that why you're looking at the builders' ads?"

"Got it in one."

"Look, I don't want to stick my oar in, but most of the builders who are any good don't need to advertise in the paper. There's a guy I went to school with who's OK…I could give you his number?"

"Would you? That would be very kind."

"No, not kind – ulterior motive. I want you to settle in here if you're going to come to church – there's precious few of us under forty and we could do with bringing the average age down a bit." Before I can answer the café door opens again.

"Be back in a tick," says Owen, and flies behind the counter.

# Chapter Three

My mental image of a Yorkshire builder was a rotund man in a cloth cap who would exhibit a great deal of sucking of teeth when confronted with my barn. I certainly didn't expect Richard Wainwright to be tall, dark and handsome with a couple of days of designer stubble and a gold hoop in his left ear. But then I didn't expect a naked swimmer to be reading the lesson in church either. It's clear I'm going to have to abandon my southern prejudices sooner rather than later if I'm going to fit in here. But I still can't help feeling we should all be running around downing mugs of tea you can stand a spoon up in, not drinking skinny lattes.

In this aspect of his behaviour Richard doesn't disappoint. I am already making the second pot when he reappears from his prodding and poking in the barn, drapes his long body against my kitchen doorframe and says:

"I can do it, but it's going to cost you."

"I expect it to cost me," I grin at him. "It's a wreck I want to turn into a luxury holiday pad – I know that won't come cheap."

He wanders into the kitchen and sits down at the table. "I'll need to do a proper quote, but I reckon in the region of twenty grand. It's a lot of money – take you a while to get it back."

"I'll get it back when I sell though."

"Oh, so that's your game is it; buy – do up – sell – quick buck." He looks disapproving.

"No. It's not my game. It's my insurance policy in case I don't like it here."

He stretches back in his chair and picks up his tea. "So why did you come? I'm curious."

"Well, you mustn't tell anybody, but I'm on the run from an international drug smuggling cartel and I thought they'd never find me in Great Fencote."

"Hmm…I wouldn't be so sure. You don't know what evil walks the streets of Northallerton. Only last week someone was prosecuted for putting the wrong sort of yogurt pot in their recycling bin – it was all over the papers." We both burst out laughing.

"Seriously, love," he carries on, "if you don't want to say then that's your business. No-one round here's going to mind."

"I was just trying to make it sound more exciting than it is. My husband ran off with his secretary, that's all."

"It happens. My wife left me for a pen pusher at the council. Said she'd had enough of muddy boots all through the house. Each to their own, I suppose." He shrugs.

"The funny thing is," I continue hesitantly, "that when it happens to you, you feel like it's never happened to anyone else. When someone else says it, you realise just how common it is."

"Human nature, love. We're not cut out to be monogamous. We get bored and we move on, that's all there is to it. Still, if you get lonely and fancy a shag..."

"Let's see what sort of builder you are first," I snap. Maybe a little too tartly, so I put on a smiley face and continue, "I want to know if the muddy boots are worth it."

Richard roars with laughter.

But I don't want a shag, although I spend some time thinking about it later, sitting on the bench by the pond, gin & tonic in hand and William dozing at my feet. What I want is time; time on my own to heal, like it says you need on the advice pages of the magazines I've started buying. Time to work out where I went wrong, if I'm honest, because although I have an inkling, I'm not completely sure.

You see I wasn't very good at telling Neil I loved him – or maybe I just wasn't good at loving him full stop. I thought that being his best friend would be enough; I thought that after the passion had gone it was all you had left and you just had to get on with it. We had settled much too young into a middle aged rut and it had only taken a whiff of excitement to break our world apart. If only we'd been able to talk about what we both wanted then we might have been OK. But I've never been much good at that sort of thing.

I'm just not very good at loving people full stop. After my father died I was the bitch from hell to my mother, but I suppose in my defence I thought I had good reason. I loved my father to distraction so I couldn't understand how eager she was to replace him; I didn't find out about her money worries until much later. Looking back it's little wonder she couldn't confide in a thirteen year old ball of anger and it's probably the reason we've never been close since.

I didn't cope very well with her constant stream of boyfriends and suspect I managed to put a fair few of them off. I sulked, I stropped, I wore a uniform of black leggings and shapeless sweatshirts. I had lots of girlfriends but didn't go near a boy myself – anything male had become the enemy. I left school as soon as I could and got myself stuck in a dead end job in a pet shop.

By the time Derek started going out with my mother I was becoming heartily sick of the way I was. Derek was a straightforward and thoroughly nice man who told me he wanted to be part of our lives but not to replace my father. No-one had ever said that before. He also helped me in a practical way by lending me the money to go to a private secretarial college. I say lend, but bless him, he never asked for it back. Instead he teased me and said it was nice to have a young lady about the house instead of a feral cat.

Out went the spiky haircut and back came my natural curls. Out went endless mooning around to Smiths' records and in came going to parties with my friends. I got a proper job at a motor dealer and shortly afterwards a proper boyfriend, Neil.

Was ours a marriage of convenience? I still don't know. It certainly seemed convenient that he proposed when Mum and Derek were planning to retire to Spain. Like I say, I'm not too good at loving people; I suppose after losing Dad it seems too much of a risk. But that doesn't mean I didn't miss Neil; at first, anyway.

Just being in Yorkshire makes it easier to move on and after my second G&T I am brave enough to ask myself whether I actually want Neil back. If his car pulled into the drive, and he started to cross the lawn, I know William would race towards him. But would I? Would I want to go back to playing second fiddle to the man and his dog, to be the perfectly manicured corporate wife, and rush home from my own stressful job to cook the tea and iron his shirts? And have him grunt and heave on top of me after a few glasses of wine on a Friday night?

I reach down to scratch William's ears.

"Come on, supper time," I murmur. He looks at me gratefully and stretches. Just at this very moment, being a single woman means another gin and a fishfinger sandwich for tea. Bliss.

# Chapter Four

The door of the church creaks as I push it open and I wince; I was hoping to make a quiet entrance and slip unnoticed to a seat at the back. As I pick up a prayer book from the pile on the font I notice Owen waving to me. Despite myself, I smile. He slides along his pew and gestures to the space next to him. I bow my head briefly towards the altar then join him, noticing that the wood is still warm from where he has been sitting. I catch a wholesome whiff of mint shampoo.

"Hi there," I whisper.

"Hello to you, Alice." His voice is smooth like honey with very little trace of an accent, but if he went to school with Richard then he must be local.

An elderly man two rows in front of us starts to turn around but his wife slaps him on the arm and his head swivels forwards again. I am desperate to laugh, but I dare not. I glance surreptitiously at Owen to find him looking for the first hymn in his book.

Owen is dressed in chinos and a sports jacket with the palest of green shirts underneath. His lime tie is a blaze of rebellion in the otherwise muted outfit and the whole thing doesn't quite come off. He just has to be single; no right thinking woman would let him out of the house like that.

"Nice tie," I tell him.

"You don't scrub up so bad yourself."

The organ begins to pump out music and we stand as the vicar emerges from the vestry.

During the hymn I have time to examine both the vicar and my surroundings. The church is compact, with a low, beamed ceiling. Light streams through the window over the altar, illuminating a royal blue carpet which has seen better days and a highly polished communion rail. There are about twenty people spread out across the pews and Owen was right; apart from us and the vicar there seems to be no-one under retirement age.

I hazard a guess that the vicar is about forty, but it's very hard to tell because although his face is unlined and his sandy hair cropped short he has a large bald patch in the middle of it. He's so academic he almost loses me during the sermon but I warm to him when he takes the oldest of his parishioners' communion to their seats.

I'm not really used to the order of service and I struggle to follow without it being too obvious that I don't know when to sit or kneel. It is quite some years since I've been to church but I thought it would be a good way to get to know people. I don't quite have the courage to walk into the pub on my own and I wonder idly if the age profile there would be any younger.

Half way through the second hymn I feel a sharp poke in my side. I look down to see Owen offering a packet of Polos.

"In case you get the urge to cough during the sermon," he whispers. For a moment I think he's having a joke at my expense, but he looks very serious. "Go on," he urges. I take one, and he pops a sweet into his own mouth before stuffing the packet back into his trousers.

At the end of the service I stand to leave. "Thank you for looking after me," I tell him.

"I haven't finished yet. There's coffee in the vicarage now and it won't do you any harm to come and meet everybody."

Of course he is right. None of the people who seemed so daunting in church are the least bit unwelcoming; away from the pulpit Christopher exudes warmth and we soon fall into conversation about his work. He explains that he looks after three local churches, not just St Andrew's, and he and his wife Jane have been in the parish for almost five years.

"Three churches? I expect that keeps you busy."

"Not as busy as it should. It's so hard to get people to take an interest these days, especially the young families. They turn up at Christmas if we're lucky, but that's about all. And I'd far rather be doing christenings than funerals."

I nod. "I bet you have a fair few of those."

"Luckily not in Great Fencote. The last one was Owen's gran – and that was over a year ago."

Right on cue Owen materialises beside us and tells me he has to leave.

"Sunday lunch at Adam's mother's. If I go then they can't argue – not too much, anyway."

I raise my eyebrows "Tin hat time, then?"

He grins. "It's not her fault – it's a generation thing. She's never really come to terms with him being gay so she thinks I'm a good influence because I'm not." He presses his hand onto my arm. "See you soon," he says, and then he is gone.

By the time I leave the vicarage it is almost one o'clock. I have promised to help out at the village fete in two week's time and almost agreed to join Jane's book club. Catching up on a bit of serious fiction would make a nice change; I've become far too hooked on glossy magazines.

It is another particularly warm day and I am drawn to the river. William and I retrace our steps to sit on the grassy knoll. William pants and I shield my eyes from the sun. The water glistens and shimmers. Close to the bridge, the heron is motionless, waiting for a fish. I realise I have come here to think about Owen.

It is hard to relate the extremely polite and well-scrubbed man to the strangely elemental river creature, and it fascinates me it is the same person. I gaze into the Swale and enjoy the memory of the muscles in his shoulders and back working through the water, and the whiteness of the soles of his feet as they the surfaced every now and then.

Eventually I drag myself to my senses and pull William briskly back along the path. But I can't shake the sensuousness of the memory, although it is unwelcome. I can do without this sort of longing; I tell myself sharply that I need to get a life.

If getting a life means going to the pub, then it is Richard who provides the opportunity when he phones a few days later to say he has my quote ready and it might be better if we discuss it over a drink at the Black Horse in Kirkby Fleetham. And perhaps have some supper too, because it would save each of us having to cook for ourselves. A very practical man is Richard.

Practical; and good looking. But of course he knows it and that's never held a great deal of appeal for me. He's good fun though and we enjoy a bit of harmless banter in his van when he picks me up.

As soon as we reach the bar a youngish man wearing a checked shirt turns away from his conversation and looks me up and down. "Very nice indeed, Dick," he nods. "Brunette for a change, I see."

"Alice is a client, Matt," replies Richard. "I've brought her here to discuss work."

"You didn't take my old ma out to the pub when you did her chimney."

"That was just a small job. I'm going to have to ply Alice here with drink just so she doesn't faint when she sees how big my quote is."

"Your quote...that's a new name for it."

"It's not one I've heard before, either," I chip in.

There is a momentary silence and I realise that perhaps in The Black Horse women are seen but not heard, but the landlady quickly comes to my rescue.

"Makes a change from them boasting about their tools," she says, raising her eyebrows. "Lovely lads though, not an ounce of lead in their collective pencils, but they wouldn't hurt a flea."

"Hey, Liz, that's not fair," Matt protests.

"Of course it isn't," she replies, then turns to me. "Now Alice, what can I get you? Have what you like – if Richard's going to fleece you for a job, you'd better start getting your money back now."

In the end we don't even talk about the quote. We sit at the bar and have a couple of drinks, chatting with the others. Then Richard's mobile rings and he wanders outside to answer it, leaving me all on my own in the middle of a slightly uneasy silence.

"So, how did you meet Richard?" Liz asks.

"Owen Maltby recommended him."

"Really?" She sounds a bit surprised but before I have time to ask her why, Matt chips in.

"I'd steer clear of that weirdo if I were you." He says it as though he means it.

"Oh come on, Matt," Liz carries on, "be a bit charitable – it wasn't exactly normal him being brought up by his gran and that."

"Ugh." Matt shudders. "But he's so creepy – all that so-called charming."

So called charming? What's wrong with being charming? Just because Owen is gentlemanly and polite…I am about to wade in on his behalf when Richard breezes back into the bar.

"Come on, Princess, I'm starving – let's order something to eat."

Nine o'clock comes and goes and it becomes apparent Richard is in no fit state to drive me home. Even if he offered, I wouldn't particularly want him to – I don't want to end up in the nearest ditch. High summer or not the sky is already darkening and I decide that if I'm going to walk then I'd better make a move.

I slide down from my barstool. "Right – that's me done – I'm off home."

Richard looks up from his conversation about football. "Shall I take you?" he offers without a great deal of conviction.

"No, I'm fine on my own. I'm not exactly going to get lost, am I?"

"What about the ghosties and ghoulies?" Matt asks.

"I'm not worried about those," I scoff.

"Well what about Dick getting his leg over?"

"Now that does sound scary. See you guys around." I give Richard the briefest of pecks on the cheek and make my way out into the night air.

First, it's colder than I expected and second, I'm drunker than I thought I was. I tug my pashmina from the bottom of my handbag and wrap it around me before setting off down the road.

I am fine within the street-lit security of Kirkby Fleetham but once I walk past the national speed limit sign I find myself in almost total darkness. Across the fields I can see lights coming from the farm buildings at the other end of the village green to my house and I focus on them. It's only a mile or so and it won't take me very long.

The road dips away towards the beck and all of a sudden I lose sight of the lights. It is very dark and I start to think of Matt's ghosties and ghoulies – and then of deranged axe-men hiding in the hedge and every tiny movement in the undergrowth makes me jump. It certainly isn't the same as walking home between the pools of yellow streetlight in Reading; it's not only the darkness, it's the silence too – or rather every sinister rustle and squawk that breaks it.

Finally I hear the comforting throb of an engine and as I approach Great Fencote a car rushes past and I press myself into the hedge. Something catches my pashmina and it rips a little as I tug it away. The sweat feels clammy under my top and my mouth is instantly dry but I convince myself it's only a bramble or a piece of barbed wire. I wrap the pashmina back around me but then worry a spider might have attached itself to the fabric, so I give it a shake and stuff it into my bag.

At last the village green is ahead of me, the lights from the farm re-appearing to my right. From the opposite direction a tractor lumbers along, and as I reach New Cottage its headlamps illuminate a figure sitting under one of the trees on the green. With a start I realise it is Owen. I turn to look again, but that part of the green is in darkness for a moment or two until the lights from a second tractor swing round. There is no-one there.

My hand is frozen to the metal latch on the gate. If Owen had been sitting under the tree then he couldn't possibly have jumped up and hidden so quickly. The tractors rumble on to the farmyard and there isn't enough light to see anything on the green now, however hard I peer.

I stand motionless for an age, watching for a movement among the shadows. In the distance the tractor engine cuts out and I hear voices, and a metallic sound as a barn door grates open. My hand is stiff from clinging to the latch and on the village green all is quiet and still. I open my gate and crunch up the drive.

## Chapter Five

My legs catch in the sheet that has somehow wound itself around me. I close my eyes but all I see is every last detail of the way the tractor lights picked out the paleness of Owen's face and hair and the baggy cream shirt he was wearing. I sit up in the darkness and plump my hot little pillow, but that doesn't work either.

There's something else, too. In that strange way your mind hops about when it refuses to sleep I remember the woman by the freshly filled grave in the churchyard. And Christopher telling me there have been no funerals in Great Fencote for over a year. The inconsistency looms over me at three in the morning and I am still awake when sky loses its blackness and the first red-grey streaks of dawn appear.

In the sunny light of day, however, it seems a relatively simple matter to clear up so I attach William to his lead and make my way up the village to the church. It is still early but there are signs of life from a few of the other houses; an open curtain here, the sound of the radio there. I find myself wondering if Owen lives in one of them.

William and I walk straight past the church porch and around the back of the building, but there I stop; there are a few old gravestones near the path, but by and large the area is an overgrown meadow, long grass dotted with buttercups and the occasional poppy.

I am standing exactly where I was when I came across the grieving woman but this morning it's brighter and my eyes aren't swimming with tears. I scan the churchyard for anything which could look different. Close to the far boundary is a lumpy patch of brambles even now deep in the shadow of a tall fir tree. Could I have mistaken it for someone kneeling? I narrow my eyes, squint at it, and decide it is entirely possible.

Having solved one mystery I return to the village green. It is a long, narrow triangle of grass with Ravenswood Farm at its apex and New Cottage (among other properties) at its base. About half way up a metalled track cuts across it, and between my house and the track is the tree where I thought I saw Owen.

My confidence in my detection skills is boosted by my trip to the churchyard but I still can't work out whether someone has been sitting under the tree recently or not. William sniffs around for a bit then cocks his leg. He isn't exactly helping.

"You're not much of a snoop dog," I murmur, and he looks up at me, big brown eyes trusting and completely uncomprehending.

I make a circuit of the tree wondering how Owen could have seen me and jumped up to hide behind it before the second tractor came. But why would he have done that? Why would he have been there at all? It is the 'why' that's been making me feel so uneasy for most of the night. Time and time again Matt's voice came back to me, calling Owen a weirdo and creepy. What if he is? What if he's some kind of stalker? Could I have got him so very, very wrong?

I convince myself, somewhat conveniently, that the only way to find out is to see more of Owen and to make up my own mind. A trip to Caffé Bianco is clearly in order but it takes me the rest of the morning to pluck up the courage.

By the time I arrive the café is half full but there is no-one to be seen at the counter. I ring the bell and a voice belts out from the kitchen

"Won't be a minute."

After a few moments a pasty looking man with a shaved head appears, wiping enormous floury hands on a white tea towel. "What can I get you?"

"A skinny latte and whatever cake you recommend."

"They're all good."

"I'm sure they are, Adam – Owen's told me what a great cook you are."

He grunts and turns away to start the coffee, then grabs a plate and shoves the nearest piece of cake onto it.

"Where's Owen today?" I ask.

"He's sodded off to London and left me on my own. God knows how I'm going to cope if it gets busy at lunchtime."

Adam won't cope, I can see that. He'll get stroppy with indecisive little old ladies and have customers running from the place in droves, never to return.

"I'll help."

He looks brighter for a moment but then he says "No, you can't. Owen says we've no money for extra help."

But I'm already half way behind the counter. "Then you can make me a cake instead. Now find me an apron and bugger off back into the kitchen."

His look is one of unqualified relief as he disappears. But I don't have time to think about it because the café door swings open and a bevy of office workers walks in. I have no time even to study the coffee machine; still, I've seen it done a hundred times before and it can't be that difficult.

Two hours later the place is deserted and I am on my knees. Adam would never have managed on his own and quite honestly it was irresponsible of Owen to leave him; surely he knows Adam isn't exactly a people person? He's alright with me though; in fact he's very sweet. As I dump the last of the dishes into the washer I feel his heavy hand on my shoulder.

"You go and have a sit down, pet. I've got some cheese scones freshly baked – we'll have those and a cup of tea."

A few minutes later he eases his bulk onto the chair next to mine. It's not that he's fat – just what you'd call a big lad; tall, muscular, broad-shouldered, ever so slightly going to flab. He is in total contrast to Owen's pristine neatness.

"I gotta thank you," he mutters, not looking me in the eye, "but

I don't even know who you are. Let alone why you did it – but I'm right glad you did."

"I guess I owed Owen a favour – he was very kind to me in church last Sunday."

Adam nods. "Then you must be Alice."

"Yes, yes I am."

There is silence while we munch our scones; tangy cheese and mustard tingle together on my tongue. More for something to say than anything I ask:

"So will you need me tomorrow?"

"No. Owen should be back by then. I put him on the train after we closed yesterday and he promised me faithfully he'd be home tonight. I'll bloody kill him if he isn't."

I smile. "It's always as well to have Plan B." I scribble my number on a paper napkin. "If he doesn't show up, then call me."

I am more than half way back to my car before I realise that Owen wasn't even in Great Fencote last night.

## Chapter Six

Wednesday morning comes and goes and I receive no call. I am a bit sorry, to be honest; I enjoyed the hustle and bustle of the café – it made me realise how much I miss regular contact with people. Before my divorce I worked in sales – used cars, to be precise – in a big, busy showroom just off the A4.

I miss my job and I miss my friends but there's no point in dwelling on it. I came up here quite deliberately to make a fresh start. While I wait for the kettle to boil I gaze out of the kitchen window, watching a blue tit swing to and fro on the empty birdfeeder. Its disappointment makes me disproportionately sad; it probably has a family to feed somewhere. I scribble 'birdseed' on the bottom of my shopping list.

I wrap my mug of tea in both hands and drift from room to room, trying to work out where to start. The paintwork in the utility is grubby and chipped and there's a loose floorboard in the dining room which squeaks every time I step on it. I shiver – the room is north facing and it's never warm. I decide to go upstairs and empty some of the boxes littering the spare bedrooms.

I achieve order of sorts but by early evening my back is aching and William is sulking because he hasn't had a walk. When I pull on my jacket and show him his lead he leaps around so much it is hard to fasten it to his collar.

Eventually we set off down the lane towards Little Fencote. As we round the corner opposite the church William spots a man some yards ahead of us walking a golden retriever. He can't help himself but bark, and when the man turns around I am pleasantly surprised to see that it is Owen.

He waits for us to catch them up. "Well hello, Alice," he says, "I didn't know you had a dog," and again I am struck by the smoothness of his voice.

"William, this is Owen." I introduce them rather formally then look down at the retriever. "And this is?"

"She's called Kylie."

"Kylie!" I don't want to snigger when he looks so embarrassed. "Well I suppose..."

"She's Adam's dog," he cuts across me. "I'm just the mug who has to walk her while he cooks the tea." He laughs, but he looks a bit cross, and I wonder if Adam did have a go at him about being left on his own in the café.

We walk in silence down the lane. I had planned to turn right at the end, but wonder if I should go whichever way Owen doesn't and leave him to his mood. When we reach the T junction he pauses.

"Fancy a walk around the trout pond?"

I hesitate. "Isn't it private property?"

"Not when you went to school with the owner's son."

"Did you go to school with everyone around here?"

For the first time this evening he smiles. "Oh, probably."

As we walk up the track to the pond I am struggling for something to say.

"So, how was your trip to London?"

"Adam said you helped out in the café."

"I'll do anything for some of his cake," I laugh, but it sounds a little false. "Now don't let him forget he promised me one."

"I think he's already on the case. Adam may not be the ideal waiter, but he's a man of his word – take it from me."

There is a pontoon across the pond which leads to a small, overgrown island. We walk across, the dogs' claws clinking on the wooden planks. At the far end Owen stops.

"We can let them off their leads here. They can't go anywhere except back past us – or into the water. Does William swim?"

"Not from choice."

"Well that's alright then."

There is another awkward silence while the dogs nose around the undergrowth so I ask, "How was your lunch on Sunday?"

Owen looks surprised, but all the same sounds pleased I remembered. "It was OK, actually. Thanks for asking."

I can't help but sneak a surreptitious glance at his trim body. He is wearing a pair of faded jeans with a cheesecloth shirt out over the top of them. One of the buttons has come undone and I catch a glimpse of his flat stomach. It makes me want to reach out and stroke the tiny golden hairs so before I start to blush I blurt out:

"Have you ever swum here?"

It is a stupid, stupid question given how shallow the water is and from Owen's point of view it's come from nowhere. Damn.

"Not swum, but I've paddled. My grandmother used to come here to collect herbs when I was little and it was a great place to play."

"It must have been lovely growing up in the country."

"It was pretty much perfect, yes." His head drops and he leans on the railing of the pontoon, looking into the water. I follow his gaze. Two fish swim below us, flickers of silver just under the surface.

Before I even think what I'm doing I'm touching his shoulder. "Owen, are you alright?"

He nods. "Fine, yeah. No, really, Alice – I am. Just a bit tired – sorry not to be great company." He straightens and my tentative hand falls away. "Now come on, I must try harder to entertain the lady." He slaps the back of his knuckles in mock playfulness. "Did you know? This pond holds over three hundred trout – isn't that amazing? The farmer grows potatoes, too – the fish and chip man I always call him."

"Owen – you don't have to try to entertain me, you're fine just as you are."

He looks sideways at me, his face half hidden by his hair. I try to read his expression, but then his phone rings.

"No – OK – on my way back now. I bumped into Alice – wanted to show her the island...ten minutes, no more."

He turns to face me. "My tea's nearly ready – I'd better go."

Before I can even call William, Owen whistles so loudly beside me it nearly bursts my eardrum. Kylie appears, panting, with William a few paces behind her.

Owen looks at me, an impish smile on his face. "Sorry. But you didn't think I was going to stand here yelling her name, did you?"

I start to laugh and he gives me the briefest of hugs before putting Kylie on her lead and we set off down the pontoon.

## Chapter Seven

Increasingly, Owen is taking up my thoughts. I feel a bit uncomfortable about that business on the village green, but the more I see of him the more I like him. But does he like me? I can't be sure. Did something happen on the pontoon, or am I building up a little friendly hug to be more than it was just because I want it to be? And why do I want it to be? It's much too soon to be thinking about a new man – much.

Anyway, by Saturday night I have plenty else to think about. Richard calls saying that if I want he can start on Monday – someone else has let him down over a job at the last minute. I am half way through agreeing before I stop short.

"What's wrong, Alice?" he asks me.

"It's just there's so much crap in the barn the previous owners left," I wail.

"I'll give you a hand to clear it tomorrow if you like. We can take it down the dump in my van."

"Oh Richard – could you? I'd pay you extra, of course."

"How about you cook us a roast dinner instead? I never make one for myself – there doesn't seem much point." He pauses. "I take it you can cook?"

"Yes...not sure about the standard of my Yorkshire puddings though."

"Don't worry about that. Aunt Bessie's will do – as long as there's plenty of them."

So that's me told.

Sunday morning is spent clearing out the barn. There's nothing we can do about the old freezer – the council will have to take that away – but otherwise numerous cardboard boxes, a chest of drawers eaten rotten by worm, a rusty lawnmower and various other broken tools are piled into Richard's van and taken to the municipal tip.

It is almost three o'clock by the time we come back.

"I'm beginning to get hungry, love," he tells me. "Why don't you go and get cleaned up then you can start on dinner. I'll finish off out here."

I look down at my grimy jeans and dust-covered T-shirt – he's right – I'm certainly not in any fit state to cook a meal.

After a quick shower I feel more human. I run a wide-toothed comb through my curls and pull on some clean trousers and a strappy top. Automatically I take my lip gloss out of my make-up bag; I usually wear it because shiny lips detract attention from my less than perfect eyes, but should I be dolling myself up now? Richard has been flirting with me all day and I don't want the awkwardness of having to turn him down.

I am half way down the stairs when I hear voices in the driveway. It's Owen and I instantly regret the lack of lippy.

"I just popped round to make sure Alice is OK," he says. "We missed her in church."

"Too much to do here, mate. I'm starting work tomorrow and she wasn't anywhere near ready."

"Is she around?"

"Upstairs somewhere I think. Listen, Owen…not sure how to put this tactfully, but three's a crowd, if you get my meaning."

I quite literally feel my jaw drop. There is a pause in the conversation before Owen continues, "I didn't realise you and Alice…"

"That's OK, mate, you weren't to know. Thanks for the introduction by the way – see you around." Two sets of feet crunch along the gravel in different directions.

How dare Richard send Owen away like that? How dare he lie to him about our relationship? I am about to race through the front door and after Owen, but I stop. I actually need Richard; or rather, a builder – one who will do a decent job. I clench my fists hard, what's left of my nails after this morning digging into the palms of my hands. Calm down, Alice, don't be too hasty. You can always square it with Owen later.

So I retrace my steps and swap my top for a clean, but drab, old sweatshirt. In the kitchen I put my mind to making possibly the most disappointing roast dinner Richard has ever eaten. It seems a waste of good beef to overcook it, but everything I put in front of him is in the style – and quantity – of nouvelle cuisine. With no seconds. And positively, positively, nothing for afters.

I am still wondering how to put the record straight with Owen when Adam calls next morning to tell me my cake is ready. Richard and his carpenter are already hard at work in the barn, measuring up for new windows and having animated discussions about load bearing joists. Richard has taken his disappointment with his Sunday dinner very well, all things considered, and is his bright, breezy and cheeky self.

"I'm going into town," I call to them. "Do you need anything?"

"Can you pick us up some pasties for lunch?" he yells back. "I daren't ask you to make us sandwiches – you'd probably cut the crusts off or summat."

I am still smiling as I walk down the alleyway to Caffé Bianco; Richard has hide as thick as a rhinoceros – an admirable and enviable trait. I glance through the café window and notice Owen cleaning tables. He is side-on so he doesn't see me, his fair hair flopping down and forming a curtain between us. He stops for a moment, gripping a table edge, head bent, and then he is on the move again, carrying a tray back towards the kitchen.

I wait until he disappears before I go into the café.

"Anyone home?" I call.

"Won't be a tick, Alice. On my way." To my surprise and disappointment it is Adam who shouts back; and Adam who appears moments later, carrying an oblong cake box.

He sets it down on the counter and grins. "There you go."

"What is it?"

"It's a cake, you dumb ha'pporth."

"I meant, what sort?"

"Open it up and see."

I ease the lid off the box. Inside is a cake in the shape of Superwoman, only with a letter A emblazoned across her chest instead of an S.

"Oh, Adam," I gulp.

He looks at me in panic. "For chrissakes don't blub, woman."

"Sorry." I sniff and look at him purposefully. "Right – I don't suppose you do pasties, do you?"

"Don't normally, but I can do. When d'you want them for?"

I grimace. "Today. I've got the builders in and they've asked for some for lunch."

"Can you give me an hour or so? I can knock a few up."

"You don't mind?"

"I like doing summat different. Come back about half eleven."

Owen doesn't even come out of the kitchen to say hello. Surely he isn't avoiding me because of what Richard said yesterday? There must be another reason – maybe the phone rang or something. But my fears are confirmed when he isn't in the café when I collect the pasties, and it makes me feel indescribably, if inexplicably, sad.

# Chapter Eight

I wake up in the night because I hear someone crying. Or at least, I half wake up, because if I'd woken up fully it might have made me more uneasy. It's an odd noise, not a child's wail, but something part way between sobbing and keening, and I can't work out if it's a woman or a man.

I poke my head out of the open window to see if I can pinpoint where it's coming from. The night is still with barely a rustle from the trees. One of the horses in the field behind the house coughs and I wonder if perhaps that is what I heard.

I stumble back into bed but as my head hits the pillow the crying starts again, very softly now and further away. Maybe it's coming from a nearby property; whoever it is sounds as though they are at the depths of despair but I just want to go back to sleep. I can't exactly go knocking on doors to find them, can I?

I put my head under the pillow to shut out the noise and it sort of works. My shoulders and back relax into the mattress and eventually I feel Owen's arms around me and hear his sweet voice telling me not to worry, it will all be alright. I am safe and loved in a dream.

# Chapter Nine

I completely forget my promise to help at the fete until Jane turns up on Thursday morning to finalise the rota.

"I can be there all day," I tell her. "I'll just need to pop back to see to William, but otherwise I'll do whatever you need me to."

"Oh bless you, Alice. There aren't very many of us and some of the older ladies find it a bit much if it's hot." And she dashes off next door to collect the bottles Mr Webber has promised for the tombola. Jane is always dashing somewhere with a great deal of purpose and I feel a stab of envy.

By nine o'clock on Saturday morning my blouse is already sticking to my back – I didn't know the weather could be like this in Yorkshire. I make sure William has plenty to drink then set off up the dusty lane to Kirkby Fleetham, the hum of bees in the dog roses accompanying me on my way.

Kirkby Fleetham village green is a spacious arc of parched grass on the road to Great Fencote. Normally populated by old men with dogs, this morning it is a hive of activity and I make my way between the cars unloading all manner of goodies and tat to the relative sanctuary of the marquee. It smells of musty canvas, cakes and potting compost, but away from the glare of the sunshine it exudes a sepulchral calm.

My job is to help a wiry lady called Margaret with the book and plant stall. Despite her wrinkled face and salt and pepper hair Margaret pulsates with energy, her small dark eyes always on the lookout for something new. She has a pair of glasses on a gold chain around her neck, but I never once see her put them on although I do catch her peering myopically at the prices on some of the books. But as far as the plants are concerned, she knows everything and more.

I, however, know nothing and Margaret turns out to be very good at explaining it all. Understandably, given she's a retired teacher. Originally from Newcastle, she came to Northallerton as a new graduate, married, moved to Great Fencote, was widowed in her forties, and has lived in the village ever since. All of this I discover within about fifteen minutes.

"I'm next door to your friend Owen," she tells me.

My friend? That's news to me. "I expect he's a good neighbour," I offer by way of a suitably bland reply.

"Oh yes, he's always been a sweetie, right from when he was a little lad. His grandmother was so proud of him, but I used to say she only had herself to thank for bringing him up properly."

I am curious to find out more about Owen's childhood but I don't want to appear nosey, and anyway, we have a sudden influx of customers clamouring for some of Margaret's dahlias. All the pots are neatly labelled but I still almost get myself into a muddle.

"You're not a country girl, are you?" Margaret laughs.

I shake my head ruefully. "I don't know what I'm going to do with all that garden."

"If you don't mind me asking, if you don't like gardening why did you buy a house in an acre of land?"

"My husband was keen on it." It's no good – I have to bite the bullet at some point. "But he left me, so now I'm on my own. I couldn't have carried on living in our marital home – I wanted a fresh start."

"Oh Alice, you must be feeling so let down. I felt a bit that way when Walter died, but at least he didn't do it deliberately – or let's say I don't think he did." There is a twinkle in her eyes and it leavens her sympathy. I like that a lot.

I smile at her and open up just a little bit. "At first I wanted to string his unmentionables from the nearest lamp post, but I'm over that now; I'll survive."

"Of course you will – human beings are very resilient."

Two small children are browsing the books and our conversation is once again interrupted while Margaret helps them to choose and I flounder my way through the sale of some more plants.

Once the rush dies down Margaret continues, "Of course, you have just the right house for a female survivor."

"Why's that?"

"It was built by a woman. Not in the physical sense, of course, but she owned the land and had the property put up to her specification."

"Wow – that must have been unusual back then."

"Almost unheard of. She was a businesswoman too, the village cheesemaker."

"So that would explain the barn – she must have needed somewhere to keep her cattle. Fancy that, a single woman making her way in the world three hundred years ago."

"She didn't stay single – she married a farmer called Charles later in life and they had a son, but I don't know what happened to her after that because a family called Stainthorpe lived in the house for generations – right up until the 1960s."

"How on earth do you know about the lady cheesemaker? It was so long ago."

"From Owen's grandmother – she had so many stories. I wish I'd written down what she told me; the tradition of oral history in our villages is almost dying out."

"She sounds like an interesting lady."

"She was. She died only last year and she's left a real gap in the community; she was very knowledgeable."

"What, about local history?"

Margaret shakes her head. "More than that – she was a wise woman all around. What she didn't know about herbs…and people, for that matter…we do all miss her, Owen especially."

"He's a nice man, isn't he?" I venture, and Margaret nods.

Towards the end of the afternoon the atmosphere at the fete changes. The mostly empty stalls are cleared away and our marquee is commandeered as a beer tent. Christopher, our vicar, and the landlord of The Black Horse roll in the barrels and set them up on a trestle while Liz polishes the glasses.

I am hot, tired and dusty and longing to sink into the bath, but as I help Margaret to pack up what's left of the books I feel a tap on my shoulder.

"Hello, Princess. Not leaving, are you?" It's Richard.

"Well yes, I am."

"But you will be coming back? Go on; make an old man happy..."

He smiles and I smile. A party is a party and the bath can wait. "Give me an hour to finish off here and walk William..."

"And another hour to make yourself look beautiful."

"Cheeky bugger," I toss my curls theatrically. "That will take about five minutes."

As I make my way back onto the field later, one of the first people I see is Owen. He is helping out on the coconut shy. His shirt sleeves are rolled up and he looks relaxed, but I have the impression that the moment he sees me he crouches low to a small child in a pink dress and starts to explain to her in some detail what she should do.

The locals from The Black Horse have formed a group part way between the marquee and the barbecue. Richard breaks off his conversation and comes to meet me, wrapping a proprietary arm around my shoulder and leading me towards the bar.

"No G&T tonight, love – will you drink beer instead?"

"Yes, go on. It'll make a nice change – it's so hot." Secretly I am rather relieved; if I'd spent all night drinking gin I would probably have got very drunk.

Famous last words. The beer tastes innocuous enough, but maybe it's the heat, or the fact I only have a couple of sausages to eat, but by the time dusk falls I'm feeling distinctly worse for wear. I know I'm pretty pissed because the jokes Richard and his mates are making are getting funnier and funnier, and I can hear myself laughing louder and louder. Gross.

Doubly gross when Richard starts pawing my bottom through my skirt. I don't want to tear him off a strip in front of his friends so instead I decide it's time to go home.

"I'll walk you back," offers Richard. I'm a bit surprised but I reason he must feel guilty about leaving me to fend for myself last time. I can do with an arm to lean on anyway; let's say the edges of my world are feeling a little blurred.

We are not far down the lane when he stops in a farm gateway and takes me in his arms. There is still enough light for me to see that his eyes are dark with passion. He is incredibly good looking and I am momentarily flattered – he sees it in my face and it spurs him on.

"Oh, Alice." He is breathing beery fumes all over me as he makes a slobbering attempt to kiss my lips. I turn away and try to wriggle free. "You know you want to," he continues, his arms wrapping more tightly around me. His hold feels just on the wrong side of affectionate. Too late, it puts me on my guard.

"Richard – cut that out," I manage to slur.

He ignores me and spins me roughly around so that my back is against the gate. I am feeling cornered and it's hard to breathe so I react violently when his hand makes its way under my skirt.

"Get off!" I yelp and struggle to free myself, but his whole body pushes me harder against the gate. The more I thrash about the more firmly he holds me and all of a sudden I realise I am completely trapped – he is just too strong. The bars of the gate are cutting into my back and I find myself screaming, "For the love of God, Charles – no!"

Richard pulls away slightly. "Who's Charles?"

I grab my chance and use the space between us to knee him firmly in the groin before taking myself off down the road as fast as my wedges will carry me.

I don't get very far. I am too drunk to run and soon my chest is bursting with every step. I sit on the parapet of the little bridge over the beck to take stock. I'm alright really; OK, my ribs feel a bit tender but I tell myself there's no real harm done.

I hear footsteps coming down the road. My first instinct is to run, but what if the footsteps started running too? It has to be Richard – the tread is definitely male, and I can feel my teeth chattering. Perhaps if I duck down by the stream he'll walk on past and I can hide until he's gone. But what if he's waiting for me when I get home?

I decide my only option is to face him off. Fuelled by Dutch courage I call out "Who's there?"

"It's me, Owen."

I am so relieved I almost wet myself. Literally.

"What the hell are you doing creeping around after me?"

He has now come close enough for me to see him. "I'm not creeping around," he says, with some exasperation "I'm just making sure you get home alright, because Richard's obviously not gentleman enough to do it."

My anger with Richard, Owen, and men in general bursts out. "Why should you care, when you've been avoiding me all week?"

"Avoiding you? I don't know what you mean."

He sounds so sanctimonious I could scream. And I do (almost). "Of course you do – you hid in the kitchen when I came to collect my cake, for a start."

"I did not. I had a meeting."

"You didn't. You were clearing tables just moments before I came in."

"Then I went straight into the office, put on my jacket, and went out of the back door."

"To avoid me."

"To go and see the bank manager, not that it's any of your business."

"Like it's none of your business how I get home."

He draws a sharp breath. "No, I don't suppose it is. However, as we are both walking in the same direction, are we going to stand here arguing all night or are we going to get a move on?"

Stubborn as I feel, I can't stand here for much longer – I need to go to the toilet for one thing, and my head's swimming for another. Besides, I won't really feel safe until I'm in my own house with the door firmly locked behind me. Without another word I start walking and Owen falls into step beside me. I say beside me, but that's not so easy for him because I'm swaying all over the place. A little way further on my foot catches on something and I almost trip up, but his hand is there to steady my elbow.

"Woops-a-daisy," he says.

"Woops-a-daisy? No-one in the real world says woops-a-daisy anymore."

"Now you're misquoting one of my favourite films."

"Notting Hill?"

"That's right..." and somehow we chat about it all the way to my back door.

Inside, William is scratching and whining. "Somebody's missed you," Owen comments.

"He's been on his own too much today," I say, fishing in my bag for my key.

Once the door is open William leaps up to welcome me. I am surprised he doesn't race straight to his favourite drainpipe but when I flick on the light I can see why; he's messed all over the floor.

I turn to Owen. "Poor dog – he never asked for any of this, he never asked to come here." A maudlin tear runs down my cheek.

Owen places a warm hand on each of my shoulders. "Alice, I'll clean up. You go to bed and sleep off that beer. No argument. OK?"

I don't even thank Owen. I rush upstairs to have a pee but never get back down again because I start to feel sick. And to be sick. And finally to fall asleep (I prefer that to the thought I pass out) on the bathroom floor, cuddling a towel.

I have no idea how long I am there but it is still dark when I wake. I haul myself up against the chill of the radiator. Am I going to throw up again? I don't think so, but I feel lousy and I want my bed. I manage to stand and stumble back to my bedroom. The beam from a full moon slices my pillows and I make my way across the room to shut the curtains.

A movement in the garden catches my eye and I try to focus better to peer out. To my absolute amazement, Owen is coming out of the small door at the side of the barn. He closes it behind him and then he hesitates, his head bent. He passes his hand over his face and looks briefly to the heavens, the wetness of his tears glistening in the moonlight. Then, very slowly, he trudges away.

# Chapter Ten

Not one single fibre in my body wants to move. I roll over slowly and my stomach lurches, but I can hear William whining and I can't let him down again, poor dog. My feet find the floor and that makes my head thud even more. With a superhuman effort I finally stand up.

At the bottom of the stairs I spy my spare keys on the mat. Owen must have locked the back door and put them through the letterbox. I leave them where they are. My own keys are nestling on top of my handbag which I'd slung on the garden room shelf. I grope for them as William capers around and finally I'm able to let him out into the sunshine.

I lean on the door frame and watch him sniff his way up the border, praying he doesn't find any decomposing wildlife to roll in. Last night is pretty hazy but I can't fathom Richard's behaviour – I wouldn't have thought he had an aggressive streak in a million years. And then there's Owen – kindness itself, but why was he sneaking around my barn in the middle of the night? Perhaps neither of them are quite what they seem; or maybe I'm just a really bad judge of character.

William might be enjoying the sunshine but every ray is finding its way behind my eyes and sending needles into my skull. I know the only way to clear the poison from my body is to drink loads of water but it's too hard to face. I shut William back into the garden room and fall asleep on the sofa.

I feel a tiny bit more human when I wake again but it's early afternoon before I manage to stir myself properly, eat some toast, wash and dress. My priority has to be to thank Owen for his kindness – and try to find out what he was doing creeping around my barn. But that's a tough one because in the sober light of day I can't be completely sure I didn't imagine it.

I know where Owen lives from the evening we took the dogs to the pond; one of a terrace of Victorian red brick villas next to the church. There's every chance he won't be in but I'm still strangely nervous as I walk up the short path to the door. Partly because I'm no longer certain I have the right house; the front window is swathed in a frilly lace curtain and there is a flock of Lladro geese on the windowsill.

But it is Owen who opens the door and when he sees me his smile reaches right to his eyes.

"Alice! How are you feeling?"

"A lot better than I did this morning thanks – still a bit like I've been poisoned though." I laugh a bit louder than I mean to.

"I expect you do."

"I don't want to disturb your Sunday; I just wanted to thank you for being so kind last night."

"It's no problem, really." He hesitates for a moment. "Do you have time for a cup of tea?"

"That would be lovely if it's not too much trouble."

"Of course it's not. Ads has fallen asleep listening to the cricket on the radio and it would be nice to have some company. You make yourself comfy in the front room and I'll pop the kettle on."

He holds open the door to the living room then disappears. The lace curtains and china geese were only the start of it – there are ornaments everywhere; dogs, cats, birds – on the mantelpiece and on the shelves in the alcove next to the fireplace. There is even a china cabinet against the back wall, with a rose-bud patterned tea service as its centre piece, the cups and plates surrounded by miniature animals.

The overcrowded feel of the room isn't helped by the sofa and easy chair being covered in an old fashioned tapestry-like fabric. And linen antimacassars – and those silly little bits that cover the arms so they don't get dirty either. The whole place is like stepping into a 1950's time warp.

I perch on the edge of the sofa just as Owen breezes in and pulls a table out of the nest just behind the door.

"Now would you like anything to eat? Has your tummy settled OK?"

"I had some toast earlier thanks, but I'm not sure I could face anything right now."

"Just the tea then. Sugar?"

I shake my head, thinking how very sweet he is and how much I am beginning to like him.

It isn't long before he comes back with two mugs of tea and sits down at the other end of the sofa. I am suddenly aware of the gentle murmuring of Adam's radio in an upstairs room.

It is Owen who breaks the silence. "Margaret said you were a great help to her yesterday."

"Hindrance, more like – I know nothing about plants. But she's a lovely lady, isn't she?"

"Yes. She's lived next door for as long as I can remember – I'm lucky to have such a good neighbour."

I pick up my mug and nurse it in my hands. "You've always lived in the village then?"

"Pretty much." He pauses. "What about you, Alice, where are you from?"

I take a sip of my tea but it tastes a bit odd; like the china's tainted by something. More likely it's my taste buds. "Reading. Very suburban, me; it's taking some getting used to living in the country. But I like it," I add hurriedly, "I'm just not sure about the beer."

"That fete beer's lethal – it's about eight percent alcohol."

"Eight percent? No wonder I felt ropey after a couple of pints."

"Pints – you're brave."

"Well, Richard bought them for me and I didn't know how strong they were."

Owen raises an eyebrow. "They're impossible, those lads. They like a joke, which is fine, but they don't always think through the consequences."

"You looked after me though."

I wish I hadn't said it because Owen looks away.

"Paying me back for helping Adam out in the café, was it?"

He smiles and nods eagerly. "You could say that, yes."

We chat for a little longer but I can't find a way of asking him why he was in my barn. By the time I leave I feel very much better, but even so Owen gives me his phone number in case there is anything I need. I use it when I get home to text him another thank you, but even though I wait for quite a while there is no reply.

## Chapter Eleven

The next morning I'm surprised to hear a tentative tap on the garden room door. I'm not expecting anyone; thankfully the builders have disappeared off somewhere else for a few weeks so at least I'm spared having to look Richard in the eye.

I open the door to see Margaret gazing out over the lawn.

"Good morning," I chirp.

"Good morning, Alice," she replies. "I hope you don't mind me popping around, but Owen said you weren't too well yesterday and I thought I'd just make sure you're alright today."

"I'm fine now thanks." I hesitate. "As you're here, would you like a look around the garden?"

Her face lights up with a maze of suntanned wrinkles. "That would be marvellous."

At the word garden, William stands and stretches. "Come on then," I tell him, "but no showing me up by digging in the flowerbeds."

Margaret bends down and scratches his ears. "So this is William," she says. "He is rather handsome." The dog looks up at her adoringly.

As we make our way around the property Margaret positively bubbles with advice, most of which flies straight over my head. It is beginning to dawn on me that gardening is something I'm supposed to do now that I live in a village and as I've never been much interested before it's going to be another rather steep learning curve.

As we progress along the borders Margaret is amazed at the variety of plants. Most of them are becoming choked by weeds but I have to admit they're still very pretty; blues, pinks and whites in all shapes and sizes, fighting their way out from a tangle of green.

"Help yourself to whatever you'd like," I tell her. "It looks as though there's far too much here."

"I have the opposite problem to you," she laughs, "you've got too much space and I've not got enough of it. I've even encroached on Owen's garden to grow the cut flowers for church."

"Isn't Owen much of a gardener?"

She shakes her head. "He doesn't have time, dear. That young man works so hard – he has no time for a life of his own at all."

I nod. After all, the café is open six days a week. I suppose the rest of his time is spent walking Kylie for Adam and being nice to waifs and strays like me.

At the very end of the plot, half overgrown, we come across some raspberry canes. Margaret is ecstatic.

"These are late ones, Alice, and it looks like you'll have a terrific crop – as long as you put nets over to keep the birds off."

I look at them dubiously. "And do something about those nettles."

"That won't take you long, dear, as long as you've got a good pair of gloves," and I know I have another job to add to my ever growing list.

It is as she's waxing lyrical about the greenhouse that it occurs to me. "Margaret," I say, stopping her in midstream, "If you wanted it for your plants I'd be more than happy. I'll get someone to fix the glass and it'll be fine."

Her face lights up. "Alice – really? I've never had space for a greenhouse myself."

"Of course." I indicate the rest of the area with my arm, "and if there's any other part of this wilderness you could use..."

"You wouldn't mind me trekking through your garden unannounced?"

"Not at all," I reply. "You could even check up on how badly I'm doing with the raspberries."

Her look of unrestrained delight fills me with genuine pleasure. "You are an absolute sweetheart," she tells me. I don't think I've ever been called that before.

## Chapter Twelve

All the magazines say that soft furnishings are the most exciting part of doing up a house, but I can't say I'm that that interested so I end up mooching inconclusively around Northallerton for more than half a morning. Probably out of desperation, the woman in the haberdashery suggests I take away a book of swatches to think about over a cup of coffee. She makes me realise that I've been avoiding Caffé Bianco, but at the same time it just isn't in me to go anywhere else.

The door is propped open to let in the breeze – or maybe let out the heady mix of coffee and baking. It's certainly drawn a few people in; a handful of young mothers have pushed two tables together in the corner and barricaded themselves in with pushchairs. An elderly couple gaze out of the window, not talking.

Adam appears when I press the bell on the counter.

"On your own again?" I ask him, wondering how on earth Owen could have possibly seen me come in and hidden himself away.

"Owen had to go to Leeds. He won't be back for hours."

"So d'you need a hand?"

He looks down at the counter. "I do really. But Owen said I mustn't ask you again."

"Why ever not? Did I do something horribly wrong last time?"

"Not a bit of it. But he says if we can't afford to pay you..." a smile twitches on his lips, "and he said there must be a limit to the number of cakes a skinny little tyke like you can eat."

But I am already behind the counter and stowing my handbag on the shelf under the till. "Well, if Owen whinges, tell him I owed him a favour. If you need me again, you can always pay me in pasties – when the builders come back I'll need hundreds of those."

Later that evening I text Owen: 'Hope you didn't mind me helping out but I felt I owed you one after the weekend'. There is no reply; clearly his old fashioned politeness doesn't extend as far as the digital age.

But on Sunday, when I arrive in church, Owen smiles and slides along his pew to make room for me. I was planning to sit with Margaret but it would be rude to refuse his invitation.

"Sorry I didn't reply to your text," he whispers "I've been so busy…but it was nice to hear from you."

I am about to ask how you can be too busy to send just one text but then I notice the dark circles under his eyes.

"Owen, are you OK?"

He pushes his hair back from his face and looks at me but he doesn't say anything, even so I have the weirdest sensation that the dark centres of his devastating blue eyes are speaking to me, and they are saying 'no Alice, I'm not – but there's just no way I can tell you'. In the privacy of the pew I give his hand a little squeeze, and to my surprise and delight he gives mine a little squeeze back.

By the time we are drinking our coffee in the vicarage I am wondering if I imagined the look. We help Jane to pass around the biscuits and cups, with me still a little shy and Owen being generally delightful to everyone. He is a charming man and I can see that his fellow parishioners adore him. It strikes me that perhaps he is still trying to be the little boy his grandmother was so proud of and I can't decide if that makes his niceness all the more genuine or just a little bit plastic.

I am cross with myself too, because I am increasingly drawn to Owen and I don't want to be. I quite deliberately spend a long time talking to Jane about her children and then make a quick exit through the back door. Not quick enough – I am only half way down the path when I hear Owen call me.

"Alice?"

I turn around.

"I was going to ask you – d'you fancy taking the dogs for a walk later?"

I feel myself starting to smile and Owen is grinning back.

"Yes, I'd like that."

"Me too. Meet you outside the church at about six?"

"Perfect."

And I look forward to our walk all afternoon.

Given that we arranged to meet by the church, when I look out of the window I am a little surprised to see Owen sitting under the tree on the village green. I glance at my watch – it's ten to six; maybe he's decided on a different route and is waiting for me there instead. I hurriedly swap my dirty T-shirt for a soft v-neck sweater, slap on some lip gloss and race downstairs to attach William to his lead.

I swear it only takes me a few minutes, but by the time I walk down the drive Owen has gone. I pause at the gate, puzzled, but then I see him walking towards Kirkby Fleetham, with no dog. I am about to call his name but something stops me. Instead I make an attempt to pull William to heel and we start to follow.

Only then Owen calls *my* name; from somewhere down the road behind me. "Alice – where are you going?"

I swivel around to see Owen and Kylie approaching from the direction of the church. I turn back towards Kirkby Fleetham, but the man I thought was Owen has disappeared around the bend. The beads of perspiration on the back of my neck trickle under my jumper.

"Owen," I ask him, "do you have a double?"

He laughs. "Not as far as I know. Why?"

"Are you sure? It's just that I saw someone very like you sitting under the trees over there, and then he started to walk that way."

"I think I'd know if I did have one, I've lived around here most of my life, remember."

"He was so like you I started to follow him – that's where I was going. But it wasn't you because you're here, and anyway, he was wearing a cream shirt." I grind to a halt, looking at Owen's navy fisherman's sweater.

"Well that settles it," he replies. "I don't even have a cream shirt. Plenty of the white ones I wear for work, but no cream."

We walk back through the village and I try to put the man under the tree out of my mind. There must have just been a passing resemblance: he was probably only a walker taking a rest in the shade. I refuse to remember the time I thought I saw Owen under that tree before. I'm not exactly going to be sparkling company if I start dwelling on that.

But Owen himself seems a bit pre-occupied. We chat as we walk through the village, but after a while fall into silence and I can't work out whether it's a companionable one or not. When we reach the fork in the road he asks me if I'd prefer to go to Scruton or back to the trout pond. I choose the pond because I can let William off his lead.

This time I sit with my legs dangling over the edge of the pontoon, pretending to look for fish. The evening sun warms my back and the shadows cast by the bushes on the island shimmer and lengthen over the water. I half close my eyes and they merge together, looking almost like the outline of a low building. A faint smell of honeysuckle wafts by on the breeze.

After a while Owen sits down next to me, his knees tucked under his chin.

"Thanks for helping Adam on Wednesday, but you didn't have to."

I look sideways at him. "Is that 'didn't have to' as in 'I don't want you to do it again'?"

He shakes his head. "It's not that simple."

"Then what is it?"

He doesn't answer so eventually I continue, "Adam said something about not being able to pay me, but truly I..."

"We're struggling, Alice, that's the honest truth. But I didn't want anyone to know."

"It's not Adam's fault; I think it was out before he realised."

"Well I think he was being manipulative, just so he didn't have to serve any customers."

"He's not good at it, Owen. Surely you realise..."

"Of course I know – I'm not blind to his faults, or stupid."

His glare is enough to silence any thought of replying. After a little while I stand up; I am bitterly disappointed – I thought Owen wanted to enjoy my company, not tear me off a strip and push me away. I walk out onto the island and call William, praying it's not one of his moments of selective deafness. Luckily he emerges quite quickly from behind a shrub looking bedraggled and happy.

"Come on, it's supper time," I tell him, and he wags his tail as I bend down to put his lead back on.

Owen is still sitting on the pontoon, hugging his knees, and is the very picture of desolation. Looking like I feel, in fact. It makes me stop behind him.

"You've been so kind to me, Owen. I really, really want to help. But I just feel like I'm intruding."

He shakes his head without looking up. "I'd like you to help as well, but we can't pay you so there's no point in even talking about it." The man is stubborn as a mule. Inside I am pleading with him to let me help at the café; I'm so lonely on my own in the house all day. But all I say is goodnight, and I start to walk down the pontoon.

"Alice," he falters, "I'm so sorry. I didn't mean to end up talking about work and spoiling the evening."

I shrug my shoulders. "You've nothing to be sorry for. It's your business, after all. If things aren't great it's bound to play on your mind."

"I shouldn't be putting it all on you though – it's not fair if I ask you to come for a walk then all I do is whinge."

I crouch next to him again. "Owen – I don't want you to put on an act with me. It's OK to share how you feel, be who you are."

"Now you're being much too kind, if not a little foolish." He punches my arm playfully and scrambles to his feet. "Come on, let's go home – you promised William his supper a full five minutes ago and I swear I can hear his tummy rumbling."

# Chapter Thirteen

Not sleeping well is becoming a habit. I wake with a start in the velvety darkness and my mind instantly switches to worry mode, the proverbial monsters from under the bed shifting and groaning and keeping me awake. I turn on the light, pick up a magazine, change my mind, put it down again. Not once, but several times. It is daylight before I doze off again.

So it is late next morning when William and I make our daily circuit of the garden and Margaret is already hard at work clearing the greenhouse. I watch her for a few moments, thinking how unlike my perfectly coiffed mother she is; straight hair cropped close, wiry arms tanned from being outside so much protruding from the sleeves of a floral blouse that has seen better days, her whole being vibrant with energy and good humour.

She stops work for a moment and spots me. "I thought I'd make a start before it gets too warm," she explains.

I look guiltily at the raspberries. "I'll come out and join you when I've given William his biscuits."

Margaret and I work for an hour or so, with William snoozing under a nearby plum tree. It's good to be doing something physical and even better that I'm not alone.

After a while Margaret gives up on the tangle of brambles in the greenhouse and comes over to help me.

"They're ripening beautifully," she says. "You really do need to think about buying those nets."

"I'll get them this afternoon. Only goodness knows what I'll do with all the fruit if I do manage to keep the birds off them – I've never made jam in my life."

Margaret snorts. "Well don't ask me – I can never get mine to set."

"Perhaps I'll give them to Adam so he can make some raspberry tarts for the café."

"He'd certainly make the best of them – he's such a talented young man. Misunderstood by a lot of people around here, but then looking like a skinhead and keeping himself to himself doesn't exactly help."

"So he doesn't get involved with the life of the village in the way Owen does?"

"Well no, but then he's not from around here."

"From his accent I thought that he was."

Margaret laughs. "You're obviously not tuned into the local subtleties yet. Adam's from Leeds – Owen met him when he was at university there."

"I didn't realise they went back that far. Judging by the paintwork on the café, I assumed the business was pretty new."

"It is. They only started it at Easter. Owen's a pharmacist by profession, you know, only he gave it up when his grandmother fell ill so he could look after her. Once she died he never went back to it. I don't know why."

"What was wrong with her?"

"She had cancer and it was a nasty drawn out business for both of them. It's lucky that Adam moved in straight afterwards because Owen would be very lonely on his own."

"Are you lonely on your own, Margaret?" I ask.

"Sometimes. But I just get on with it. Why, are you?"

I hesitate. "I...I don't really like to think about it. I'd rather keep myself busy, you know, so I don't have time."

She reaches out and pats my hand. "It's much the best way, dear."

I know she's right. But I also know I need more than just activity; I need to find something to do that will use my brain. As I carry the nettles to the compost heap it strikes me: Owen's problems with the café have provided me with the perfect opportunity to help him and to help myself at the same time.

I reach Caffé Bianco just before closing time; the last customers are going out just as I am coming in.

Owen looks up from the counter and smiles. "Hello, Alice. What can I get you?"

"Skinny latte please." I delve into my bag for my purse but he stops me.

"Oh no, this one's on the house. We're shut, anyway."

"Owen..."

"No argument." He turns to the coffee machine. "You couldn't put the sign to closed and pop the bolt across for me, could you?"

Adam drifts out of the kitchen. "I could do with a coffee too. Alright, Alice?"

"Fine thanks. You?"

"Better now. Started the day with a hell of a hangover though. Not good for a Monday."

"You can say that again," Owen snaps.

"Oh, don't go on. You know why it happened – now just leave it, alright?"

"But every time you..."

"OK, OK – so I'm lousy at choosing boyfriends – there's no need to rub it in." Adam sounds quite vicious, and there is an uneasy silence while Owen makes two lattes and an espresso for himself.

"I've come to talk to you about an idea I had to help the business," I falter, "but if now's not a good time..."

"Oh, Alice – you are sweet, but you shouldn't worry about us," says Owen a fraction too carelessly.

Adam snorts. "Don't bullshit, Owen. All you ever do is moan about how bad things are, and how we'll struggle to be here next month."

"We won't be if I can't persuade the bank to give us some breathing space."

"Won't trade pick up over the summer, with the tourists and that?" I offer.

"Well it might if we weren't stuck down an alleyway in the back of beyond," grumbles Adam.

"It's not the back of beyond," Owen retaliates. "It's on the main footpath to the biggest car park – and anyway it was the only place we could afford."

I don't want this to escalate into an even bigger argument so I step in quickly.

"So what we really need to do is let people know you're here."

Owen folds his arms. "We can't afford to advertise, we haven't got any money."

"You're like a fucking parrot these days," Adam shoots back, "'we haven't got any money, we haven't got any money'". His mimicry of Owen's posh accent is cruelly accurate.

"Hey, cool it guys. This isn't getting us anywhere and it's beginning to piss me off."

Adam fiddles with the handle of his mug and Owen straightens a pile of paper serviettes. Neither of them looks at me.

I take a deep breath. "OK, there are things we can do very, very cheaply to promote the café; things I can do at home on the computer for the price of a few reams of coloured paper and a printer cartridge. Leaflets for car windscreens, discount vouchers, loyalty cards – all sorts of stuff. Please let me try – you've both been so kind to me."

"That sounds great," says Adam. "We can offer a free coffee when they buy a cake or summat..."

"I don't think we need to be that generous," I smile.

Owen opens his mouth to speak, but Adam cuts across him, "If you say 'we haven't got any money' I'll thump you."

"I wasn't going to say that. I was just going to say thank you."

Adam puts an enormous arm around his shoulder and gives him a squeeze. "Good lad."

I am half way to the car park when Owen catches up with me. I hear his footsteps running so I turn to wait.

"You shouldn't have had to have witnessed that," he tells me, "I apologise. For both of us."

"I understand. It's a stressful situation."

He pushes his hair back, running his hand over his head in what is becoming a familiar gesture. "You're not wrong. It seems like I'm perpetually tired, just trying to work out what to do. And I'm afraid I take it out on Adam when I shouldn't. Especially when he's just been chucked by someone he was beginning to care about. I ought to be more patient with him I know, but..."

"If there are times you can't talk to him about stuff, then you can always talk to me."

"Thanks, Alice. I really do appreciate it." And he hugs me; a proper hug, not one of his little quick ones, a real hug where I feel the warmth of his body through his shirt. As I walk away my heart begins to sing. Most inappropriately, so I tell it in no uncertain terms to shut up.

# Chapter Fourteen

I am most surprised to see Richard's van pull into the drive. I haven't seen hide nor hair of him since the night of the fete, but on a practical level I wasn't expecting to, knowing he was waiting for the damp proofer before being able to get any further with the barn. All the same, at the back of my mind was the nagging thought that I might have lost my builder.

Apparently I haven't. "How you doing, Princess?" he calls as he crunches across the gravel.

"Good, thanks. You?"

"Busy as hell with this dry weather. But I am free this evening – fancy coming out for a bite to eat?"

I hesitate. The night of the fete is very much unfinished business between us but somehow I don't want to be the one to bring it up. Our eyes meet, and all of a sudden Richard looks more than a little uncomfortable.

"Look, I can understand if...well..." he tails off for a moment before starting again. "Look, can I just come in for a minute?"

I nod and lead him as far as the garden room where I perch on the edge of my desk while Richard stands in front of me, looking rather like an exceptionally tall and dusty schoolboy.

"Alice, about, you know...I could say it was the drink but I'd rather just tell you I've never, ever done anything like that before and hope I never do again."

He looks so wretched I try to make light of it. "You've probably never had to."

He smiles fleetingly. "I'm not that irresistible – wish I was. But honestly, I…well, you know, I'll understand if you want to find another builder. I mean, I might have hurt you and it might be hard to have me around the house after that."

"I might have hurt you, kneeing you in the groin."

"Thankfully I was too drunk to feel very much, although I did wake up with a hell of a bruise on my thigh."

"Well let's just say I won't give you another one unless you deserve it."

"Deal." We shake hands solemnly. "D'you want to come out then?" he asks. "There's a good band playing at a pub in Bedale."

"Not tonight, Richard – I'm a bit tired. Another time, maybe?"

"Fair enough." He starts towards the door but then he says "There's just one thing, Alice – why did you call me Charles?"

"Charles?"

"Yes, when you yelled at me to stop, you called me Charles."

"Did I?"

"I wondered if Charles was your ex or something."

"No – he was Neil. And for all his faults, Neil was never aggressive."

Richard winces. "I didn't think I could be either. I may have thumped a bloke or two but I've never touched a woman in anger in my life, but there I was, trying to force you..."

"We were both very drunk."

"I've been drunker. I've been over it time and again in my own head and I still don't know why I did it – it was almost like it was happening to someone else."

"Someone called Charles, maybe?" I joke.

Richard laughs as he climbs into his van. "Let's hope so – it would get me off the hook, anyway."

# Chapter Fifteen

It is with a great deal of satisfaction I close my computer down. I pick up a sheaf of papers from my printer; red and white Caffé Bianco leaflet and loyalty card mock ups. They look clean, fresh and eye-catching and I am sure Owen and Adam will like them. I send a text to let Owen know they are ready, and wait for his reply.

In the end I wait almost a whole day. And it annoys me, because although I am busy moving my bed into the spare room ready to decorate my own bedroom and putting the nets over the raspberries, I am acutely aware that I am waiting. I keep picking up my phone to make sure I haven't missed it bleep and that exasperates me even more. I stuff it in the cutlery drawer and don't look again for a whole hour.

As I potter around avoiding the kitchen I try to make sense of it; surely if Owen really likes me he wouldn't leave me hanging on like this? And as he's not showing a great deal of interest, why am I hanging around waiting for him? I end up feeling like a sad loser and over the course of the day I become more and more miserable.

At last I receive a reply from Owen: 'Can you come to the house tonight – about 8.30?' I cheer up instantly. Bugger.

I hear Kylie bark in the distance when I ring the doorbell, then footsteps in the hall. Owen has changed out of his work clothes into a bright blue tie-dyed T-shirt and the colour really suits him. He leads me into a dining room at the back of the house.

"I hope we'll be comfortable enough in here, but it will be easier to spread things out if we work on the table." He pulls back a chair and I sit down.

"Now, what would you like to drink? Glass of wine? Cup of tea?"

"A glass of wine would be nice."

"I've got some dry white in the fridge – is that OK?"

"It would be lovely."

As I wait for him to come back I examine my surroundings and find that they are not so very different in style to the front room. The table and chairs are of the period of the house, and in a rich mahogany. The table is covered with an old fashioned chenille protector which matches the slightly faded dark green velvet curtains.

When Owen comes back he is smiling cheerily and carrying two large glasses of wine.

"Is Adam joining us?" I ask.

"No, he goes to Middlesborough on a Thursday night – there's quite a gay scene there and he enjoys it better than being buried in the country. He says hello though." He laughs, "I think he's rather taken to you, you know – it's a great compliment – he normally can't stand women."

I get the sample leaflets out of my bag and explain what I've done. Owen suggests small changes to the wording here and there and we include a voucher for a half price cup of coffee. Owen likes the loyalty card as it is; with any luck it will keep people coming back, but in reality Adam's cakes alone ought to do the trick.

Finally I pull out a poster, with a little map showing directions to the café.

"That's all very well, Alice," says Owen, "but we really need something like this at the end of the alleyway."

"Sorted – I hope." I have my fingers crossed here; I've been a bit cheeky and he mightn't like what I've done. "I've got quite friendly with the woman in the haberdashery on the corner, and she's willing to put it in her window provided you give her staff a 20% discount."

Owen is open mouthed and I back pedal rapidly. "I know 20% sounds a lot but she strikes a hard bargain. I could always go back to her though…I haven't promised..."

"Oh Alice, it's not that at all – you're wonderful, really you are. How on earth did you think of doing that?"

I shrug my shoulders. "I've worked in selling all my life and it feels like I've always known this sort of stuff. It comes naturally. Anyway," I carry on quickly, "how do you want to tweak the poster?"

We talk for a little longer, and when everything is finalised and I've finished my wine I stand up to leave. I say everything, but there is still a small piece of card in my pocket and I can't decide whether to give it to Owen or not. But he seems a bit less tense than he has been of late so I decide to risk it. It's a little trick I read about in Psychologies magazine.

"I've got something for you," I venture, and I press it into his hand.

He reads it out loud: "This too will pass."

"For when you're having a particularly shitty day. Stuff it in your pocket and remember it's there."

"Alice, that's so sweet of you…it might just help me to keep everything in perspective and stop me taking it all out on Adam. He really doesn't deserve it."

"We normally do take things out on the people closest to us."

He smiles a wry smile. "Yes, worrying, isn't it? Sometimes… sometimes the harder you try with someone the more you tie yourself up in knots." And I wonder if maybe, just maybe, he might be talking about me.

"Perhaps the answer's not to fret about it too much," I suggest, knowing only too well it's easier said than done.

Owen offers to walk me home and we stroll in silence back to New Cottage. I am half way up the drive, some yards away from him, when I turn to say goodnight.

"Come here." His voice is different; soft, low, yet commanding in a way which sends shivers down my spine.

I retrace my steps and he hugs me; tenderly but firmly, and then he drops a gentle kiss onto my cheek.

I find myself saying, "Don't disappear on me" – but I don't know where the words come from.

"I'll try not to." He touches my shoulder and smiles, and then he is gone. I raise my fingers to my cheek as I watch him walk up the village.

# Chapter Sixteen

Although I never realised it, in suburbia there is a constant hum, even at night; distant traffic, the muted burble of TVs, the footsteps of late night dog walkers – and it is all quietly comforting. Out here, well, there's nothing.

If it really was nothing then I could get used to that; the trouble is the long stretches of nothing punctuated by sudden alarming noises which always wake me up. At first the screeches and screams completely unnerved me but when I mentioned them to Margaret she explained they were owls or foxes, so rather than being irrefutable evidence of murderers under my bedroom window they are just a pain in the neck.

It doesn't help that it's so muggy I have to sleep with the windows open. It's an invitation to every bug in Yorkshire and most of them buzz and some of them even bite. After weeks and weeks of rural sleep deprivation I am starting to feel decidedly grouchy.

Most mornings I'm a bit of a zombie so it is no surprise that I'm staring blankly out of the kitchen window when I hear a scrunch of tyres on the gravel. I'm not expecting anyone, but soon I hear Richard's voice calling.

"Yoo-hoo, Princess, are you there? I've brought Bob to have a look at the damp proofing work."

"How do you always know when I've just put the kettle on?" I yell back, trying to stir myself. "Come through to the kitchen."

After our cup of tea I open the big barn doors to let the light stream in and William and I follow the men as they walk around inside, looking critically at the cobwebbed walls and scratching around in the cracks in the concrete floor.

"This will all have to come up," Bob explains. "Then I'll put a plastic membrane underneath and inject a chemical damp proof course all round the walls."

"It doesn't seem that damp to me," I venture.

"No, love, but the air can get through it now. You have it all cosy and sealed in, and you'll soon have a problem. Just re-concreting the floor might make the place damp. Best do the job properly."

I'm not completely convinced but Richard is nodding and I have to trust his judgment; anyway, I'm feeling particularly crabby so it's better to keep my mouth shut.

It's too hot for much in the way of lunch so William and I spend a few hours in the garden. The area destined to become the patio for the holiday let is out of the afternoon sun so I attack the weeds until my arms are raw with scratches from the brambles. One cut is quite deep and stings like hell. After a futile hunt for the Savlon I grab my keys and handbag and head for Boots in Northallerton.

On the way back to the car I find myself in the alleyway that passes Caffé Bianco. I have heard nothing from Owen since that wonderful kiss on the cheek last week – it seems beyond him to reply to a text – but even so I have half a mind to pop in to see him if he's not too busy. When I peep through the door Owen is leaning on the counter, deep in conversation with a skinny blonde. I turn away before he notices me.

When I get back to the car I positively throw my handbag into the footwell and slam the gears into reverse. I am about to pull out when I catch sight of myself in the rear view mirror. The months of stress are taking their toll and I am confronted by a pair of sunken brown eyes peering miserably at the wrinkles forming around them. The rosiness in my cheeks has been replaced by an unhealthy pallor and there is a nasty spot on the side of my nose. No wonder Owen prefers talking to the skinny blonde.

I take my foot off the clutch and the car stalls. Hot tears well up behind my eyelids. But after a few moments I tell myself to get a grip; I only look so rubbish and feet so grotty and ratty and confused about everything because I am so tired. I make a split second decision; straight back to Boots to buy the most expensive face pack they have and a packet of Sleep-Eazee. And there's no way I'm walking past Caffé Bianco.

## Chapter Seventeen

The first time I wake it's pitch black. The hours of true darkness are very few at this time of year and if I don't go back to sleep then I'm in for a long one. For a while I stare at the ceiling, trying not to think of anything very much but focusing on my breathing. When that doesn't work I indulge myself in a little fantasy of being held in someone's (alright, Owen's) arms. When that doesn't work I remember the sleeping pills in my handbag.

They must have an effect because I doze off for a while, but then I wake with a jump, feeling completely disorientated. There is a noise which seems to be coming from somewhere inside the house, but after grappling with it for a few moments I realise it isn't inside at all; it's the crying I heard before but now it sounds very close.

Wide awake, I sit up and listen, but once again I can't pinpoint the sound. It seems louder when I lean out of the open window, but I can't tell where it's coming from. The sobs are truly heartbreaking; someone's in real trouble somewhere and I hope they have someone to comfort them. Rather selfishly, I also hope that even if they haven't they'll shut up.

I close the window and crawl under the duvet. The crying doesn't seem any quieter and I stick my head under the pillow, which works to a degree, but just as I am dropping off the weeping reaches a new crescendo. As if that isn't enough it wakes William and he starts whining. I yell at him to pack it in. There is peace (from him at least) for about five minutes, and then he starts up again.

I fling back the duvet and stalk down the stairs, almost tripping over my handbag. I pick it up, march into the garden room and let William out. Daybreak is seeping into the sky and I watch him race across the lawn to cock his leg on a tree. He seems undisturbed by the crying now, but it sure is bothering me. I wonder if taking more sleeping tablets would block it out and I read the label on the packet; you can take up to eight pills so I down another six with alacrity.

I know they won't work straight away so I follow William across the garden. He is sniffing around in the long flowerbed that stretches towards the pond. I can still hear the crying but it doesn't seem to be coming from a neighbour's house; if anything the sound is eddying around and I resolve to follow it.

William and I walk towards the little orchard, but the noise becomes fainter and we retrace our steps until we are standing between the garden room and the barn. Here the crying seems to be bouncing off the buildings and the noise intensifies until I can hardly bear it. William starts to whimper and I begin to feel uneasy – and then I begin to wonder if it can possibly be coming from inside the barn.

My desperate desire to make the noise stop is stronger than my growing fear. Keeping William to heel I walk up the side of the barn and open the small door. But inside all is quiet, just the peaceful munching of the two cattle as they chew the cud. No-one crying at all. Very gently, I close the door.

When I realise what I have seen I am rooted to the spot. But I don't dare open the door again to check if the cows are still standing in their stalls, and if the sweet smell of fresh hay still permeates the air. My hand is locked onto the handle, but I am too scared to turn it, and still the crying goes on and on. Then William licks my bare leg and I am galvanised into action, running back into the garden room and slamming the door.

William flops onto his rug and looks at me expectantly; he's after a biscuit. As I pull one from the box on the shelf I notice the sleeping tablets. I have to shut out that noise or I'll go mad. I give William his treat, fling a few more pills down my throat, and curl up next to him. His fur is soft and warm. Under my hand his little heart beats solidly.

## Chapter Eighteen

At first I can only feel, and hear. William wriggles out from under my arm and starts to bark; a corner of my brain realises he wants to go out but I am incapable of doing anything about it. So I am thankful when I hear the garden room door creak open. But I'm not grateful for long, because Margaret is calling my name and shaking me. I want to tell her to go away but for some reason I can't speak. She must understand what I want though, because after a little while she leaves.

My peace isn't meant to last. I am hauled into a sitting position but my head lolls forwards and I can't lift it to see who's holding my shoulders.

"Alice – Alice – how many of those bloody tablets did you take?" I register the fact that it is Owen's voice, but I can't answer. He holds me upright with one hand while his other finds my pulse. He swears – uses the f-word in fact, and then says something about mustard.

"Don't like mustard," I try to mumble, but I lose track of what's going on, except that Margaret is holding me up and she won't stop talking. "Had to stop the crying," I tell her, "please let me sleep." But she won't, and the next thing I know Owen is forcing some disgusting liquid down my throat. I gag and spit it out.

He shakes me gently. "Alice, can you hear me? This is really,

really important." His voice is urgent so I try to concentrate. I also try to lift my head and open my eyes to look at him, but I only have a very narrow range of vision.

He is speaking again. "You've taken too many tablets and they're making you ill. You have to drink this; it'll make you very sick, but if you don't I'll need to call an ambulance and they'll take you to hospital and pump your stomach out. You don't want that to happen, Alice, do you?" I manage to shake my head.

"Good. Now come on, I'll hold you up." He shuffles to my side and props me against his shoulder. "Now drink." He tips the glass into my mouth again and I take the liquid down. Then I am vomiting into a bucket I didn't know was on my lap and William is barking and snarling.

"Get that bloody dog away from me!" Owen yells, then William's claws drag along the floor and Margaret murmurs

"It's OK, fella, Owen's only trying to help her, ssshhh..."

Her remonstrations don't work and I guess she takes him outside because the barking becomes quieter. I am exhausted by it all and lean against Owen.

"Come on Alice, talk to me, you must stay awake."

"So tired...the crying..."

He drops a kiss onto the top of my head. "Oh, you poor angel, and I've been such a selfish shit, wrapped up in myself..." He reasserts himself. "Alice, talk to me. Do you know who I am?"

"Owen."

"That's right. And where do I live?"

"Next to Margaret."

"And what's my café called?"

He questions me relentlessly and after a while it becomes easier to answer. He feels my pulse again and I am aware of his body relaxing a little beside me.

"Margaret told me you're a pharmacist."

"Yes, I was."

"Why did you stop?"

"I'll tell you in a minute. But first I'm going to take you upstairs to bed, because you need to rest."

I try to smile. "I thought I wasn't meant to go to sleep."

"There's a difference between sleeping and falling unconscious. You chucked up a fair few of those pills, your pulse is normal, and you're more with it now."

"How do you know?"

"Because you're asking me the questions."

He wriggles around until he is kneeling beside me and puts his arms under my thighs and back. He lifts me easily for such a slightly built man and carries me through the dining room and up the stairs. He pauses at the top for a moment, then sees my unmade bed through the open door in front of him and puts me gently down on it, covering me with the duvet.

He sits on the edge of the bed and holds my hand. I open my eyes properly and look at him; his face is pinched and pale and there are dark circles under his eyes, but I still get lost in that incredible blue – it is almost as though I am hypnotised by it as I fall asleep.

From the moment of waking I am aware I am not alone in the room. I can't work out why, but when I open my eyes and see Margaret sitting by the window reading I remember and inwardly cringe with embarrassment.

"Margaret," I say, and she looks up from her book. "I am so sorry for all the trouble I put you and Owen to. Really I am."

"That's OK, Alice. We're just kicking ourselves for not noticing how low you'd become. Some neighbours we turned out to be."

I am puzzled for a moment but then the penny drops. "I didn't take the tablets deliberately," I explain. "At least, not for the reason you think. It's just I haven't been sleeping well and I was getting pretty desperate." It doesn't sound like a particularly convincing explanation.

"You said something about stopping crying – it made us think..."

"It wasn't me crying, it was someone else."

"Someone else?"

I haul myself into a sitting position. My mouth feels like a hedgehog has been sleeping in it, but there is some water by my bed and I take a sip.

"It's someone nearby. I've heard them before, a few weeks ago, but last night they sounded really distraught. I got up and tried to trace where it was coming from but I couldn't pin the sound down. It was weird."

"It couldn't have been an animal, could it?"

"I did wonder the first time I heard it – I had a friend who had a Siamese cat that cried like a baby – but last night it was a definite sobbing, and it never sounded like a child anyway."

Margaret frowns. "How very odd."

I wonder whether to tell her what I saw in the barn but decide against it. Instead I swing my legs over the edge of the bed.

"I think I'll go and clean my teeth and have a shower."

"Are you sure you're up to it? Owen said you'd feel very wobbly and you were to stay in bed until he got back."

"I'll be careful, I promise. I don't want to cause you any more grief."

Owen was right; I do feel rather weak and feeble so I take the precaution of not locking the bathroom door. As I haul the long T-shirt I sleep in over my head realisation dawns that it was all I was wearing – no underwear, no nothing. I was in such a state too; the chances were that I was fairly indecent. I look down at my naked body in horror.

The shower exhausts me and afterwards I sit up in bed sipping my water, trying to chat to Margaret. Footsteps crunch on the gravel and she peeks out of the window.

"It's Owen," she tells me. "He said he'd be back as soon as the café quietened down."

We hear William growl, and before I even have time to blush Owen's head appears around the bedroom door. "Can I come in?" he asks.

I manage to smile and Margaret nods.

He sits down on the bed. "So, how are you feeling, Alice?"

I have to put on a show for him – just have to. "Better, much better, thanks. You and Margaret – you've been wonderful – I don't know what would have happened without you."

"Well I do, and I break out into a cold sweat every time I think of it." He laughs but it sounds false. "William hasn't forgiven me for making you sick yet, but it's a small price to pay." He indicates a bag in his hand. "Right – are you feeling hungry? Because Adam's baked you some lavender shortbread which should be nice and gentle on your tummy."

"Well isn't that kind of him," exclaims Margaret. "I'll make some tea to go with it."

Once she leaves there is a silence and as usual I feel I have to fill it.

"Owen – there's something I need to explain. You both thought I took those tablets deliberately, didn't you? Well that wasn't the case. I was just desperate to get some sleep. I took a couple, but that didn't work because…well…it just didn't. Then William wanted to go out and I read the bottle and it said you could take eight so I..."

"No more than eight in a twenty-four hour period, probably."

I feel about five years old. "Oh," is all I manage to say, but then a thought strikes me. "Is there anything in them that could be hallucinogenic?"

"Perhaps. Those over the counter remedies aren't sweeties after all. It really pisses me off that people think they can help you but can't harm you – they can be very powerful and people just don't realise."

"I guess I thought that," I mumble.

"Well don't buy any more. If you have trouble sleeping then get up and make yourself a camomile tea or something." He sounds quite grumpy.

I stretch out my hand and cover his. "Owen, I am so sorry. You don't need this on top of everything else."

I have the impression he's about to say something, but Margaret comes in with a tray of tea and plates and instead he starts fussing with the shortbread.

# Chapter Nineteen

Owen and Margaret clearly didn't buy my explanation about the tablets and have decided I need watching. I am curiously ambivalent about their assumption; on the one hand it is acutely embarrassing, but on the other it's quite nice to be made a fuss of for a change.

Margaret spends most of the next day working in my garden and popping in and out of the house, so I tell her I'm planning to go to Leeds so that she doesn't feel she has to do it again. Of course, then I really do have to go, but apart from getting lost on the ring road, I actually enjoy my day in the big city and treat myself to a very expensive facial at Harvey Nichols.

In the evening Owen calls and we take the dogs for a walk to Scruton. He is cheerful, solicitous and charming; when he hears I've been to Leeds he makes me laugh with stories about his student days, but he can't hide the black circles beneath his eyes.

On Friday they bring Adam into the campaign and he drops by for an hour on his way back from work to deliver a batch of pasties for my freezer and to ask me to supper the next night. It is he who tells me how busy the café has been and asks if I'd mind helping out on Monday because Owen won't be around. I have the feeling it's another ploy to keep me occupied and under observation, but I am very happy to accept.

I dress up a little for supper on Saturday; nothing over the top, but it's nice get out of my decorating gear and put on a skirt and a fancy T-shirt. Margaret is invited too and I can't see her turning up in her gardening trousers. I've been hanging wallpaper in my bedroom all day, so it's lovely to sink into the bath for an hour, dress in clean clothes, grab a bottle of wine from the rack and make my way up the village.

William is invited too but he instantly disgraces himself by emitting a low growl when Owen opens the door.

"You really must cut that out," I tell him, "Owen was helping me, not hurting me. Can't you get that into your thick head?" But I guess spaniels aren't exactly noted for their intelligence.

Owen takes it in good part and leads me to a small patio at the back of the house, where the table is set and Margaret already has a glass in her hand. Kylie is lying in the shade half way up the lawn and I shoo William off to join her.

Owen disappears into the kitchen leaving Margaret and me alone. We wander up the garden to look at her flower bed and I am amazed at the array of scent and colour. Stocks, towering gladioli, gerberas in soft, muted colours. I have a strong suspicion she also knows how to arrange them properly.

Closer to the kitchen is a large border given completely over to herbs. I don't pretend to recognise many of them, but the bed is neatly tended and each plant carefully labelled.

"Do you grow these as well?" I ask Margaret.

"No – this bit's down to Owen."

"I expect Adam finds them useful in the kitchen."

"Actually, they're nothing to do with Adam. They've been here as long as I can remember. Owen's grandmother..."

Owen materialises beside us and thrusts a glass of wine into my hand. "Dry white, isn't it?" he asks.

"I was just admiring your herbs."

"Oh, they're very much the poor relation next to Margaret's glads. Come on, let's sit down – Adam's getting some of his gorgeous nibbly bits out of the oven."

The food is excellent. The nibbly bits turn out to be melt in the mouth savoury palmiers and tiny cheese straws. Next there is pasta, with a creamy sauce full of delicate herbal flavours and shreds of parma ham. The dessert is naturally the piece de resistance; mille feuille packed full of fresh apricots and peaches, nestling in the lightest whipped cream I've ever tasted.

"Where on earth did you learn to cook?" I ask Adam.

"When Owen and I were sharing a flat in Leeds, at first I didn't have a job so I watched loads of daytime TV and found I was really interested in the cookery programmes. I managed to find work as a kitchen porter in a restaurant and I absolutely loved it. Luckily the owner had a bit of faith in me and sent me on day release to learn how to be a pastry chef. I worked for him until Owen's gran got ill, then I got a job as sous-chef at Crathorne Hall so I could be around to help Owen out. I learnt an unbelievable amount there and ended up doing the cakes for their afternoon teas. It's what I'm best at, but I still like doing other things."

"You're so lucky having a job you love."

"I know. I just wish Owen..."

"I do love the café, Adam, you know that."

"But you're wasted there."

"It's what I want to do."

Owen clenches his jaw and I'm scared they are about to argue, but Adam just pats his hand and says, "Sorry mate. I didn't mean to be ungrateful," and Owen offers to make some peppermint tea. I am surprised when he walks over to the herb patch and picks the mint fresh, but I don't know why I should be. If the herbs were his grandmother's he's probably been doing it all his life.

I have drunk just a fraction too much wine and I lean back in my chair. Adam and Margaret are talking about a TV programme I've never seen and I let my mind drift, trying to imagine what Owen's childhood was like. I half close my eyes and I can see a fair haired boy following an old woman along the herb garden. They seem to be playing a game where she hides the labels on the plants and he tells her what they are and I find myself drawn in, intrigued. I can hear the whispering of their voices, but not catch the words. Then Owen puts the teapot and mugs down on the table with a clatter and I wake up.

# Chapter Twenty

Adam picks me up just after eight on Monday morning.

"You're bright and early," I say as I jump into the car.

He snorts. "I've already been into town once – Owen got the six o'clock train."

"Where's he gone?"

"London."

"He went before, didn't he? Does he have friends there?"

"No; it's business."

"What, to do with the café?"

In response, Adam turns up the radio. "It's too early for all these bloody questions," he tells me. Perhaps he's not a morning person.

Within a couple of hours he is perfectly cheerful. I prepare the café for the day then help him to make sandwiches ready for the lunchtime take out trade. Adam explains he'd really prefer each one to be made to order, but now the café is getting busier it's just not possible. He's not wrong; from eleven o'clock onwards I am rushed off my feet, but I wouldn't want it any other way.

By the time Adam and I wash up and put everything away it's pretty late.

Adam leans back against the kitchen table. "Fancy a quick pint?" he asks.

"I do – but I really can't leave William any longer. Margaret was popping in to let him out at lunchtime, but he won't be very happy by now." I have a sudden thought. "Perhaps we can walk the dogs to The Black Horse instead."

"I'd like that. For a moment there, Alice, I thought you were going to turn me down because you had a date."

I have a vague suspicion his question might be loaded. I pick my words carefully. "No date, no boyfriend."

"Really? Owen thought you and Richard..."

"He's not my boyfriend," I snort. "He's not my type at all."

Adam can barely keep the look of triumph from his face.

# Chapter Twenty-One

I wait outside with the dogs while Adam goes into the pub for the drinks, the evening sun warming my bare arms and face. For the last hour or so I have been positively fizzing inside, wondering if Adam's rather artificial question could possibly mean what I hope it does. I am eager to turn the conversation towards Owen and when Adam sits down opposite me I lose no time in asking him how they became friends.

"The stock answer is when Owen was at uni in Leeds. But the full version is rather longer, and not something either of us talks about."

"Oh, that's OK, I didn't mean to pry," I say, trying not to sound too disappointed.

"No, I am going to tell you, because I want you to understand what a special guy Owen is. He's a bit tired and stressed at the moment – it's making him moody, but it's not his fault – and I wouldn't want you to get the wrong impression about what he's really like.

"I didn't settle very well at school and I was always in trouble as a teenager. By the time I was eighteen I was into drugs and got caught selling some to a young lass so I ended up in prison. That's where I met Owen. Not that Owen was inside, obviously, but the Christian Union at Leeds Uni ran a prison visiting programme and Owen signed up for it.

"Prison was awful for me. I'd thought I was tough, but life inside for a young gay man was brutal, to say the least. But I had a good social worker who put me forward for this visiting. The first bloke they sent was a complete arsehole, really condescending, and I nearly didn't give it another go, so I was ready to fight back all guns blazing when Owen turned up.

"At least, I'd meant to, but instead of some bigoted do-gooder I was confronted with a little lad trying to stop his voice from shaking as he pushed a bar of chocolate across the table and said 'I didn't know what to bring – if you'd prefer something different next time, let me know – if you decide you want me to come again, that is'. His whole attitude was so unlike the guy before; there was no question that he didn't see me as an equal, and that persuaded me to give it a real go. I was pretty desperate for a friend, anyway.

"When I look back on it now, Owen was the first person who had been genuinely interested in me for who I was. He was such an innocent he'd never met anyone remotely like me; and I'd never met anyone like him either. Well, Alice, he's kindness personified and once I began to realise there were no hidden agendas, I let myself trust him and we got on like a house on fire.

"My release date coincided with the start of Owen's second year and before I even came out we'd decided we were going to share a flat. Owen had plenty of student friends but he was far too serious to get involved with all the normal horseplay and he said he wanted a life outside the university as well.

"We had really high hopes but initially it was a disaster. I'd expected Owen to have all the time in the world for me but the reality was that he had to study very hard. I didn't have a job and I soon fell back in with my old crowd and old ways. I don't know, maybe I was pushing Owen to make me his number one priority and show the sort of commitment I felt for him. Only back then I wasn't canny enough to realise it.

"It came to a head one night when I came back to find him waiting up, absolutely furious. He accused me of taking drugs, and when I denied it he actually ripped the sleeve off my shirt to expose the needle marks. I was gobsmacked – I didn't know he had it in him. The next thing I knew he was throwing my stuff onto the landing and we were yelling at each other like a couple of banshees until one of the neighbours came out and told us in no uncertain terms to put a sock in it or he'd throw a bucket of cold water over us.

"It made me realise how much I had to lose. We sat up all night and well into the next day, talking about what we both needed to do to put things right. I agreed to go on a rehab programme, and he agreed to give me all the support I needed while I did it. I promised not to see my old friends again, so I wouldn't get drawn back into crime. He explained he couldn't watch me rip my life apart – he was training to be a pharmacist – he knew more about drugs than most people, after all.

"And he stuck to his word – despite all the studying he had to do he was always there for me. You see, Alice, without Owen I'd have just pissed my life away. And I'm not the only person around here who owes him a great deal."

"How so?"

Adam shakes his head. "That's for him to tell you when he's good and ready. All I've done is share my story, not his."

My voice sounds very small. "I'd like to hear Owen's story, get to know him better..."

"You care about Owen, don't you?"

I nod. This is no time to lie; not to Adam and not to myself.

"Not in a just-good-friends sort of way?"

I nod again.

"Well thank fuck for that."

I start to giggle uncontrollably. Then Adam joins in with a horrible noisy cackle that makes William jump up from my feet and bark. So we laugh even more, until the tears are rolling down our cheeks. I finally manage to stand up.

"Come on," I tell him, "time I was getting back – William's hungry."

As we round the last bend into Great Fencote I am surprised to see Owen striding along the edge of the green towards us.

"Adam – it's Owen."

"Where?"

"There, you idi..."

But when I look again, Owen isn't there. With a horrible sense of déjà vu I break into a run, dragging William behind me. The only place Owen can be is behind one of the trees and I am determined to prove to myself he's there. I keep them in my line of vision as I run – it's only a couple of hundred yards – and when I get to the green William and I circle them. No Owen. No-one there at all. But then William lets out a low growl.

Adam has caught me up. "Alice – what are you on about? I'm not picking Owen up from the station until eleven o'clock tonight. He'd have phoned me if he was getting an earlier train."

"I saw him, Adam, I know I did. He was walking towards us, under the trees."

"It must have been a trick of the light, pet."

But I know it wasn't. I also know that I don't understand what I've seen – it makes no sense. I am fully awake, I have taken not a single tablet and I have drunk all of half a pint of beer. I say goodnight to Adam, feed William, and start to cook my supper, all on autopilot.

If it hadn't happened before it might be different. But this is the third time; and two of them in broad daylight. I turn off the heat under my pasta. All the elation of the early evening has disappeared. What the hell is going on?

## Chapter Twenty-Two

If I couldn't get my head around it last night I'm doing no better this morning. I take my coffee to the bench by the pond, determined to think this through logically. Who, or what, have I seen on the village green a total of three times now? The thought it might be a what occurred to me at about three in the morning, but in the bright light of day I remember that I don't believe in ghosts.

The obvious answer is that it is Owen, and he was playing some kind of trick on me, but I cannot begin to imagine what it might be. It's still in the back of my mind that Matt called him creepy, but it's so much at odds with the story Adam told me that I can't believe he's right.

So I decide I need to focus on what I do know: twice I have seen Owen when he is supposed to be in London, but I only have Adam's word he was actually there. However the other time it couldn't have been Owen; it might have been him sitting under the tree, but he couldn't have been walking towards Kirkby Fleetham when he was calling me from the opposite direction.

So I have the facts, but they don't make sense. Surely I can't be imagining Owen's there? Did just talking about him with Adam make me want to see him so much he materialised in my mind? Is my fondness for Owen bordering on obsession, even? Now that is a very worrying thought and I push it away, but all the same I am aware I'm thinking about Owen and hoping my phone will ring pretty much all day.

My phone does ring the next morning, but it's Adam telling me he's made another batch of pasties and asking if I can pop around to the house this evening to collect them. It is only after I hang up that I wonder why he doesn't just drop them off like he did before.

When I arrive Adam bundles me inside.

"You've got time for a quick drink, I hope?" he asks.

"Yes, that would be nice."

As we pass the bottom of the staircase he yells, "Owen, Alice is here," and without waiting for a reply he leads me into the garden.

It takes an age for Owen to appear and Adam is getting fidgety. The penny begins to drop he is setting us up, but before I can say anything Owen strolls through the kitchen door and with a nonchalant "Hi Alice" throws himself down on the chair next to Adam. I almost laugh because he is so obviously freshly washed and shaved. But I changed myself, and put on some lip gloss; we are both trying really hard – too hard, probably.

Once Adam disappears it is difficult to keep the conversation going. Looking around for inspiration I spy the herb bed.

"Margaret said your grandmother planted the herbs and that you look after them now."

"Some of them pre-date Gran, even. See that rosemary – it was planted by her grandfather when they first came to the house."

"Really? I didn't know it lived that long."

"It's unusual, I admit."

"Want to give me a guided tour?" It's something to say.

We wander along the herb bed and Owen tells me the names of the more unusual plants. The evening air is filled with their scent as he rubs his hands over them, stroking them almost, to release their perfume. I notice how gentle his touch is and my insides turn almost liquid. We crouch close, next to the camomile, but I'm not really listening to what he's saying because all I want is for him to make love to me.

I stand up. "Margaret said there wasn't much your gran didn't know about herbs. Was she a good cook?"

"Yes, she was." He hesitates before carrying on, looking at me as though weighing me up. "But she used the herbs for other things."

"Like what?"

"Medicines" he says, not taking his eyes off mine.

"Medicines? Did they work?" I am now genuinely interested.

His face takes on a stubborn mask, like it did when he was trying to stop me working at the café. "Of course they did."

"So is that why you became a pharmacist?"

He gapes at me. "You spotted the connection. I don't think anyone else ever has – except Gran, of course."

I shrug. "It seems logical."

For a moment I think he is about to say something else, but he closes up and we walk back to the table in silence. The moment of intimacy has passed, but I can still smell the camomile. Even as he walks me and my bag of pasties home it fills my nostrils. There is no hug at my garden gate, but when he says goodnight there is a whole world of unsaid words in his eyes. Sadly, neither of us has the courage to speak.

## Chapter Twenty-Three

Adam clearly isn't going to let things rest there. It is quite early next morning when I receive a text: 'Owen didn't ask you then?'

'Ask me what?'

'I'm going to wring his fucking neck.'

I am still laughing to myself when my phone rings and Owen's number appears on the little screen.

"Good morning, Owen," I say. "How are you today?"

He sounds distracted. "Fine…fine…Alice – would you like to come out to supper with me on Saturday night?"

"I'd love to, really I would." There is a silence at the other end of the phone. "Owen?" I venture "Is Adam by any chance standing next to you with a gun at your head?"

"No – a kitchen knife in my kidneys actually – and don't think I'm joking." Suddenly we're both laughing and I can hear Adam's cackle in the background. I think it's going to be alright.

On Saturday afternoon I am like a teenager getting ready for a first date. I change my mind several times about my outfit but in the end decide on the same skirt I wore to church when Owen said I scrubbed up well. I also choose quite a tight embroidered T-shirt and my very best underwear; at least that way I feel sexy underneath even if I'm a bag of nerves everywhere else.

When Owen arrives he is smartly dressed in navy chinos and a shirt striped in the exact blue of his eyes. They are such a deep blue, almost purple in fact, and are by far his most striking feature. He's not conventionally good looking, I don't suppose, but seeing his generous lips break into a smile or those devastating eyes appear as he pushes his hair away certainly puts butterflies into my stomach.

He takes me to a pub high up on the Moors. It seems to be in the middle of nowhere but the tables outside are packed with people admiring the stunning views. We make our way through the chatter to the quiet calm of a low beamed bar, where Owen knows the manager.

"Friend of Adam's," he tells me. "He'll look after us."

All the way in the car Owen has chatted constantly, pointing out local landmarks, and now we are busy choosing our food and ordering drinks, but I know there will be a moment when an uneasy silence falls. It does, and as I don't want to talk shop, or about myself, or appear too nosey about him, I ask what his grandmother was like.

He puts his head on one side. "It's a long time since anyone's asked me that," he replies. "You see, everyone I know knew her too; we've always lived here..." he trails off, gathers himself then continues with a false brightness. "I think the last person to ask me was Adam, and that must have been about ten years ago. He was quite anxious about meeting her for the first time."

"I expect he was."

Owen looks a little surprised at my comment.

"Adam told me how you met. The full, unexpurgated version with no punches pulled."

"Wow – he must trust you."

"I hope he does, but I think he had an ulterior motive. He wanted to make sure I knew what a great guy you are." If anyone is going to push the conversation in this direction I know it has to be me.

"Adam's horribly biased," Owen laughs. "I hope you didn't fall for his pack of lies."

Hidden beneath his joking I half sense a hollow ring of truth. But I'm not going to be put off.

"Hook, line and sinker," I reply, trying to hold his gaze. "After all, it was you who told me that he's a man of his word."

Owen looks away and fiddles with his knife. "I thought…I thought you were seeing Richard and..."

"I was never 'seeing Richard' in the way he made you think. I overheard what he said to you that Sunday when you came to see how I was. I was so mad at him; I was cooking him supper and I spoiled it quite deliberately I was so cross. I haven't a clue why he said it."

"Well I have and she's called Maria. It was a long time ago but I guess it still rankles." He sighs and runs his hand over the top of his head before carrying quickly on. "Basically I'd been out of college a year or two and I'd just come back here to live. I worked for Boots and they moved me to the Bedale branch. I met Maria on the bus; she lived in Leeming Bar and worked in Bedale too, and we'd have a chat every day – she was really friendly.

"In the end I plucked up the courage to ask her out. I've never been much good at that sort of thing, as you might have noticed, but I made myself do it. She told me she had a boyfriend and had to finish with him first. I didn't have a clue that boyfriend was Richard until about a month later when we walked into The Black Horse and there he was. It was awful – a real scene – I'd never been in a fight before and I didn't come off too well. But I thought it was worth it because I was madly in love with Maria. As was Richard.

"Of course, eventually she went back to him and they married. It didn't last – I think they both had roving eyes, to be honest. Richard and I rub along OK nowadays, he even invited me to the wedding but at the time I was too cut up to go. So I suppose Richard thought he'd be getting one over on me if he said he was going out with you."

"Wow – he's got some memory – that's one long-time grudge to hold."

"Oh, I don't think it's a grudge, exactly." Owen looks a bit uncomfortable for a moment but then our food arrives and he skilfully changes the topic to safer, more general ground.

Although I'm nervous I am determined not to drink too much

and disgrace myself again. However I've still had enough to make me feel just a little bit brave by the time Owen drops me home.

"Why don't you go and park the car and then come back for a nightcap?" I ask him. When he agrees I tell him he'll find me by the pond.

It is late dusk, so as well as the brandy bottle and a couple of glasses I carry out an old glass oil lamp I bought on some forgotten holiday to Spain and rest it on the edge of the decking. It is hard to light with William capering around my legs, but I manage it by the time Owen crosses the lawn. William, rather rudely, stiffens and growls.

"Cut it out, you stupid dog," I murmur, ruffling his ears. "How many times do I have to tell you?"

Owen laughs, "I don't think he's ever going to forgive me, you know."

"Give him time." I pick up the bottle, "Is brandy OK?"

"Lovely – a real treat."

I pour us both a generous measure. "Tonight was a real treat for me too; thank you so much for dinner, Owen."

"My pleasure." He wanders over to the edge of the decking and looks out towards the Moors, a distant wall of bleakness fading into the last of the dusk. "They look even more dramatic in this light."

"I was saying to Margaret that I'd like to explore them."

"If you like, I'll take you. There are some wonderful walks – so good that William might even call a truce."

We are standing very close, so close I can feel his warmth, and I look up at him. I can see that he is weighing up whether or not to kiss me and I so want him to. The light has faded fast and the oil lamp is so dim that I can barely see his features, yet I know what is in his eyes; and they are saying that it is all too complicated.

"Why is it too complicated, Owen?"

He jumps out of his skin and stares at me in amazement. His voice is hoarse. "How did you know what I was thinking? Did I say it out loud?"

I shake my head. "I…I can't explain. I just knew. It's not the first time…sometimes I feel I can see what's written in your eyes." I turn away from him. "Oh my God, that sounds so naff."

He touches my shoulder very gently. "What would you say if I told you that ever since I was a small boy every time I've walked past this house I felt it would be important to me, and that right from the first time I saw you, I felt like I've known you forever? And if that doesn't sound naff, I don't know what does."

I fiddle with my brandy glass. "It's funny you should say that about the house. The first time I walked up the drive – when Neil and I were just looking, really – it was like I was coming home. Maybe that's why it was a good place to lick my wounds."

"Are you still licking them?"

"Is that why you think it's too complicated? I've got too much baggage?"

Owen shakes his head. "Not you, Alice. I don't know – it feels so right, but all the same it's…I don't know..."

He tails off and I seize the advantage, wrapping my arms around his waist and stretching up to kiss him, but to my amazement he twists his face away. I am amazed not only because of his words, but because I can feel the beginnings of an erection filling against me.

"Owen?"

"But it is too complicated. There's so much I haven't told you, so much..."

I have never seduced a man before but then I have never wanted one the way I want Owen. It is uncharted territory, my mouth is dry and my hands are trembling, but all of a sudden it is as though a previously undiscovered part of me is guiding me home. Very gently I stroke his cheek.

"Then you can tell me now – we've got all night."

My fingers move down his neck and under the collar of his shirt. He is motionless, holding his breath. I trace the line of buttons slowly towards his navel, lingering on the softness of his skin between each one.

"Oh, God, Alice – don't make it any harder..." he whispers, but I smother his protest with another attempt at a kiss, and this time he does respond, his lips cool and firm on mine, his tongue sliding along the edges of my teeth. My hands slip under his shirt and his back is smooth and warm beneath them. He kisses me again, with more purpose. He's not resisting any more.

# Chapter Twenty-Four

It is beyond the grey of dawn and the first weak rays of sunlight slant across the window. Owen's breath is light and steady next to me, and I luxuriate in the moment of not waking alone. I turn my head towards him; in sleep he looks almost boyish, the worry lines gone and his hair sticking up in crazy spikes.

I lie on my back and close my eyes but I don't want to sleep; I am enjoying having him close to me, and thinking about the night before. That was a bit of a revelation, to be honest. After our uncertain start in the garden, after our first explosive quickie on the sofa in the snug, when we actually made it into bed Owen turned out to be the most generous lover I could possibly imagine. After years of Neil's wham-bam-thank-you-ma'am approach to lovemaking it was pure bliss.

I am so lost in my reverie I almost jump when Owen's fingers brush my face.

"Alice – you are so beautiful," he murmurs.

I turn so that I can feel every inch of him against me; my cheek against his stubble, my breasts and the curve of my stomach touching the soft hairs on his body, his prick gloriously hard against my thigh. Already it is as though I have known the shape and feel of him for years.

When we wake again it is because the church bell is tolling. We look at each other guiltily.

"I hope you're not down to read the lesson," I say.

He smiles, "Thankfully not. But it mightn't escape half the village's notice that neither of us is there."

"Is that a problem?"

"You can't avoid it in a place like this anyway. I just feel..." He bites his lip.

"Go on."

I hold his gaze and eventually he says, "Last night was wonderful, and I wouldn't change it for the world, but there are things I would have wanted you to understand first."

"Such as?"

He shakes his head. "Things that need time to explain. And although missing church isn't the end of the world I do need to get up because it's lunch at Adam's mum's today."

As he speaks he pushes me lightly away and swings his legs over the side of the bed. I sit up and tuck the duvet around me; it's not cold, but I suddenly feel naked and exposed. Owen retrieves his boxer shorts and pulls them on, then his chinos.

"I think your shirt's downstairs," I say, trying not to sound sulky and failing miserably.

He sits back down on the bed. "Have I messed up already?" He's not joking, and I realise with a jolt just how fragile his confidence is.

"Of course you haven't, you idiot. I'm just feeling a bit empty after all that closeness. Give me a hug, tell me when I'll see you again, and I'll be fine."

He is smiling and hugging me for all he is worth, and I promise I'll cook him supper on Tuesday. Tuesday – it seems nearly forever away. He kisses me and walks out of the room. I listen to his footsteps go along the landing and half way down the stairs, then stop and come back.

He pokes his head around the door. "You don't fancy taking the dogs for a quick walk this evening, do you?"

I nod, trying not to look as though he has just made my day.

# Chapter Twenty-Five

I wake alone for the first time in days and immediately miss Owen's warmth next to me. I roll over and pick up my watch – ten past eight – only eleven hours until I see him again.

I burrow under the duvet and catch a hint of his deodorant. I am reluctant to get up; I want to wallow in it for as long as possible, but it quickly fades and below me in the garden room William starts to whine. Still lost in dreams of making love with Owen I pull on my dressing gown and stumble downstairs.

I let William out and turn on the radio in the kitchen. In America the anti-abortionists are at it again. As I start to run the tap an uncomfortable realisation worms its way up from the recesses of my mind – contraception – or rather the lack of it. As the water splashes into the sink I curse out loud. What a stupid risk to take.

I need to do something – and fast. I do a quick calculation – it's borderline as to whether the morning after pill will work after five days, but Owen was a pharmacist so he will certainly know.

As I push the café door open Owen looks up from putting some sandwiches into the refrigerated display case and his face breaks into an enormous smile.

"Alice," he says, "what a lovely surprise."

We meet behind the counter and he gives me a hug and the

lightest of kisses on the lips. There are a few customers dotted around the place so it is a surprising demonstration of affection.

"I'm sorry to disturb you, but we need to talk."

He pulls away and there is anxiety in his eyes. I ruffle his hair.

"It's OK, you idiot, I only need your advice."

"Wait in the office. I'll get Adam to mind the shop."

The office is no more than a windowless cupboard off the passageway that runs along the back of the café. An old piece of kitchen unit has been fitted across the far end of it to form a desk, and on it is Owen's laptop, flanked by neat piles of paperwork. On top of one pile is a bank statement and I can't stop myself looking. I wish I hadn't; the business is overdrawn by a scarily large amount. Things obviously haven't improved that much, and what I am about to say will only add to Owen's worries. I curse my carelessness.

Owen slips into the office and closes the door behind him. "What's up?"

"Owen, you were a pharmacist – what do you know about the morning after pill?"

He only looks taken aback for about half a second, then he nods. "We have been a bit irresponsible, haven't we?"

"It's my fault, I..."

He grabs both my hands. "It's *our* responsibility, not just yours. Takes two, remember?"

He winks at me and I blush.

"Well there won't be much point in the morning after pill I'm afraid. Not at this late stage of the game." He pauses. "But if you'll trust me, then I can sort this out."

"Trust you? Of course I trust you."

"OK then, just promise me you won't spend all day worrying, and come around to see me at about half eight tonight."

"Thank you." I give him a lingering kiss and wander off to the chemist to buy about a gross of condoms.

Before I leave for Owen's I take William for a long walk around the garden then slip my toothbrush, some of the condoms and my moisturiser into my handbag. The thought of spending the night with Owen is taking my mind off puzzling over what his plans could be to deal with my potential unwanted pregnancy. Maybe he has access to some very early warning testing kit or something.

When I reach the house Owen answers the door almost before I knock and ushers me into the dining room.

"It's OK, we won't be disturbed – Adam's gone out."

"Tactful absence?"

"No. He's gone to Middlesborough. You know he always does on a Thursday." Before I can even sit down Owen ploughs on. "I can understand that an unwanted pregnancy isn't on your agenda and even though it's too late for a conventional morning after pill to work, there are alternatives." Despite garbling the words his voice sounds formal and stiff.

"What sort of alternatives?" I ask, smiling in what I hope is an encouraging manner.

"Herbs."

"Herbs? Like the ones in your garden?"

"Including some of the ones in my garden." He sounds terse. "Is that a problem?"

"No..." I find myself stammering, "It's just something I've never thought about before."

"You don't think they'll work?"

I remember him taking umbrage when he thought I was doubting his grandmother's skills so I am quick to pour oil on troubled waters. "Not at all – you asked me to trust you and I do." But somehow this isn't my boyfriend I'm talking to; it is a complete and utter stranger.

"Good. But the herbs I'm thinking about are pretty powerful, so before deciding whether it's safe to use them I need to find out about your general health."

His face is strained and his fingers are wrapped tightly around each other, flexing in and out. I try to break the atmosphere. "So do you want me to take off all my clothes and lie down on your couch, Dr Owen?"

He does at least try to smile. "Nothing like that, no. But please, do sit down."

On the table is a large wooden box, lovingly polished but wearing the chips and scars of prolonged use. I expect Owen to open it, but instead he reaches into a rucksack on the chair next to him and pulls out a notepad and a state of the art blood pressure monitor. He is very serious about all this and as he asks me questions, looks at my tongue and at my eyes, I begin to understand that this is something he is very accustomed to doing.

Eventually he opens the box. It is lined with green velvet and inside are dozens of brown glass bottles, all neatly labelled. To the left is a section for empty vials. He pulls one out and turns to me.

"I'm going to mix three tinctures; they're all uterine stimulants and they're all completely natural so they work with your body."

"So basically they irritate the hell out of my womb so that a baby can't grow."

He looks away. "It's not so different to the way the morning after pill works. It's what you want to happen, after all." He sounds decidedly huffy and I regret being so blunt.

"I'm sorry, Owen," I say, "I didn't mean it in a bad way – I was just trying to understand."

He nods. "No, no, that's fine," but his hand is shaking as he measures the liquids, so much so that he spills a great deal of the last one on the table.

"Owen, are you sure..."

"That it'll work? Of course it'll work."

"That wasn't what I was going to say. I was going to say – are you sure you want to do this?"

His eyes are momentarily wide with astonishment, but then he turns away, stoppers the vial firmly and hands it to me. "You take it in three equal doses, four hours apart. It won't taste great, so my gran would have said to disguise it in a glass of gin."

"What would you say?"

"Hold your nose and get it down you." He pauses, biting his lip. "Alice – these herbs are strong and they could give you some nasty stomach cramps. I...I'd rather be with you if they do. Would you mind waiting until tomorrow lunchtime to take the first dose, then if I could come around after work..." he trails off. He looks really miserable and I reach my hand across the table to touch his fingers.

"I'd like you there. It's a little scary, to be honest."

"No – you mustn't be scared." He is trying to sound reassuring but his voice is shaking again. He takes a deep breath. "Come on," he says, "I'll walk you home. Kylie can come too and stretch her legs." So he isn't planning to stay the night. Although that doesn't surprise me after the way he's been, it does make me feel completely and utterly alone.

## Chapter Twenty-Six

It is just before four o'clock in the afternoon and I am sitting at my kitchen table with the glass vial in my hand. It is time to take the second dose, but the first one was so disgusting – bitter and gloopy all at the same time – that I am hesitant. I am also not quite at ease with what these herbs are doing but it is far too early in the relationship to even countenance a baby. The reality is that I know Owen hardly at all – as last night illustrated perfectly.

But all the same the fact that there could be a child growing inside me is preying on my mind. The thought that I didn't have to take the stuff drifted into my head in the early hours of the morning. I've always wanted a baby and I'm thirty-five years old – I could almost hear an inner voice telling me that this could be my last chance. But I can't trap Owen in the way that Angela trapped Neil. I can't bear the thought that I would never be really sure if he loved me or if he was just doing his duty.

I play with the vial for a few more minutes, idly staring out of the window. The thought of drinking it is making me gag. In the end I decide to go down Owen's grandmother's route and drown the mixture in gin. I have to say it goes down a little better and I stir myself to prepare tea.

It is a sultry afternoon and even with both windows open there is no breeze; the kitchen is too hot before I even turn on the oven.

It won't be pleasant to eat in here and I'm loath to use the dining room, even though it's cool. I just don't like it for some reason.

The answer is clearly to eat on the little patio outside the snug and I'm sure there's some garden furniture in the loft space above the barn. It was a present from my mother so I wouldn't have dared leave it with Neil.

It is hard to see how the loft will ever become a luxurious holiday pad. The panes of glass in the windows are cracked and the beautiful oak beams covered in cobwebs. At the front end there's a nasty gash in the floor where Richard has started to experiment with load bearing joists to take the weight of the Jacuzzi. I wonder idly when he'll be coming back.

I find the little wooden folding table and struggle with it down the narrow stairs, taking it outside and setting it on the patio. As I go back for the chairs William starts to follow but gives up as soon as I enter the barn. It is far too hot for him to bother, and he slinks back to his shaded spot on the edge of the raised back lawn.

I know how he feels. The sticky heat is draining and by the time I've cleaned up the furniture all I can do is slump down on one of the chairs. William's spot is close by and I reach out to fondle his ears.

I must have dozed as I wake to the sound of Owen's voice. I open my eyes and see that he is in the scullery talking to a woman in a grey dress. I watch through the open casement but she has her back to me, so I can't tell who she is. Owen's face is tense and his words tumble out one after the other, but too faintly for me to hear what he is saying. The woman bows her head and he turns away from her, his shoulders rigid with anger.

It is at this point I realise there is no scullery, and no casement window. I bury my head in my hands and a wave of nausea rises up from the pit of my stomach. I am aware of William scampering towards the patio doors and starting to bark furiously, but I dare not open my eyes. What the hell have I just seen?

Suddenly Owen is beside me. "Alice – what's wrong?"

I shake my head, but it is beyond me to look up or speak.

His arm is tight around my shoulder, his fingers digging into my flesh. "Tell me, Alice. What is it?" He sounds desperate but I can't say what I saw – he'll think I'm nuts. Then I remember the warning he gave me about the herbs.

"It...it was just a stomach cramp...like you told me might happen." I sit up slowly. "The worst of it's over now. I'm alright really."

His grip relaxes. "I was afraid that's what it was when I saw you doubled up like that. Do you think you'd be better lying on the sofa?"

I look up properly then, towards the snug. And it is the snug, with its glazed patio door that I left open to let the air through. But I don't much fancy going in there.

"No, really, I'm OK now and it's so hot inside. There's a bottle of wine in the fridge. Why don't you fetch it and we'll sit here quietly and have a glass before supper?"

# Chapter Twenty-Seven

An hour or more after Owen has gone to work I still can't bring myself to get out of bed. I suppose we were both a bit subdued last night but apart from that he was back to his warm, loving self. No sign of the stranger who gave me the herbs to take, anyway. And no sign of him talking to a woman in a room that wasn't there.

Lying on my back watching the motes of dust rise and fall in the morning sunlight I begin to wonder if the herbs were in any way linked to what I saw. After all, when I took the sleeping tablets I imagined cattle in my barn; maybe Owen's weird herbal concoction had a similar effect on my brain?

Eventually I stir myself and spend a few hours pottering around the shady parts of the garden but achieving very little. Though I've still done enough to feel decidedly sweaty and grubby by the time I spy Richard's van pulling into the drive.

"Shall I put the kettle on?" I call out.

"That would be grand, Princess. Silly bitch where I'm working's too posh to make us a cuppa – I'm absolutely parched."

"So you knocked off early to serve her right."

"I knocked off early to come and see my favourite client – and to say that Bob can start the damp proofing a week Monday so I need to get going on that floor."

"What do you have to do?" I ask as we walk towards the barn.

"Break up that concrete and then dig down about eight inches."

Richard hauls the double doors open then turns on me in disgust. "Alice – what have you been doing in here?"

"What do you mean?" I ask in pretended innocence.

"We've cleared all this once."

"Well it's not too bad..." I start. But it is. I needed to move so many boxes and bits of furniture when I was decorating upstairs and they all seemed to end up in here. "It's pretty superficial," I finish lamely.

Richard's hands are on his hips. "Superficial, my arse."

"No, really – it's just boxes from the spare room and it won't take me a minute to carry them upstairs again."

"And that bookcase?"

"I got it down here," I mutter. But then I remember that I didn't – Owen moved it for me – and some of the heavier boxes too.

Richard sighs. "Come on then – let's shift it all back. Then I'm going to padlock those double doors so you can't mess it up again."

So we start picking up boxes and carrying them in through the garden room, up the stairs and into the spare bedroom. Last of all Richard manhandles the bookcase out of the barn and I am about to follow him when something resting on the skirting behind it and covered in thick dust catches my eye.

I pick it up and discover it is a narrow glass tube about six inches long. Rather gingerly I wipe it with the bottom of my T-shirt and am surprised to see it appears to be filled with tiny seeds.

I show Richard when he comes back.

He takes it carefully in his hand. "Where did you find it?"

"I spotted it when you moved the bookcase."

"Funny we didn't see it when we cleared the barn before."

"No, not really. It would have been behind the freezer and the council didn't come for that until later."

He crouches down next to me. "You don't know what it is?"

"No."

"It's a charm wand."

"A charm wand? What's that?"

"That's a question Owen's rather better qualified to answer than I am."

"Owen? Why?"

Richard stands up and stretches. "Because he's a charmer, Alice – not a plain and simple builder like me."

I follow him into the kitchen, where he starts washing the glass tube under the tap.

"A charmer? What do you mean?"

"Alice, do you realise that everything you've said to me over the last five minutes has been a question?"

"You start answering and I'll stop asking," I tell him as I flick the kettle on.

He finishes his task in silence then hands me the glass tube. "A charm wand is used to ward off evil spirits – and witches. Folks around here used to hang them over their doors – some still do. It's said that the witch will stop to count the seeds so won't enter the house."

"So why would Owen know about that? And why did you call him a charmer?"

"Because that's what he is – the local charmer. Or witch, if you prefer."

I have never heard such a load of rubbish in my life. "Well either that's complete crap or the wand doesn't work, because Owen's had no problems going in and out of the barn."

Richard raises his eyebrows and I kick myself. It isn't exactly public knowledge that Owen and I are an item, and I am not prepared to elaborate.

"A charmer is a white witch," he explains. "Spooky, I grant you, but not evil by any means."

"But aren't witches pagans? Owen goes to church." I am railing against this – I don't want to believe it, I really don't – but on the other hand, why would Richard be making it up?

"I don't know about that, but Owen is definitely, definitely, the village charmer. Ask anyone around here – they'll tell you."

I sit down with a bump. "So what does it mean?"

"These days, not as much as it did. But people still go to him for cures – for warts and the like, and some for more serious stuff – especially the old folks. There's a lot of them swear he's better than any doctor, just like his gran was. But it's not just that – charmers have second sight – and other skills – like making love potions. Just think, Alice, right now Owen could be putting a hex on you. Then what chance would I have?" He winks at me.

"Owen just helps people with herbs. I know that," I bluff. "And he told me about his gran doing the same."

Richard shakes his head. "There's more to it than that, I can tell you. But maybe you're already under his spell?"

I've had quite enough of this nonsense so I tell Richard not to be so stupid and divert him by asking if he wants to stay to supper.

I feel vaguely uneasy about Owen all evening. Once we've finished our meal Richard seems reluctant to leave. We sit in the kitchen and chat over a couple of beers until it is almost dusk.

As I open the back door to let him out he stops.

"What's that noise?" he asks.

I stand still and listen intently – he is right – there is a faint sound of crying and my heart begins to sink.

"It's the crying," I tell him.

"I thought that's what it sounded like, but I wasn't sure if it was an animal."

"No, I wasn't the first time I heard it, either."

"The first time?"

"I've heard it a few times, to be honest," I admit. "Someone around here must have some serious problems but I don't know who it is. Once they cried all night – it was awful."

"But you must be able to tell where it's coming from," he says as he steps onto the gravel in front of the barn.

"I never can."

We stand together in the dusk, listening. To me, the faint sound seems to be eddying around and bouncing off the buildings like it was before. I can't pinpoint it at all. Richard looks puzzled too. After a while he tells me he can see what I mean.

"At first I thought it was coming from inside the house, but it can't be. And anyway, now it doesn't seem that way at all." He furrows his brow in thought. "Process of elimination then; either it's coming from the paddock behind the barn or from Mr Webber's next door, because no-one else lives close enough."

"Well I think Mr Webber's on holiday – Margaret said something about watering his plants."

"That narrows it down then." Richard grabs my hand and I suppress a shudder as I remember the night of the fete. "Come on, we'll look in the field."

Behind the barn there is a gap in the hedge that Richard knows about and we squeeze through, William following silently at our heels. I am glad of his shadowy presence, although he seems very subdued. In the field the noise is fainter and the only form of life we can find is a neighbour's pony chewing placidly on some grass.

Richard lets go of my hand. "I give up. There's probably nothing we can do about it anyway." I agree and we walk back to the drive. "See you next week," he calls as he jumps into his van. "And don't mess up that bloody barn again."

Back in the house I close all the windows and go into the kitchen to tidy up. The charm wand is where Richard left it next to the sink. I am about to throw it away then wonder if Margaret would be interested in seeing it so instead I stuff it into my handbag. I am glad that by the time I go to bed the crying has stopped.

# Chapter Twenty-Eight

Margaret's conservatory is probably the homeliest place in the world. I edge between a lemon tree and a yukka plant which looks as though it has seen better days and perch on a battered cane chair. It is more comfortable than it looks and I sink back into its cushions. Margaret sweeps a seed catalogue and a gardening magazine off the coffee table to make space for the tray she is carrying.

A teapot under a cosy shaped like a cat, two large mugs, a carton of milk and a packet of gingernuts. My mother would have thrown a fit but I love the easiness of it all and I smile at Margaret fondly.

"I haven't had gingernuts for years."

"You do like them, don't you?"

"Oh yes, but Neil started watching his weight so I stopped buying biscuits."

Margaret looks shocked. "Really, Alice – you could still have had them yourself." She picks up the packet and shoves it under my nose. "Go on – take a couple and make up for lost time."

I nibble the edge of one as she pours the tea and I am overtaken by a wave of nostalgia; a friend's house, after school – gingernuts and orange squash – but that's all I can remember. I balance the biscuit on the edge of the tray and delve into my handbag.

"I've got something here you might be interested in, but I'm not sure."

"Alice," she laughs, "I'm interested in everything. It's what keeps me going in my old age."

"You're not old, Margaret," I counter.

"Well, only in years, and they don't matter so very much. Come on – what have you got?"

"I think it's called a charm wand." And I explain what little Richard told me about it – omitting the rubbish about Owen, of course.

Margaret holds it up to the light. "They look like wheat seeds to me. And it's very old glass – it's a wonder they haven't gone mouldy. With respect, Alice, I don't think of your barn as the driest of places."

"The damp proofing man said it was, because of the amount of air coming through it."

"Yorkshire air can be very wet – as you'll no doubt find out once you've spent a winter here. But perhaps the seeds are too tightly packed in to rot. It's quite a special thing, isn't it? What are you going to do with it?"

"I thought I'd give it to you. If you'd like it that is, and if you can find a home for it." I look at the clutter around me.

Margaret laughs. "Oh, I can always find space for another curio. I might even take it to the next antiques fair at Ripon – someone might know something about it. Folk history's fascinating."

"I remember you saying you were interested when you told me about Owen's gran."

Margaret fidgets with the wand. "Talking of Owen," she starts, and then looks at me full square. "You can't keep this relationship of yours quiet forever, you know. Best to go public with it soon if I were you, because people are beginning to talk."

"Talk? What about?"

"Oh don't look so horrified – it's nothing bad. In fact everyone's delighted you two have got together because you seem so well suited. Most of the old biddies around here have been scratching their heads about who to match Owen up with and you are the answer to their prayers."

I hang my head. "But we've been so careful. We've…we've not

really talked about it, but I guess we wanted to be sure of each other before we told anyone else."

"That's an admirable sentiment, but it won't work in Great Fencote. You can't have many secrets around here. It's not that people gossip exactly, there's just not much to talk about in the normal run of things."

"Yes, and everyone seems so very fond of Owen. I hope I can measure up to their expectations."

"Well I think you're the best thing that's ever happened to him," says Margaret firmly. "Except that you're a bit too thin."

"You can talk."

She brandishes the gingernuts again. "Well then, we'd both better have another one," and she dunks hers into her tea with relish.

# Chapter Twenty-Nine

I mention my conversation with Margaret to Owen when we are getting ready for church.

He looks up from buffing his shoe with one of my dusters. "Well we haven't been hiding it exactly, have we? I mean, I'm not sneaking in and out under cover of darkness or anything."

"No, but we haven't mentioned it to anyone either – except Adam of course. And we don't hold hands when we walk the dogs. Stuff like that makes it look as though it's a secret."

"Well it's not as far as I'm concerned. What do you want to do – ask Christopher to make a parish announcement?"

"Now you're being silly."

"Then what?"

"I don't know. I don't want to force you if you don't feel comfortable with it."

He puts the duster down and takes me in his arms. "Alice – I can't imagine what you see in me, but as long as you do then I want the whole world to know. I'm just not the sort to make a song and dance about anything, that's all."

And we walk up the village hand in hand.

If I have much of a Christian faith it is what was instilled into me by my father. He used to sometimes take me to church as a child and up until I was about nine or ten he knelt by my bed with me while I said my prayers. I think the last time I really prayed was at his hospital bedside, desperate for him to regain consciousness after his coronary. But he never did.

It somehow feels right to be in church with Owen; I have an inkling his faith is very strong, and kneeling next to him or listening to his beautiful smooth voice tell the congregation about the words of the prophets seems to strengthen my own belief. We sing 'Love Devine All Loves Excelling' and I catch him glancing at me between verses. I feel content and complete.

All the same it seems a little odd that our relationship is suddenly public; Christopher beams at us as we chat in the porch and I am peculiarly conscious of Owen's long fingers entwined with mine. I am glad we are not going for coffee at the vicarage today.

As we walk onto the road together Owen laughs, "Our ears will be burning for at least the next hour – we've just become Great Fencote's front page news." He kisses the tip of my nose. "I'll just get changed then I'll pick you up in twenty minutes."

I have been longing to see North Yorkshire's famous coast. Our trip is not to Staithes or Whitby; Owen says it's best to see them in the autumn when the summer crowds have gone, so instead he takes me to the beach just north of the Moors where he used to go as a child.

Skinningrove is not pretty or twee; it's an ordinary village that used to be a fishing port and just happens to have a beach. Tourists don't often find their way here but a good smattering of locals do, although even on a sunny Sunday you could hardly call the large stretch of sand crowded. Almost as soon as we set down our bags and rug Owen starts to strip off.

"Let's swim before lunch," he says, his head half in and half out of his T-shirt.

I look at him as though he is quite mad. Yes, the sun is shining, but there is a devilish breeze whipping across the North Sea. I don't even want to take my sweatshirt off, let alone the rest of my clothes.

"It'll be lovely once we're in," he urges, but I remain unconvinced.

"You've been brought up to it" I tell him. "Last time I swam in the sea was in Spain and it was a good deal warmer than this."

"It's alright for them that can afford fancy holidays," he says in his best Yorkshire accent.

"It wasn't a fancy holiday – my mother lives over there."

He stops undressing for a moment and looks at me. "You never said."

I shrug my shoulders. "William and I will come for a paddle while you have your swim."

As I watch him plough through the waves the sun disappears behind a rogue cloud. Owen's comment about not telling him my mother lives in Spain is starting to smart. There's plenty he hasn't told me. Not only the things he said he wanted me to know before we became lovers but has never mentioned since, but also the herbalism stuff – I refuse to call it charming. Perhaps they are one and the same.

But those herbs must have worked because I have my period – another reason I don't want to swim and I probably should have told Owen. He seemed very confident about the treatment but I guess deep down he's worried about an unwanted pregnancy too.

Initially I can't fathom out how to broach the subject but I stumble upon a way that evening as we are kissing and cuddling on the sofa in the snug. Reluctantly I pull away.

"I should have said," I mumble, "I've got my period. I don't know if it makes any difference to you..."

"There's more than one way of making love to you, Alice," he whispers and my insides turn into a lovely sticky goo.

"At least it means we don't have to worry about a baby anymore," I plough on, but as soon as I say it I know I should have kept my big mouth shut because for a split second Owen freezes.

"What's wrong?" I ask him

"Nothing." His voice is calm, but when I look in his eyes I catch a fleeting glimpse of something surprising – fear. But it can't be, surely.

"Look, I sensed you weren't happy giving me those herbs – I gave you the option to back out – we…we could have chanced it..."

"No, Alice, no we couldn't. We did the right thing for us." He emphasises the last word in a peculiar manner.

"I mean, I probably wasn't pregnant anyway..." I want to prolong this conversation, get to the bottom of it. But Owen clearly doesn't, because he starts kissing me again, and in a way that demands my complete and undivided attention.

# Chapter Thirty

The tinny piece of non-descript music that is Owen's ringtone wakes me. He leaps out of the bed and fumbles in the pocket of his abandoned trousers for his phone.

"Shit – no alarm…give me five minutes and I'll be there." He turns to me. "It's ten to eight – I've got to go," and he starts flinging on his clothes as I struggle to come to. I fail miserably, and in just a few moments he's kissing me goodbye and promising to send me a text.

The banging of the front door disturbs William and he begins to whine so I haul on my dressing gown and wander downstairs to let him out. He races across the drive to the lawn and I follow him, my bare feet luxuriating in the dew covered grass. I watch as he sniffs along the edges of the flower beds but my mind is with Owen. Once again he has avoided talking about something important and I am beginning to think it's more than a habit.

I am just wondering whether or not I feel resentful when I hear a van pull up outside and the big gate push open. It can only be Richard – but I have no time to run inside the house without him seeing me before he reverses up the drive and jumps out of the cab.

He looks at me, laughing. "Not sure the bed-head look suits you, Princess."

"It's none of your business," I grumble.

"I like my clients well turned out," he winks. "Babydoll nightie would have been fine; towelling dressing gown's a real no-no."

"Fuck off and die."

Richard starts unloading his tools. "No chance of a cup of tea, then?"

"You know where the kettle is. I'm going to have a shower."

"If I bring you up some tea, can I watch?"

I have to laugh. And laughing makes me feel so much better.

Richard warned me that today would be noisy, but the sound of the pneumatic drill is getting me down. At some point someone put a thin skin of concrete on the barn floor and what's left of it needs to be broken up before Richard can start the digging. William follows me around the house whimpering occasionally, so I decide to take him for a long walk.

I put on my sunglasses and a long sleeved shirt then pack water for both of us in my little rucksack before we set off towards Kirkby Fleetham. William is happy to meander, sniffing the hedgerows in the hope that if he finds something interesting I'll let him off his lead to chase it. You'd think he'd know me better than that; I've never been able to shake off the feeling that he just might not come back if I give him his freedom.

On the other side of the village the footpath hits the river on a massive bend. Here the Swale cuts deep into the countryside and we scramble down the bank to the water but William can't quite reach it to take a drink. Instead I pour some out of my bottle into his plastic dish and he gulps it down. We wander along the river bank for a while, past the stone bridge, but he is starting to pant and his heart really isn't in it. He's not a young dog, after all, and he is wearing a very thick coat. I wonder idly if I should have him clipped.

We walk downstream past Owen's swimming spot and turn into the wood by the beck where it is cooler. As we come out the other end, to my astonishment I see Owen standing next to the stream a couple of hundred yards away, shoulders hunched and staring into the water. But it's lunchtime; how on earth could he have left the café? What the hell has gone wrong?

I am about to call him but something stops me. At that very moment my phone vibrates in my pocket. When I pull it out there is a text from Owen asking me to supper tomorrow night. The figure on the bank hasn't moved; he certainly hasn't been texting. Then I realise what made me hesitate; this Owen is wearing a cream shirt.

I start to drag William along the path but the other Owen turns and walks purposefully across the field in the direction of New Cottage. I am determined to catch up with him and find out for once and for all what's going on – especially as he's heading towards the corner of the garden by the pond where there is no possible way through the fence. I quicken my pace, but William lets out a yelp; his lead is caught around his paw.

I bend down to free him but in doing so lose sight of the other Owen. I stand up so abruptly my head starts to spin; for a fleeting moment the hedge around the garden disappears and the scene seems to shift. I blink and look again; it's all back to normal. Except that there is no Owen. Nothing between me and the hedge except the low tussocks of grass.

# Chapter Thirty-One

Margaret and I are working in the garden. Well, Margaret is working; I am managing little more than a pretence of digging dandelions out of the lawn. I had another bad night, you see. Not only was I puzzling about seeing the other Owen disappear in the middle of a field but the crying came back again. And it was relentless. On and on until I had to plug my iPod firmly into my ears to drown it out. But of course then I couldn't sleep because of the music. As dawn broke I got out of bed and set about making an eight hour playlist of songs to snooze to.

I am finding it very hard to accept there are things happening around me that I don't understand. I am not a great believer in the paranormal, but a disappearing Owen and untraceable tears definitely come into that category – if only by definition. They are outside of normality; at least, I can't find a normal explanation for them.

It can't be all in my mind; no-one else has seen the other Owen – indeed, Adam said he didn't see him, but Richard has certainly heard the crying. Perhaps he's the person I should talk to about all this but as he's always clowning around it's hard to find the right moment.

As if on cue he appears at the bottom of the lawn and makes a beeline for Margaret and me.

"I hope you're coming to say you've put the kettle on," I call.

He doesn't reply, and as he gets closer I notice he's looking very pale.

"Richard, are you alright?"

"Yes..." he is unusually hesitant, "but I've found something in the barn I think you should take a look at."

"What is it, Richard?" Margaret asks.

"I...I'm not sure. At least...well...you see what you think."

The school teacher in Margaret takes charge and Richard and I trail after her down the garden. In contrast to the bright day outside the electric bulb is bathing the barn in an unhealthy yellow glow.

"Where am I meant to be looking?" asks Margaret.

"Over there; just beyond the side door. Be careful – there's quite a step down to the part I've already dug."

Margaret strides forwards but I hold back. Whatever it is, if it's made a big bloke like Richard go white I'm not sure I want to see it. From a safe distance I watch Margaret bend down and use her hands to scrape away some soil. She is between me and the whatever-it-is, and I am quite happy for it to stay that way.

After a few moments she looks up. "It's a tiny skull," she exclaims.

"Do...do you think it's human?" Richard asks.

"Yes. And so do you, don't you?"

He nods. "I could have easily crushed it with my spade, but it looked so white against the dirt I stopped."

"I wonder if it's just the skull, or whether there's anything else?" Margaret sounds genuinely curious and she starts to prise away more earth. After a few minutes she asks if I have a small trowel.

"It's in the greenhouse," I tell her.

"I'll get it." Richard disappears; glad to be out in the fresh air probably. I seem to be rooted to the spot, watching Margaret scrape at the bare earth with her stubby fingers.

When Richard comes back he hands Margaret the trowel then stands next to me. He touches my arm. "You alright?" he whispers, and I nod. We watch Margaret work. After a while she starts using her fingers again, and then points excitedly into the hole.

"Look – another bone."

"Margaret, I think you'd better stop." To my surprise, my voice sounds calm and assured.

Reluctantly, she stands up and brushes her trousers down. "I suspect you're right, Alice. I just got a bit carried away."

"What do we do now?" Richard asks.

"I have no idea," I tell him crisply, "Which is why I'm going to call the police and ask them."

I don't feel very crisp by the time the police have come, and gone, and come back again with a forensic expert; I feel a bit like a wilted lettuce. But it is good news of sorts; they're not treating it as a crime, they think the skeleton is far too old for that and they're going to contact the county archaeologist to see what he makes of it.

Finally on my own I close the big barn doors to keep William out and approach the hole in the floor for the first time. The early evening sun slants through the window at the far end and the skull is almost luminous caught in its rays. What I can't get over is how very small it is; about the size of the Tiny Tears doll I had when I was a kid.

The question is; how did it get here? It is one I cannot even begin to answer. I contemplate the hole for a while longer then William starts to bark so I turn away and out into the sunlight.

Owen is standing at the back door. When he sees me he rushes across, anxiety all over his face.

"Are you alright, Alice? I bumped into Margaret and she told me what Richard found."

I wriggle my way tighter into his arms and smile up at him. "It's been a bit hectic here this afternoon, but I'm fine, really. Come and take a look."

I shut a very disgruntled William in the garden room and Owen follows me into the barn. I crouch down at the side of the hole.

"Richard said he was lucky not to smash the skull. It would have been a shame; it's so tiny and so perfect. Look – you can even see the shoulder bone poking out – Margaret had a bit of a dig around with a trowel. But what really puzzles me is how it got here. I guess maybe if the archaeologists can date it then we might have an idea. They're going to try to send someone tomorrow. But it's all very strange, isn't it?"

I wait for a few moments for Owen to reply and when he doesn't I look up, surprised to find he isn't even there. I go back outside and am even more astonished to find him gripping the drainpipe that runs next to the barn door and throwing up.

"Owen, whatever's wrong?" I wrap an arm around his shoulder. His body is damp with sweat and when he raises his face it is almost grey, with beads of perspiration dotted across his forehead. There is no time for me to read his expression before he retches again. His knuckles are white as he grips the drainpipe.

After a while he straightens and leans away from me onto the barn wall, his eyes closed, trembling ever so slightly.

I squeeze his shoulder. "Let's go inside."

We make our way across the drive, through the garden room and into the snug, where I make him lie on the sofa. The trembling has become shivering and I pull the throw off the easy chair and wrap it around him like a rug. I don't know what to do next, so I sit on the floor and stroke his hair.

After a while he murmurs, "I'm sorry, Alice."

"There's nothing to be sorry for." I kiss his forehead, finding it damp and clammy. "Is there anything I can do? Get you a drink of water, maybe?" He is silent. Then inspiration strikes. "Some peppermint tea to settle your stomach?"

He smiles unconvincingly. "Can you make it half and half with camomile?"

I ruffle his hair as I stand up. "Of course I can."

When I come back with the tea he is sitting on the edge of the sofa.

"Alice, you are so kind and so lovely. I don't deserve you."

I am about to make a joke when I realise he is deadly serious.

"That's crap," I tell him.

He doesn't reply, but stares down into his mug.

I try again. "What made you say that?"

"I'm such a fucking waste of space. I come here to make sure you're alright and look what happens? One look at the…the..." He is biting his lip hard and I put my hand on his knee. "I bet Richard didn't throw up," he finishes bitterly.

"Actually, Richard was pretty upset," I tell him. "But this isn't anything to do with Richard; we're talking about you. And you have no reason to beat yourself up over this."

"But Alice, you don't understand; I'm no help to you and all I do is hurt you."

"Owen – you've never hurt me." As I say it I know that it's a lie, but only a little white one. Anyway, not being that great at texting or calling back isn't a huge fault in the great scheme of things.

"No – but I will, I..."

He sounds panicky and it unnerves me. I cut across him, "What on earth makes you say that?"

"It's just inevitable, it's..." There is something close to fear in his eyes and it is a look I've seen before.

"No, it can't be inevitable." I am trying to stay calm. "But do you think you can explain?"

"Oh, Alice – I'd so like to…but I can't…I'm so..."

He puts his hand over his mouth and rushes past me in the direction of the downstairs toilet.

It takes a while for Owen's stomach to settle and even longer for me to persuade him to stay, but eventually he agrees. Which is why, when I wake in the middle of the night on my own, I feel a bit disorientated. As I come to I can't remember whether Owen went home or not, but then I hear the crying and I am filled with foreboding.

I pad onto the landing. It is clear the sound isn't up here, although it does seem to be coming from inside somewhere. Without turning on the light I grope down the stairs to the dining room. When my bare toes touch the floorboards they feel cold as stone.

I pause. The crying seems further away and Owen is nowhere to be seen. I cock my head to one side, listening. After a few moments I hear the soft click of the kitchen door opening and closing, and Owen's footsteps across the tiles. The sound carries the memory of the night after the fete when I thought I saw him come out of my barn.

Owen appears in the dining room and jumps out of his skin when he sees me.

"What are you doing here?" he asks.

"Looking for you."

"I...I just wanted some fresh air."

I am about to ask him if he can hear the crying when I realise the house is silent. Except for William snoring in the garden room. Owen looks pale and his eyes are sunk back into his head.

"Are you OK?"

He nods. "Just really tired. Come on Alice, let's go back to bed."

## Chapter Thirty-Two

I take my coffee to the decking next to the pond to wait for Dr Graham, the archaeologist, to arrive. I want to get away from the house and feel the sun on my back.

Owen went off to work this morning as though nothing was wrong, but I took him a coffee while he was shaving, and the eyes looking out from the mirror were lifeless and ringed with black. What if the crying has been Owen in my barn all along? But it can't have been – that night I opened the door and saw only cattle he certainly wasn't there…but was that real, or was it the effect of too many sleeping tablets?

And if it is Owen, then why? I've seen a sadness in him, certainly, and more than once, fear as well. But what has shaken me most is his absolute conviction that he will hurt me; he almost sounded intent on making it a self-fulfilling prophecy.

I hear a car pull into the drive and I jump up from the bench to welcome my visitor. Dr Graham isn't the venerable old gentleman I expected but a prematurely balding man of about forty, tall and skinny, wearing cords and a black polo neck jumper.

He shakes my hand warmly and I offer him coffee.

"Later, perhaps," he says, smiling. "I'd like to take a look at your find first."

I show him into the barn and he kneels next to the hole in the floor. "My, oh my – that little skull looks perfect," he exclaims.

"There's a shoulder bone poking out too," I tell him. "I hope the whole thing's intact."

"My first guess is that it might be." He looks up over his shoulder and grins. "But in archaeology we're not really meant to guess, so don't tell anyone."

"Then what will you do?"

"There's no doubt we need to lift the skeleton and have a bit of a dig around to see if we can find out anything about its context."

"Its context?"

"Yes. How it relates to the building around it, if there's anything else buried with it. It might help us to get a date, and maybe even some clues as to how it got here."

"It would be nice to know. But what happens to it afterwards? I…I'd like to think it could have a proper Christian burial." This is Owen's idea actually – he mentioned it just before he left this morning – and somehow it does seem the right thing to do.

"Don't worry, Miss Hart, we do treat burial sites with the proper respect."

"But afterwards? I'm sure it's not important enough to be kept in a museum..."

"We don't know that at the moment. But if it's not of historical significance there is nothing to stop you disposing of the body as you wish."

'Disposing' is such an awful word, like it's going to be thrown into the dustbin. "But it's someone's child," I find myself whispering.

Dr Graham smiles again. "I'm sorry. I didn't mean it to sound harsh. Let's have that cup of coffee and I can explain the whole process to you."

The house is empty and lonely after Dr Graham leaves and I want someone to talk to. I pick up the phone and dial Richard's number; he'll be interested to hear what's going to happen, I'm sure. But my call goes straight to voicemail – he must have had another job to fit into today. And I know Margaret has gone to York with a friend. I look at my watch; if I eat a sandwich really slowly, then do a few chores, it will be about three o'clock before I get into Northallerton and the café should be a bit quieter by then.

Actually, it isn't. There is quite a queue so I slip behind the counter and ask Owen if he wants a hand. He looks absurdly grateful.

"You couldn't clear a few tables, could you?"

I grab a tray and a damp cloth and get to work.

It is a full fifteen minutes later that the dirty plates are stacked in the dishwasher and the queue has dwindled to a couple of elderly ladies dithering over which cake to choose. I stand next to the coffee machine and listen as Owen takes them through what's on offer and then, with a great deal of charm, guides them towards the Victoria Sponge. I am sure the reason these old biddies come here is because of Owen; he never rushes them, he is unfailingly polite, and he has that special way of making customers feel they are the only person in the world. If they weren't about seventy I might even be feeling jealous.

Finally he turns towards me and I can see the lines of tiredness etched into his face.

I squeeze his hand. "How you doing?"

"Better for seeing you." He gives me a brief kiss on the cheek. "How did the visit from the archaeologist go?"

I start to tell him but another customer comes in, and then another, so my account of what is going to happen next becomes disjointed as we make drinks and serve cakes. I thought Owen might stop me helping but he doesn't and we work seamlessly together while in the lulls I tell him that one of Dr Graham's team will come next week to excavate the body and the area around it, before taking the finds away to their lab to be examined and dated.

"Finds?" Owen asks, "Does that include the baby?"

"I think that is the baby."

"Did you ask about burial?"

"Yes. If it's not of historical significance then we can do as we wish."

"And if it is?"

I am puzzled by his anxious tone. "Well, it won't be, will it?"

"How do you know?"

"It seems pretty unlikely..."

"So does finding the skeleton of a baby in your barn at all."

Another customer comes in and I have to concede that he is right.

A little while later Owen says, "I think we should talk to Christopher about this."

"Christopher?"

"He's the vicar, after all. He might have a view. Or...or perhaps be able to say a few prayers or something before they start the excavation."

There seems no harm in doing as he asks.

# Chapter Thirty-Three

The evening starts well enough. Christopher and Jane are fascinated to hear how Richard found the little skeleton and the archaeologist's plans for it. As Christopher opens a second bottle of red Jane asks if she can bring the children to see the excavation.

It is only when Owen says, "It's not a sideshow, it's a burial site," that I realise how little he's contributing to the conversation.

"I don't think the fact that it's a burial would bother them too much..." Jane starts, but Owen cuts across her.

"That isn't what I meant. I meant that it should be treated with respect."

"Jane only wants to bring the children to look," I tell him. "It would be very educational for them." I know I sound awfully prim but it certainly isn't up to Owen who I let into my barn and who I don't. There is an uneasy silence.

"They will treat it with respect, Owen," says Christopher, easing the cork out of the bottle. "It's the way they've been brought up."

Owen looks suitably contrite. "I'm sorry. I didn't mean to be rude. But anyway, that's not how I meant it."

Christopher puts the wine down and leans forwards, interested, rather than confrontational. "Then how do you mean it?"

"It's just the way everyone's behaving. First Margaret having a good poke about in the hole; then the archaeologist labelling the poor child as 'a find' and threatening to cart it off to a museum somewhere…it's not right."

"I'd have said it was the normal thing," I reply.

"Maybe, by some people's standards, but it's not *right*." Owen takes a deep breath and I notice his hands are shaking as he pours wine first into Jane's and then into my glass. "Look, however long ago it was someone buried a tiny child in unconsecrated ground. Now that child deserves a proper, Christian burial. Not to be treated as…as…well, a sideshow is the best word I can think of."

"Owen," I try to take his free hand, but he pushes me off. "They did say we could give it a proper burial once they'd finished."

"As long as it's not of historical importance. That's all that matters to them; not that it's a tiny human being."

"We do need to discover the historical context, though," says Christopher. "Only then will we know what's appropriate to do."

"What d'you mean, appropriate? Are you refusing this child burial?" Owen is bristling with indignation.

"Listen, Owen. The first thing that needs to be determined is when the baby died. For all we know, it could pre-date Christianity."

I shake my head. "The archaeologist was fairly certain that it couldn't pre-date the barn. Although of course he can't be sure until they've excavated it properly."

Christopher steeples his fingers together. "Well if that's the case, then we're dealing with a predominantly Christian era, certainly. However..."

"Then what's the problem?" Owen bangs the wine bottle down on the kitchen table and Christopher looks genuinely shocked.

"Owen, this is really important to you, isn't it?"

"It should be important to all of us. We all call ourselves Christian, after all."

Christopher ignores the slur. "So you're saying that if we do nothing, we are walking by on the other side?"

"Yes, that is what I am saying. Yes." But it sounds to me as though it's not what Owen is thinking at all.

"Well once the authorities release the body I don't see why it can't be re-buried in the churchyard with the appropriate Christian rites."

"And if they don't release the body?"

"Then there's nothing I can do. We can't exactly stage a midnight raid on the museum, can we?" Christopher laughs and Jane joins in a little uneasily, but I don't. I even have to stop myself from edging my chair away from Owen.

"Is there nothing you can do before they take it away? Maybe say the burial service over it where it is?"

"I can't do that, Owen. For one, as you pointed out, the ground isn't consecrated, and for another, under church law they'd then need to go through all sorts of hoops before exhuming it. It just can't be done."

"It can't, or you won't?"

Christopher's voice is firm, but gentle. "It can't be done. But what we can do, of course, is pray for the baby's soul. Prayer is a powerful thing, Owen. I don't have to tell you that."

Owen runs his hand over the top of his head. "Yes…you're right. I…I'm sorry, Chris. But this is just so important."

"I know." Christopher reaches out and pats his shoulder. "Shall we say a prayer now?"

Owen nods and we all bow our heads.

"Heavenly Father, we know nothing of the child whose bones lie in Alice's barn, but like all your children, we know that this little soul deserves your peace. As Jesus said to gather little children to him, so may you gather this child into your fold, and grant him or her everlasting grace. Amen."

We fall silent. The wine tastes bitter in the back of my throat.

# Chapter Thirty-Four

Owen stretches over to silence the alarm then thuds onto his back, motionless. I prop myself up on one elbow and see that his face is deeply lined with exhaustion, his skin a dead, unhealthy-looking grey. I trace my finger along his cheekbone and down the side of his face, but he neither smiles nor opens his eyes.

"Owen, you stay there. I'll go into the café this morning."

Then his eyes do shoot open, but they are dull. "No, Alice. I can't let you do that."

He starts to sit up but I push him back onto the pillows. "You bloody well will. You look awful. What use will you be to Adam if you keel over in the middle of a busy Saturday?" Without waiting for a reply I leap out of bed and flounce off to the bathroom.

Owen may be worn out but I have woken up completely refreshed, and it isn't until I am in the shower that I realise why; there was no crying last night. Not a sob, not a sound. Thank goodness it seems to be over again. But Owen's troubles are clearly not; in fact, by taking on moral responsibility for the skeleton he's actually adding to them and I don't understand it at all.

It is no good asking Adam for advice, either. He's not good in the mornings, but even so I am unprepared for the mouthful I get when I turn up instead of Owen to go to work.

"It's alright for fucking Owen. Who's going to do the baking when I fancy a lie-in on a Saturday?"

"Owen doesn't 'fancy a lie-in' – he's exhausted."

"What the fuck do you think I am?" It isn't a question I have a satisfactory answer to, so for once I keep my mouth shut.

Normally Adam's humour improves as the morning wears on, but not today. I try to do what I can to help in the kitchen before the café opens but I am told in no uncertain terms to get out. And later there is no cheerful banter as we work and I begin to wonder whether I did the right thing after all.

Owen appears at the café in time to deal with the midday rush. He looks a little better but on close inspection I realise that he is wearing some of my concealer to hide the shadows under his eyes. He tries half-heartedly to send me away but I simply carry on working until things quieten down at about three o'clock.

"You can go with a clear conscience now, Alice," he tells me. "And thank you, I really do appreciate it."

"I know you do." I kiss him on the tip of his nose. "Are you coming around tonight?"

"I'd like to, if you'll have me."

"Just why would I not?" I tease. "Perhaps we could walk the dogs, take a picnic with us if the weather holds?"

Finally he smiles. "That sounds lovely."

"Shall we ask Adam if he wants to come?"

"Great idea."

But it isn't – far from it. When I ask Adam if he wants to come for a picnic I get a lengthy tirade about how come Owen is well enough to go out when he wasn't well enough to come to work, and how he'll have a few choice words to say about it to Owen too, once the café is closed for the night.

"Please...Adam," I beg him. "It wasn't Owen's fault. It was mine – I made him stay in bed. He looked so awful and he really isn't..."

"Shut the fuck up and get out," Adam hisses. If the café wasn't full of people I know he'd have yelled the words out loud.

I hope our picnic at the trout pond will make Owen relax a little and the way he hits the wine makes me think that relaxation is his intention too. Or maybe even oblivion. Owen is not a big drinker and he downs two thirds of the bottle in relatively short order. But it does make him more talkative and he tells me about how, when they were teenagers, he and the owner's son would camp out on the island for days at a time.

"If you look carefully in the bushes there are a whole load of old stones, like there used to be a building here. We'd try to find them and work out what it was like."

I look around the island. "Small and damp, I'd guess."

"More than likely. When we were really little we'd pretend it was a highwayman's hide out – maybe even Dick Turpin's – and have all sorts of battles with the law. It used to make Gran laugh – she'd sometimes come over here collecting wild herbs."

"Do you collect herbs from here?"

"Not very often."

He doesn't elaborate, but being me, I push on. "So where do you get your herbs from, mostly? Do you grow them all?"

"A wholesaler's in London."

"So that's why you have to go down there?"

"Yes."

Owen has gone from chatty to monosyllabic within minutes. I touch his arm.

"What's wrong?"

"Nothing."

"Owen..."

He sighs. "Look, I'm sorry. I had a nasty letter from the bank manager again, that's all."

"You don't need that when you're already so exhausted."

"No, it's just one more thing..."

There is a choke in his voice. We are sitting with our arms around each other's shoulders and he reaches across to hold my free hand just as tightly as he can. It feels complete, as though we have closed a circle between us and are therefore safe. But of course it's not real. I can't keep Owen safe from the world. The best I can do is to be there for him and I so want to tell him that I love him, but it doesn't seem to be the right time.

I am stiff with cold before he turns and kisses me. "Thanks for not making me talk," he says. "I don't think I could right now."

"That's OK. Let's go home and have a nightcap."

We have more than one nightcap, to be honest, even though we hardly speak again. We curl together on the sofa in the snug, drinking brandy and listening to a Duffy CD. When it finishes the silence is filled with the sound of sobbing.

I look at Owen in horror. "Oh no – not again."

I expect him to question me but instead he stands up and heads for the patio doors.

"Where are you going?"

"To the barn."

I unwind my legs from under me. "I'm coming with you."

He shakes his head, "I'm not sure that's a good idea."

"I don't care. I'm coming." If I do I might finally get to the bottom of what's going on.

I follow him up the garden and through the side door of the barn, edging around the hole where the skeleton is. To my surprise Owen kneels next to it, but I remain standing. Or rather I try to. He tugs on my hand so violently I find myself kneeling too.

"Show some respect," he hisses and a chill runs through me.

And then he starts reciting Christopher's prayer. Not just once, but over and over again, and, as far as I can remember, word perfect from the one time Christopher said it. From the dark corners of the barn I can smell the sweetness of the hay and hear the snuffling breaths of the animals close by. My head begins to spin with the brandy and my enforced kneeling upright and I feel I am going to topple into the grave, but somehow I stay rigid next to Owen, right until he finally says Amen. I am shaking so much it is all I can do to crawl outside and collapse face down on the cool, damp grass.

# Chapter Thirty-Five

I wake in bed when it is barely light and realise I am alone. I sit up sleepily and look around me. Owen's clothes are not on the chair where he normally leaves them; perhaps he has decided to go home. But then I hear the patio doors slide open and closed beneath me and the sound spurs me into action; if I race downstairs and open the front door I can cut him off before he goes.

I grab my dressing gown and rush from my room. But one look through the glass in the front door makes me stop; Owen isn't walking away from the house, he is crossing the road from the green and walking towards it. But then he isn't; he comes into my field of vision from the direction of the barn. It is a heart stopping moment. I open my mouth to scream but instead I watch soundlessly as Owen's face becomes a mask of terror and he turns and runs for his life.

I push open the door and race up the drive after him, then across the lawn. I am calling his name but he doesn't stop and I lose valuable ground as we pass through the orchard. At the end of the garden he vaults the fence before setting off across the field.

"Owen – Owen – please – come back!" I am screaming but I can't follow him in my bare feet. All I can do is yell and watch him disappear in the direction of the Swale and the Moors.

# Chapter Thirty-Six

I can't make up my mind how early I dare tell Adam what has happened, but at least prevaricating about that stops me from thinking about anything else. I hunch on a kitchen chair, unable to take my eyes off the digital clock on the cooker as it clicks away each minute.

It is 5.03 when I start watching the little green numbers and the hour until six is endless, but by the time quarter to seven arrives I have decided. My frozen muscles scream when I move, but I drag myself up the stairs and into the shower, get dressed, then set off up the road.

As I ring the doorbell I am praying that Owen has made his way home and will answer. But I know it is a faint hope. The house is silent; no-one comes. So I ring and ring again, and Kylie starts to bark and finally I hear Adam grumbling as he makes his way downstairs. His face is like thunder as he opens the door, but when he looks down at me his expression changes.

"It's Owen, isn't it? What's wrong?"

"He's run away."

Adam stares at me, incredulous. "What d'you mean?"

"When I woke up this morning his clothes were gone but I was in time to…to…see him run off across the field. I tried to chase after him, but it was no good…I…I didn't have any shoes on."

Adam opens the door wider. "You'd better come in."

I follow him past the vase of walking sticks and up the hallway into the kitchen. Kylie unfolds herself from her basket to lick my hand in greeting. I sit at the table and fondle her ears while Adam runs water, fills the kettle and switches it on. Ponderously he reaches for the pot and spoons tea into it. He is moving as though he has a hangover – perhaps he does. He leans on the edge of the kitchen unit and watches the kettle as it boils.

Finally he says, "I didn't mean to push him over the edge, Alice. Never in a million years. But I was angry – so fucking angry..."

"It wasn't you – something else..."

He cuts me off. "But it must have been me – those awful things I said to him yesterday evening...those awful, awful things."

I wait while he pours the water into the teapot and puts milk in the mugs. Then I ask, "What things, Adam?"

He swings around. "You mean he didn't tell you?"

I shake my head. "All he said was that he hadn't brought Kylie because you fancied taking her for a walk yourself."

"Oh shit." He brings the mugs over to the table and spoons sugar into them.

I reach my hand across and grasp his. "Whatever you said, it wasn't the final straw."

"Well if that wasn't, then what was?"

I look down at my tea. "It's a long story. Well longish. Remember the night we went to The Black Horse? When I said I thought I saw Owen on the village green but you didn't? Well, that wasn't the first time I'd seen someone or something who looked very like Owen, but wasn't."

"Someone or something? What do you mean?"

"I don't really know. It's like the crying I've heard, and now I'm sure the two are linked. Owen heard the crying too and, well, never mind that for the moment, but this morning he came face to face with the other Owen and he just turned and fled."

"But I don't understand, Alice. What are you saying? Is the other Owen a real person or a ghost?"

It is typical of Adam to have put it in such plain terms but I cannot answer him. I don't have to though, because the doorbell rings.

Adam leaps up. "It must be Owen – he's always forgetting his frigging keys."

I follow him as far as the hall. On the doorstep is a policeman and my world seems to go into slow motion – just like it does in the movies, only this is sickeningly real. The policeman is asking Adam if this is where Owen Maltby lives. When Adam nods, he asks if he can come in. He is not alone; a policewoman follows him. They always send one when there is bad news. I am rooted to the spot.

As he draws level with me Adam says to the policeman, "I'm Adam James, Owen's housemate. This is Alice Hart, his girlfriend."

"Have you found him?" My voice sounds squeaky and high pitched.

The policeman sits down at the table and gestures to us to do the same. The policewoman takes the chair next to mine and I imagine her pockets full of tissues for when I cry.

"So Mr Maltby is missing?" the policeman asks.

"Yes. Since early this morning. Why – what's happened?" Adam's voice sounds brusque; firmer than my own, anyway.

"We've had a report of someone fitting Mr Maltby's description jumping off the old bridge into the Swale. The gentleman who phoned us seemed to know him quite well and was pretty sure about what he'd seen, but of course at the moment we only have his word for it."

"So, what are you doing about it?" Adam's words eddy around my head, colliding with the memory of Owen swimming in the river.

"...Miss Hart?" The policewoman is touching my arm.

"Sorry?"

"Any arguments or such like? Any reason your boyfriend might have taken his own life?"

I force my brain back into real time and clear my throat. "Owen's been under a tremendous amount of pressure recently..." But that is all I can say.

There is a long silence.

Finally Adam asks, "So what happens now?"

"We'll let you know if there are any developments, and of course we may want to ask you both some questions later on. Does Mr Maltby have any family who should be informed?"

"None that I know of. He was brought up by his grandmother but she died last year."

I don't hear the policeman's reply. I am staring at the knots of wood in the kitchen table, trying not to think of all the years Owen has sat here drinking tea, just like Adam and I were before the doorbell rang. I want to go back to that moment again, but it won't change anything. I want to go back to first thing this morning; if only I'd just kept running across the field, not letting him out of my sight. I want to go back to...but none of it would make any difference.

Chairs scrape away from the table and Adam leads the police up the hall. On her way past the woman touches my shoulder but I don't react. I wouldn't know how to.

When Adam comes back I gather up the mugs and put the kettle on to boil again.

"The last lot went cold," I explain, but he just sits down at the table and rests his head on his folded arms. I move across and put my hand on his shoulder. "Try not to think about it, Adam. It's the only way." He doesn't answer, doesn't move. I carry on making the tea.

A few minutes later there is a tentative knock on the kitchen door. I rush to open it, struggling with the top bolt, only to see Margaret standing outside, wearing her Sunday best.

"I saw the police car," she ventures. "I came to see what's wrong."

"Owen's...Owen's..." but I can't bring myself to say it.

Adam looks up, his big round face blotchy and streaked with tears. "Owen's killed himself. He jumped off the old bridge into the Swale."

The colour falls from Margaret's face. "No," she whispers.

"We don't know that, Adam," I find myself saying. "He might still be alive, he's a very strong swimmer, he might just have fallen..."

"Oh, for fuck's sake, Alice." Adam buries his head in his arms again.

I pull a third mug off the shelf and pour some tea for Margaret. "I've only just made it," I tell her.

She sits down at the table and pats Adam's arm. "Alice may be right, you know. Owen's the last person in the world who would take his own life – his Christian faith would never allow him to. Adam, you should know that."

I find myself gratefully clutching at the straw Margaret has offered, but then Adam mutters, "But what if he was beyond reason? What if he'd lost it completely?" And I think of Owen in the barn, endlessly reciting Christopher's prayer over the little skeleton. We fall silent.

After a while Margaret asks what the police are doing and Adam tells her they're looking for him. Then she asks what we're going to do. Adam and I look at each other blankly. Finally, and somewhat desperately, she asks if there is anything she can do.

"There is one thing," I hesitate, "When you go to church, can you ask Christopher to say a prayer for Owen? Not a public one, because we don't want anyone else to know what might have happened until we know what has, but just a prayer to himself. Owen is a great believer in Christopher's prayers."

"Yes of course, Alice, and I'm sure it will help."

After she leaves Adam asks me if I really believe in all that mumbo jumbo. I say that I think I do, but it doesn't matter what I believe, but what Owen does. So I tell him about our drink with Christopher and Jane on Friday night, and then what happened in the barn just hours before Owen disappeared.

When I've finished Adam looks at me bleakly. "So he had totally lost it then?"

I nod. "I think so, yes. Even before he saw the other Owen; even before your argument; so you needn't start blaming yourself."

"Alice, I will always blame myself. You see, I told him I wanted out of the café, out of his life. I threw every good thing he's done for me over the years back in his face. And d'you know what? He just stood there and took it. I wanted him to fight, to yell back at me, but he didn't. He just waited until I'd run out of steam and then he asked me to give him another week or so, just so he could work out how to unravel it all. And then he went upstairs to get ready to go to see you.

"But I couldn't leave it there. I was even angrier that he didn't seem to care I was leaving so I stormed after him. But when I got to the top of the stairs I could hear him sobbing. Like a little child – like he did when his gran died – and if I'd been any sort of friend I'd have gone right in there and hugged him. But I didn't. I just grabbed a beer and went to watch television."

I want to say to him 'There are always things that we think we should have done' but somehow I can't form the words.

## Chapter Thirty-Seven

I use William as an excuse to go home. Adam and I are not doing each other any good; he is drowning in guilt and grief while I am trying to pretend this isn't happening. Although he looks forlorn, alone at the kitchen table, I sense his relief when I leave.

In total contrast William jumps up to lick my hands before racing across the lawn. I follow him half heartedly, and all I can do is wonder why I didn't just keep running after Owen. Surely tearing my feet to shreds would have been nothing compared to the way his world was tearing apart. After a very short while I can stand it in the garden no longer, and lead a reluctant William back to the house. I can't even look at the barn.

Being inside isn't much better. I wander around like a ghost. For a long time I stand at the dining room window, gazing at the village green, willing at least one of the Owens to appear, but of course no-one does. A few cars whizz past, blatantly ignoring the thirty mile an hour limit like they always do, and then a couple of cyclists, but no Owen.

The room is chill and I hug my arms around me. I am longing for my shawl; my grey dress feels thin and inadequate, and yet it's the one I always wear. My hand reaches for my stomach, so recently bereft of the life inside it and the dark emptiness threatens to engulf me. I am not gazing at the village green, but at the farmhouse beyond. It is so achingly familiar with its low thatch, but its homely comfort is too far in the past for me to reach.

I jump out of my skin when Richard's van pulls into the drive. I feel disorientated, as though my mind slid off somewhere else. It must be shock, I tell myself, and stride through to the garden room to open the door.

Richard looks as though he has aged about ten years. The lines around his eyes are not laughing, but are etched deeper into his tanned skin.

"I came to say how sorry I am about Owen," he says, looking down at his trainers.

"How do you know?"

"It was me who saw him on the bridge. Alice – I would have stopped him if I could, I tried to go after him, I..." He is twisting his keys round and round. What he says hits me like a bow wave; if it was Richard who saw Owen jump, then there can be no mistake.

I grip the doorframe. William licks my hand. Richard continues to stand there.

"Come in," I say. "Then you can tell me exactly what you saw."

For about the hundredth time today I make a pot of tea and spoon sugar into the mugs. Richard doesn't complain and we sit down at either side of the little kitchen table.

"So – what happened?"

"Didn't the police tell you?"

"Only in outline. Richard, please, I need to know."

"There isn't much to tell. I was coming back from town at about quarter to six this morning. I'd...well, I'd bumped into an ex in the pub last night and one thing kind of led to another." He pauses. "But anyway, I was crossing the new bridge when I saw Owen on the old one. I knew something wasn't right straight away because he was standing on the parapet. I mean, I know he's a strong swimmer but he understands that river – he'd never dive in from there – and besides, he was fully clothed.

"As soon as I got to this side I stopped and shot out of the van. I called out, but maybe I shouldn't have because it was then he just leant forwards and tipped himself into the river. It sounds fanciful, but for a moment, before he...he did it...he looked just like an angel. His arms outstretched, his fair hair and white shirt..." Richard swallows hard.

"I absolutely pelted down the bank. I knew he'd be hurt, but I thought at least I could jump in after him and try to stop him from drowning. But by the time I got there I couldn't see him. Nothing in the water at all – not even a ripple. I guess the current's quite fast under the bridge but I keep going over it again and again in my head; if there was anything else I could have done."

Richard paints good pictures with his words. I think of the funny stories he's told me about his other clients; odd how you think of irrelevant things at stressful times. But something about the image isn't right – I replay the scene in my mind and suddenly I hit upon it.

"Owen wasn't wearing a white shirt," I blurt out. "He was wearing a brown fleece."

"What about underneath?" Richard sounds cautious.

I think hard. Had Owen taken the fleece off yesterday evening? No – he'd put it on; when he arrived he'd been carrying it – and wearing his blue T-shirt.

"A blue T-shirt."

"Perhaps he went home to change?"

I shake my head. "No. Richard – he ran across those fields in such a state..." I stop mid sentence. "The shirt couldn't have been cream, could it?"

"Yes, very easily. Or any light colour. I didn't really get that good a look; it was just the impression of an angel stayed with me."

"What you saw could very well have been an angel. To be honest, I don't rightly know what it was, but it wasn't my Owen."

So for the second time today I launch into the story of the other Owen and how I think it's somehow linked to the crying we heard. Richard listens without comment, his big hands wrapped around his mug of tea.

When I finish he says "So this other Owen, as you call him, he's always wearing a cream shirt, is he?"

"Yes. Not white – a really definite cream."

"Then I've seen him before. One night last week when I was driving home I passed him in the lane coming up from Scruton. I beeped my horn and waved but he didn't acknowledge me. I just thought it was Owen being a miserable sod, to be honest."

It takes a moment for what he says to sink in. "So you've seen him too?"

"Looks like it. But Alice, what is it we've seen? A ghost?"

"I don't know, I..." My hand flies to my mouth. "Adam! We've got to tell Adam it wasn't Owen you saw – he's breaking his heart up there. Come on."

"Perhaps you'd better go on your own. I'm not right comfy with Adam, you know."

I grab his wrist. "Oh no, Richard, this is no time for a bout of homophobia; Adam mightn't believe it if I tell him, but he'll have to believe a firsthand account."

When we arrive Margaret is sitting with Adam in the kitchen. She offers us tea but I refuse, saying I'm drowning in the stuff. Adam is so dazed he doesn't even question why Richard is there but Margaret looks at us expectantly.

"Richard was the one who saw Owen jump off the bridge – but now we've talked about it we've realised it wasn't Owen at all."

At this point Adam does acknowledge Richard. "Crap, Alice. He's just saying that to get into your good books now Owen's gone. He's had the hots for you since the day you arrived."

"No – it's not like that at all. It was me who realised it couldn't have been Owen because the person Richard saw jump was wearing a cream shirt."

"You mean there were two people throwing themselves into the river this morning? Get real, Alice."

I want to shake him. "Adam – what Richard saw was the other Owen. I didn't see where he went because I was too busy trying to catch our Owen, but he must have headed for the river too."

"The other Owen?" Adam is more thoughtful now. "I suppose if you can see him, and Owen did, then there's no reason why Richard shouldn't..."

"I've seen him before, too," Richard interrupts, "only I thought it was our Owen at the time – I was just a bit surprised when he didn't acknowledge me."

"Excuse me," butts in Margaret, "what on earth are you on about?"

So for the third time today I tell the story of the other Owen.

I expect Margaret to be highly sceptical but she isn't. In fact, she passes no judgement at all, just nods occasionally, and when I have finished starts on a tale of her own.

"Owen's gran used to tell a story about a young man who killed himself by jumping off that bridge. I couldn't get it out of my mind in church – I kept thinking that Owen must have known the story too and perhaps that was what had put the idea into his head."

Richard looks ashen. "So you think it could have been this other guy's ghost I saw?"

Margaret nods.

"What else do you know about him?" I ask, but my voice comes out hoarse.

"Well the story goes that he fell in love with a girl who was secretly engaged to someone else. The lad had always been a bit wild, but he went completely off the rails when he found out he couldn't have her, drinking and wenching, as they put it then – it was even said he fathered an illegitimate child but he never acknowledged it. Still he tried to persuade the woman he loved to marry him but she would not break her word to her fiancé and in the end he drowned himself in the river."

It's only a story but the hairs on the back of my neck stand on end and I start to shiver. A chill creeps through me from head to foot.

Margaret asks if I'm alright and I shake my head. "I think I'll just go home and have a lie down. It's probably delayed shock – I'll be OK."

She reaches over the table and squeezes my hand. "That sounds like a very good idea, Alice."

Back in my own bedroom I draw the curtains against the sun. On the floor next to the window is Owen's T-shirt – he didn't even stop to put it on. I pick it up and bury my face in it. It smells of his sweat, and the washing powder he uses, with just a hint of his deodorant. It smells just like Owen and I cannot bear it. I cannot bear to think of him out there, somewhere. I cannot bear to think of him suffering. But more than anything, I cannot bear to put the T-shirt down and I sit on the side of the bed, waiting for the tears to come. But nothing happens.

I put my face to the T-shirt again. I picture Owen washing the tearstains from his face yesterday evening then pulling it over his head. He'd done a good job – I hadn't noticed he'd been crying and he hadn't told me – not anything about the row with Adam. The familiar hurt surges up with a vengeance; I love him so much, but I know him so little. And yet – I know him so well, too. Sometimes, I feel I even know what he isn't saying. But not this time. When it all came falling down on top of him, he didn't tell me and he ran away from me. How can I mean anything to him?

I want to shelve the hurt but I can't because it's almost physical. It is gnawing into my stomach and chest like a rat. I didn't know emotional pain could feel this way. I hug the T-shirt to me, trying to make the feeling so acute that the bubble will burst. I can hear Owen's voice telling me that it was inevitable he would hurt me and I wonder if even then he was planning to kill himself.

The thought brings me to my senses; it wasn't Owen who jumped from the bridge this morning. I don't know what it was, but it wasn't Owen. But as for where he is...I would sell my soul to the devil just to be able to answer that one.

I sit on the bed for hours, but I don't cry. Eventually I start to feel cold so I crawl under the duvet. I fall into an exhausted sleep and – rather inevitably – I dream about Owen.

I am watching from a window as a mob of people banging pots and pans surround him, chanting words I can't quite make out. In the middle of the crowd are two teenage boys on stilts, but one of them has flowers in his hair and they are bumping and grinding their bodies together like some lewd circus act. Owen is ignoring them and trying to push through the mass.

His way is barred by the boys on stilts and two women grab him from behind while some of the men pull his leggings from him and lift up his shirt to expose him to the crowd, who are now pointing and jeering loudly. I feel my face glow crimson – I have never seen a man's intimate parts before and I am burning with shame. I turn away from the window and feel myself falling, falling forever into a blackness where all I can hear is the thudding of my heart.

## Chapter Thirty-Eight

This morning is happening to two Alice's at the same time. There is the practical, business-like Alice, sitting in Owen's kitchen with Adam, trying to work out what we will tell the police and what we won't – and there is the totally messed-up Alice who cannot quite believe that pain can be so sudden, so intense.

Luckily the business-like Alice is winning, because it is the last term you could apply to Adam. He's all over the place – a total mess, inside and out. Unwashed, unshaven – I don't think he even went to bed, given he's wearing the same T-shirt as yesterday. His face is puffy, his eyes red-rimmed – he has been shedding enough tears for both of us.

I take command. We have to decide how much we are going to tell the police. Owen is so private he won't want them to know anything about his life. Obviously we can't breathe a word about the other Owen and there is no way I'm going to let on how Owen was about the baby in the barn. So just what are we left with as a plausible explanation for him taking off like that, and as far as they are concerned, taking his own life?

We can only come up with one thing. "The pressures of running the business," says Adam. "The hours he puts in when he shouldn't be wasting his life fucking waiting tables." He buries his head in his hands "It's all my fault."

"No, Adam, it's not. It was so many things, one on top of the other, it wasn't just the row you had on Saturday and if anything it was my actions that started..."

"You did the right thing. You saw how shattered Owen was when I refused to. I should have done something weeks ago, but..."

"Listen, Adam. We can't keep blaming ourselves – it's pointless. We've just got to do what we can to protect Owen's interests now. We've got to find him, Adam – we've got to make him come back. If we just sit and wallow we'll get nowhere. Maybe...maybe the police would even help if Richard did tell them he wasn't sure..."

"Oh Alice, of course they won't. You just don't get it. They're only interested because they're looking for a body. We've got to hope they'll actually find Owen alive along the way – or some clue to his whereabouts anyway. Otherwise he's just another missing person and they'll do sod all."

"What do you mean, some clue?"

"I...I dunno."

But the police do find something. When they arrive to take statements from Adam and me they bring the items that the diving team took out of the river. The policewoman pulls out four little clear plastic bags and lays them on the table in front of us. In the first bag is a bunch of keys I recognise as Owen's.

"They're Owen's keys." My voice is almost a whisper. The key to the front door of this house, the ignition key to his Peugeot, and the two little keys that look like they open cupboards or boxes. All attached to a battered York Minster souvenir key ring. I look at Adam.

"That's his phone, too," he says, pointing to another bag.

"Lots of people have Nokia 7110s." I don't want to believe it; I've been texting Owen on and off and I can't bear the thought that he won't receive any of my messages; then I really would have no way of contacting him.

Adam picks up the bag. "It is Owen's. See where the bottom corner of the case is cracked? He dropped it down the stairs in the multi-storey in Leeds. It fell into three pieces, but it still worked when he put it back together. He was amazed. He told me about six times..." He tails off, choking back yet more tears. He has so many memories of Owen to haunt him. I only have a few weeks' worth – he has years.

But instead of crying again he looks straight at the policeman and starts to talk. "Owen and I run a business and to be honest the money side of things isn't great– we only started at Easter and he's worked all hours..."

"You both have," I interrupt.

"Yes, but all I have to do is bake. Owen does everything else. It's been a terrific strain..."

There is a silence and then the policewoman asks, "Did either of you think he might have tried to take his own life?"

Adam doesn't answer. Did I? Did I even consider it before? "No." It's the truth, but my voice doesn't sound as firm as I want it to.

Once the ordeal is over I walk back down the village to New Cottage. Margaret is in the garden and she gives me a big bony hug.

"Come on," she says, "there's plenty to do in the greenhouse."

It is while we are re-potting spidery looking bits of green she assures me will grow into lupins that Margaret asks me whether I will be helping Adam in the café from now on. The question stops me in my tracks.

"I hadn't thought about the café," I admit.

"Well you should. Adam can't mope at home all day and anyway, it's his and Owen's livelihood. He shouldn't waste all their hard work now, but neither can he run it on his own."

"But how are we going to look for Owen if we're running the café?" I ask.

"How are you going to look for Owen anyway? Where would you start? He could be anywhere, Alice – anywhere."

"But we've got to try."

She puts her hands on my shoulders. "Alice, child. He's run away because he doesn't want to be found. Not at the moment, anyway." Margaret is so wise, but the words hit home like hammer blows, starving me of air. Something ugly wells up behind the lump in the top of my chest; not a scream, not a howl, not a sob. Margaret takes me in her arms and rocks me. I can smell the moist potting compost, I can hear the birds singing, but I really do not want to feel.

In the evening Christopher turns up. He's wearing his dog collar under his jumper so I guess it's an official visit. He stands at the front door clasping and unclasping his hands.

"I just wondered how you are?" he ventures.

"I don't know," I answer truthfully.

"No news about Owen?"

I look into his anxious face and remember that he and Owen are good friends. I shake my head, "But come in, I shouldn't keep you on the doorstep."

I lead him through the chill of the dining room and into the kitchen. "I was just going to have a glass of wine – will you join me?" Actually, I'd been going to have about half a bottle of gin so perhaps Christopher's arrival has saved me from myself.

I give him the bottle to open while I find the glasses. He looks at the label.

"Owen liked this one, didn't he? He'd often bring a bottle over if he had an evening to spare."

"It is one of his favourites, yes."

"He was quite knowledgeable about wine. We used to talk about all sorts of stuff," Christopher carries on. "He was one of the few people who never lost the art of conversation."

It is only then I realise Christopher is talking about Owen in the past tense. I set the glasses on the table and turn to face him. "Owen isn't dead," and as I say it I pray for it to be true.

"He's not? You said you hadn't had any news."

"We haven't. Well, they haven't found *him*. They've…they've found his keys and his phone – but not Owen."

"Alice, I don't want to take away your hope, but in the long term it might be better to face facts."

"There are no facts."

"Margaret said someone saw him jump off the bridge. If that's the case..."

"They were wrong."

"Alice..."

I don't hear what he says because it suddenly occurs to me how I must sound given Christopher doesn't have the full story. But how would he react to the whole story? He might still think I am deluding myself...but it's worth a try.

"It was Richard Wainwright who saw it happen," I interrupt, "but we now know he was mistaken. The person...whatever...he saw, was wearing a light shirt. Owen wasn't."

"So you're saying Richard saw someone else?"

"Or something." So once again I embark on the tale of the other Owen, finishing my story with a rather limp, "I don't expect that sort of thing fits in too well with a Christian view of the world."

"That's where you're wrong. As a Christian I have to accept there are many things we don't understand; how echoes reach us from another time or place, for example. To be honest the idea fascinates me."

"Echoes from another time or place? That's a good way of putting it. Maybe that's even what the crying is."

"The crying?"

So I start again, this time with the story of the sobbing. How I first heard it, then how Richard did, and how it came back with a vengeance just after the baby's body was found. But then I grind to a halt and pick up my glass, swirling the wine round and round, watching the legs form and drain away.

Christopher is looking at me quizzically and finally he asks, "Do you feel able to tell me the rest?"

I gather my thoughts. "Owen is a great believer in the power of your prayers."

"That's comforting to know. Especially as I will be saying a lot more of them until he's found."

I take another slug of wine and plunge on. "Remember the prayer you said for the baby on Friday night? Well on Saturday I heard the crying again. Well, I had on Friday too but I didn't say anything to Owen but I think, looking back, maybe he had as well, I can't be sure...But anyway, he said he was going to the barn and I begged to go with him and he made us both kneel by the grave and he just said your prayer over and over, like a man possessed… I should have known something was badly wrong then, but I…well, I really let him down."

I am amazed how much of a relief it is to say the words out loud. Perhaps because Christopher is a priest I feel his knowing might give me some sort of absolution.

"I'm sure you didn't," Christopher murmurs.

"I'm sure I did. I was just so…I don't know, shocked isn't the word, or scared…by what he was doing, once he'd said Amen and let go of my arm I just crawled out onto the lawn. After a while he came and picked me up. And he was totally himself again, worried I'd get wet with the dew, but I couldn't handle it at all. He wanted to hug me, but I wouldn't let him. I…I had to force myself to take his hand to go back inside. I…I don't think we even spoke. But I should have known. I should have talked to him, not let my own fears get the better of me. He must have thought I'd abandoned him too."

"Too?"

"He'd had a row with Adam. He didn't tell me about it, though. But now Adam's beating himself up and I'm telling him not to, while all the time…Listen, Christopher, I know this isn't completely my or Adam's fault, but..."

"You can't help the way you feel. It's natural, under the circumstances."

"I know that too." I try to smile at him. "Anyway, tomorrow we're opening the café again so with any luck we'll be too busy to dwell on it."

"That's a brave thing to do, Alice."

"Margaret talked us into it. Said it was no use moping and Adam needs to make a living. I thought Adam would be dead against it, but he seems to think it's the least he can do – to make sure there's a business here for when Owen comes back."

"I think he will come back, Alice. When he's got things straight in his mind."

Assuming that his mind is capable of getting straight, of course.

## Chapter Thirty-Nine

It is just as well Adam and I turn up early to open the café. I peer through the picture window as Adam unlocks the door. The tables are clear of crockery but I can see mug rings on the nearest one and cake crumbs on the floor. A newspaper hangs off the seat of a chair.

Inside it is no better. Cups and plates are piled high in the kitchen and there are stale grounds in the coffee machine. The first thing I do is open all the windows. Adam stacks the dishwasher before he starts to bake while I haul Henry the hoover across the floor. This is the easy bit; smiling at customers will be much more difficult.

But I cope. I am familiar with the coffee machine and the till so I navigate the early morning rush with little problem. When people ask why we weren't open yesterday I apologise and blame a failure to our power supply. It's the story Adam and I have agreed. Everything is fine until one of the elderly regulars says:

"No Owen today, pet?"

I try to smile while my stomach churns. "Not today," I answer, "But you tell me just exactly how he makes your coffee and I'll do the best I can."

"Mainly milk, please, with just a little bit of that espresso stuff. I don't like it too strong." She sounds worried, so when the milk is hot we pour the coffee in together, a tiny bit at a time until it is just right, and I find I am over the bad moment. I can't stop myself from wondering how many more bad moments there will be.

The worst one comes late in the afternoon when a skinny man of about my own age comes in. He is wearing jeans, an open necked shirt, and a rather worried expression.

"What can I get you?" I ask, giving him my best new customer smile.

His reply is a question of his own. "Is this Owen Maltby's café?"

"Yes, it is."

"Is he around?"

"No, but his co-owner is." I turn to call Adam from the kitchen.

The visitor persists. "Is he not around because he's who the police have been searching the Swale for all weekend?"

"Who are you?" I try to sound arsy, but fail.

"Colin Smith, Yorkshire Post."

Before my jaw can hit the floor I hear Adam behind me. "Get out of here, you little shit."

"I'm only doing my job." Smith looks nervous; unsurprisingly given Adam's bulk looming over the counter.

"Get out before I throw you out."

The half dozen customers sitting at the tables begin to look around.

"Don't you touch me..."

Adam pushes past me so I grab his arm.

"No – Adam – he'll have you for assault." But Smith is making for the door, just as fast as his long legs can carry him.

As the door clangs shut Adam collapses into me and starts to sob. Most of the customers go back to their coffees and cakes in a typically English display of embarrassment, except for a Kirkby Fleetham farmer who leaves his wife at their table and makes his way across to the counter.

He taps Adam on the shoulder. "Come on lad, pull thyself together. Come and sit with Mother and me for a bit. I'm sure lass here will make you a nice cup of tea."

And Adam goes with him, docile as a lamb.

Instead of making a cup I get out one of the large teapots, then turn the sign on the door to closed and slip the catch. I can't face any more today. Two young mums with pushchairs hurry past me, which only leaves the couple by the window and the farmer and his wife. I fill the pot, load some parkin and flapjacks onto a tray, together with four clean cups and a jug of milk, and make my way across to the table.

Adam is calmer, listening to the farmer who is in full flow.

"...rumour in the village that it was young Owen they were looking for, but nowt was actually said. These things will get out though, in a place like this. It's not Leeds, lad."

I pour the tea and sit down next to the farmer's wife, offering cakes around as though it was a tea party.

The farmer starts up again. "So it is right then, it were Owen they're looking for?"

Adam nods. "He left Alice's place to go for a walk very early on Sunday morning and no-one's seen him since." It is a reasonable approximation of the truth.

"And Dick Wainwright saw him jump off the bridge."

"We think Richard was mistaken," I tell him, but I don't elaborate and he doesn't ask me to. Instead, his wife chips in.

"He's a good lad, Owen, always doing something for someone else. So cheerful about the place too, you'd never think..."

"He was very tired," I venture.

"I don't doubt it, pet," the farmer's wife continues. "When our Erica had shingles he were round every night to put on a poultice, but it fair took it out of him – looked so pale when he'd finished. His gran were the same; after our Paul were born and I had such a bad time, she were the only one to ease me, but she were always worn out afterwards."

"He worked too hard in the café too," Adam adds. "He shouldn't be doing it – he should be making his living from curing people – it's a rare talent and he shouldn't waste it."

The farmer shakes his head slowly. "Charming is a gift, lad, not to be used for gain. Wouldn't be right. Owen knows that – he was born into it."

This kindly couple know an awful lot about Owen, as most folk around here seem to. I am learning that lives are still conducted very much in public in these rural communities – there is little place for secrets. Which makes a total mockery of Owen being so chary about telling me.

"We just want to find him," I burst out.

"Don't you think lad from the Post could've helped?" asks the farmer. "Look, if you won't speak to him, he'll only go digging around and talk to other people. Just tell him what you've told us and be done with it. He'll get a quote from the police too, and that'll be that."

"But it won't be, will it? He'll dig around anyway."

"Well what's to hide?"

There is a brief silence then Adam says, "Nowt," very firmly.

# Chapter Forty

Adam drops me at the garden gate and I crunch up the path. William is jumping at the door before I even open it and leaps up at me in greeting, his paws scrabbling at my jeans. His ears slip silkily between my fingers then he barks and races off across the lawn. I watch, but I do not follow.

I have no way of dealing with this pain so I drink myself into a stupor. Inevitably I spend Wednesday morning struggling with a hangover. But I can smile and sell coffee with a hangover, so that's OK. It even takes the edge off customers asking about Owen once they've read the Yorkshire Post. A little bit, anyway.

I try the same tactic on Wednesday night and it is reasonably successful, but my befogged mind has trouble grappling with a call from the Archaeological Trust, saying they are sending someone to dig up the skeleton tomorrow. I agree before I've even thought about it. And then I panic. I rush into the kitchen and garble goodness knows what rubbish at Adam, who asks why on earth I don't call Margaret. Of course she is only too delighted to have the opportunity to babysit a real, live archaeologist.

On Friday I discover an additional strategy for coping. It's called mindfulness, according to Psychologies magazine, but really it's just living in the moment, and it almost works. I don't think about tomorrow, or next week, or next month without Owen, because quite frankly I can't bear to. I just think about what's happening in the here and now. Which is all very well, but it means I completely forget about the excavation until I see a strange car in my drive when Adam drops me home.

"The archaeologist hasn't left yet," I tell him, "want to come and have a look?"

He shakes his head. "Not my thing, Alice. See you tomorrow." So I walk up the drive alone.

Of course Margaret is still here. She is crouched by the hole – which is now somewhat larger – next to a slight woman with orangey-red hair.

"Oo – Alice – you're just in time – we're about to lift the skeleton."

The archaeologist stands up and introduces herself as Lucy Miller. Next to her feet is a plastic storage box generously lined with bubblewrap. It looks like a macabre cradle.

"So, how have you got on today?" I ask in my friendliest café manner, trying to force the cradle image out of my mind.

"Pretty good, really," Lucy tells me. "Margaret's been a great help. We extended the trench so that we could fully excavate the skeleton and with luck we'll be able to lift it whole. Nothing much in the way of other finds though – only this." She holds out a plastic bag containing a small brass key.

I arrange my features into a polite frown. "How odd. I guess someone must have dropped it."

"No – when we found it there were traces of fabric through the loop – something like ribbon. If you look very carefully," she points down into the hole, "you'll see another small piece there – just at the nape of the baby's neck. It was quite deliberately put there and buried with the child. It's rather sweet, really."

"But why bury a baby in a barn? Or at least, I'm assuming the barn was here when it was buried."

She nods. "Oh yes, as far as I can see it must have been. The burial is quite close to the wall – so much so that building the foundations would have disturbed it. But from the state of decay I don't think it would have been very long after; we'd need a carbon date to be sure."

"Can you do that from what you've found?"

"Well on the one hand bone's something we can date very easily, but on the other it probably isn't old enough for us to be particularly accurate."

Bone. That's all it is – a bundle of bone. Yet someone had cared enough to put a key on a ribbon around the baby's neck.

It is as though Margaret can read my thoughts. "At first Lucy thought it was an attempt to hide evidence of infanticide, or a late abortion, but the key puts a rather different complexion on things."

"Infanticide?"

"It was quite common in the late seventeenth and early eighteenth centuries," Lucy explains. "There were times of great hardship when people simply couldn't afford to raise another child. But this…I don't know…I can't be sure, of course, but my gut feel is that this baby was wanted but was stillborn – it's so small, even by the standards of the day, although why it wasn't buried in the churchyard I don't know."

I think of Owen. "When you've finished the carbon dating and that, can we give it a proper burial? Your boss said it might be possible if it wasn't of any great historical significance and I don't suppose it is."

"No, I don't think it is either. It's just one family's sad little story."

Lucy's words come back to me later. I get up off the sofa and wander into the dining room to look out over the village green. It is dusk and I have come here because I am hoping to see Owen sitting under one of the trees but the only sign of life is a bat flitting between them. After a while I slip outside. My footsteps make tracks in the dew as I walk round and round the trees, still looking.

I start to walk; back up the village past the church, past his house and beyond. The night is quiet and still; a fox barks somewhere but not even a candle gutters in a cottage window. My bare feet scratch on the rough grasses that cover the track.

I pause a little distance from the cottage. It is hunkered down behind the reeds, seeming to float on the marshy pond, its thatch stretching low to meet the honeysuckle climbing up its walls. Here a welcoming candle does burn in a window but I cannot go on – I have no reason to and an unbearable wave of grief hits me, as though it is emanating from the house itself and rising to meet my own pain.

I sink to my knees and the damp seeps through the fabric of my long grey skirt. I hug myself, and find that I am weeping and saying "My baby, oh, my baby," over and over again.

# Chapter Forty-One

It is hard to describe the total and complete exhaustion I feel as I turn the sign on the café door to closed. Words like empty, drained and hollow don't even begin to cover it. All I want to do is sleep and I am so shattered that I probably will.

But first there are a few chores that Adam and I need to do; load the dishwasher, tidy the kitchen, cash up and open the bundle of post that has been neglected since the morning. Then we're going to treat ourselves to fish and chips. I think we've earned it.

I am just lifting the drawer out of the till when Adam cries out. "Alice! Come here!"

I ram it back in and race to the office where he's standing with a postcard in his hand. "It's from Owen!" he yells and I grab it to read.

'Dear Adam and Alice,

I saw the Yorkshire Post and I'm sorry I worried you. I just needed to get away for a while. Like Alice told the paper, I went for a walk and just kept on walking. I hope you can both forgive me.

Owen.'

And I promptly burst into tears. All the uncried ones I haven't been able to shed come tumbling out and Adam envelopes me in a great big hug.

"He's OK, Alice – he's OK," he whispers.

I manage to look up, sniffling. "I know. That's why I'm crying, I think."

"You daft bint." But he hugs me tighter and lets me cry for as long as I want to, which is quite a while. Then I count the cash, and he tidies up the kitchen, all the time singing loudly and out of tune. He is so happy that when he goes to put the money in the night safe he comes back with a bottle of Cava.

"It's only a cheap one – but it'll go with fish and chips and we need to celebrate." I smile and play along with his happiness, but inside it doesn't feel right and I don't understand why.

It is only as I am getting ready for bed that the next wave of emotion hits me; a stranger, completely out of the blue. Now I know Owen is OK I can face looking at a picture of him, but when I flick to the photo library on my phone I am overcome by anger. There he is, on the beach at Skinningrove, looking exactly like Richard's angel with a halo of sunshine behind him, yet he has done the most hurtful thing possible to Adam and me, without even half a thought for our feelings.

"You selfish bastard," I yell at the picture, "How could you do this when we love you so much?" Red hot tears sear down my cheeks and I fling myself onto the duvet and howl. Never in my life have I been so angry; but then I've never loved like this either and I am even more furious with Owen for making me feel that way.

## Chapter Forty-Two

I am sitting in the office making neat piles of coins from the day's takings when suddenly the crashing of dishes from the kitchen stops and I hear Adam cry out

"Owen – thank fuck you're back!"

Owen's voice is quiet. "Ads – I'm sorry as hell, really I am."

"It doesn't matter – you're here now, and everything can get back to normal."

"Does that mean you're going to stay?" Owen's voice sounds tentative, but that isn't the word that comes to the top of my mind as he continues. "I shouldn't have done a runner, but I couldn't see past anything, you know, not without you and me here in this café, it means so much..." The word that comes into my mind is manipulative. There seems to be something less than honest in his voice.

"Of course I'll stay. Me and Alice, we've done a pretty good job..."

Owen cuts across him. "Alice – is she here?"

As Adam answers I feel panic begin to rise.

"She's in the office – cashing up."

Owen's footsteps are rapid in the narrow corridor and I only just have time to stand up and face the door before he is wrapping his arms around me and telling me how sorry he is, again and again.

His breath is warm on my hair and I nuzzle his neck, pulling myself closer into his hug. He smells different, somehow, but he feels the same; holding me solidly, rubbing his hands up and down my back, trying his best to make me feel secure. I am too scared of what I might say to speak.

"Alice," he whispers, "say you can forgive me."

"I'm just glad you're safe," I manage eventually, but my voice sounds small and somehow unconvincing. He holds me even tighter and slowly the worst of my anger starts to melt away.

Now I can look up. He touches my cheek and gently pushes my hair away from my face.

"I've missed you so much," he murmurs, "have you missed me?"

It is an unbelievably stupid question, but I nod. It is the truth – I have missed Owen more than I ever believed possible.

"Oh, God, Alice – I am just so sorry." His face is a mask of anxiety and sorrow, but there is nothing I can read in his eyes. I comfort myself with the thought it will take a while for everything to get back to normal.

In fact, we have a very normal evening. Adam cooks supper while Owen tells us about his week walking on the Moors as if it had simply been a holiday. We crack open a bottle of wine but as we are considering a second Owen says, "We'd better be a bit careful – Adam and I have an early start at the café tomorrow."

I look across the table and Adam's eyes meet mine. I am about to open my mouth, but instead he speaks for both of us.

"Alice and I have an early start. I think there's probably a few things you need to do before you come back to work; like see Margaret, for one – and Christopher. Not to mention squaring things with the police. Anyway, there's no rush for you to come back until you feel ready; we're a good team, Alice and me. And if you need longer…you know, to have a proper rest and get your head around stuff..."

Owen's eyes are pleading for my support.

"Adam's right," I tell him. There is plenty more I want to say, but I don't. If I start the anger might spill out, just when I've got it under control. I scrape back my chair. "Time for me to go, anyway."

Owen stands too. "I'll walk you home." It isn't an offer; it's a statement of fact.

We don't speak until I open my back door. William is about to fly out, but when he sees Owen he stops short and growls.

"Some things don't change," Owen says with a wistful smile.

This is an Owen I recognise. I put my arms around his waist and look up into his eyes. "Nothing has really; it's just a bit odd."

He nods. "I know, and it's all my fault."

"No – no blame." I reach to kiss him – for the first time since he came back – and he responds so tenderly and with such feeling I could weep. But I don't; or at least not until after we make love and his body is finally still, on top of mine, when all of a sudden I am wracked with sobs and there is nothing Owen can say or do to stop them.

## Chapter Forty-Three

On the outside my life is returning to whatever passes for normal. I go into the café with Adam on Wednesday, and again on Thursday morning, because Owen has to attend a formal interview with the police. He refuses to let either Adam or I go with him and he is a little pale when he comes into the café afterwards. But he helps with the lunchtime rush and all the customers seem pleased to see him. In the afternoon I serve them on my own while he sits in the office catching up with the paperwork. But after that I am surplus to requirements.

I miss the bustle of the café and with my mind less than fully occupied it has time to drift to places I haven't been allowing it to go. I owe William a very long walk but I don't want to be alone with my thoughts, so instead I make a list of everything that wants doing to the house. The sooner I finish it the better; the last few weeks have made me realise that I need a job.

I wander from room to room with my piece of paper. Progress, of sorts, has been made. Upstairs I have two habitable bedrooms and a dressing room. The next job is undoubtedly the bathroom; it's small and dated and needs a total revamp. Top of my list then.

Walking into the chill of the dining room I wonder what on earth to do with it. I don't use a dining room so maybe the answer is to take the table out and just make it into a hall. All I ever do is hurry through it anyway.

I start to shiver as I gaze around the room but it's not that cold. It must be the shock of everything that's happened but I can't let it get to me. I shake myself and stride into the kitchen to make a cup of tea and call Richard about when he can resume his work on the barn. I've been too much alone this morning – I'm not used to it. But his phone is on voicemail so all I can do is leave a message.

Instead of returning my call Richard drops around in the middle of the afternoon. William and I both rush to greet him.

"Hello, Princess," he beams. "Lady of leisure again, are you?"

I snort. "You must be joking – I'm way behind with the house – it'll never be finished at this rate."

"Ah, if only you'd called me just for my company – but I knew you'd want me to do something."

I consider telling him how pleased I am to see him but decide against it. Instead I ask him when work can restart on the floor.

"Back end of next week, I reckon. Let's see what sort of mess the archaeologists have made of it."

I unlock the barn for the first time in a week and we step into the gloom. I am about to put the light on but Richard hauls both of the big doors wide open.

"Poo – it smells all fusty in here."

He's right. To me it smells just a little of animals and straw, but I am surely imagining it. William has a very sensitive nose and he trots in quite happily.

Lucy has shovelled the earth back into her trench so the floor is fairly flat. When he found the baby's body Richard had dug about two thirds of the surface, so there's still work for him to do.

"Are you worried about finding anything else?" I ask.

He shrugs. "It hadn't occurred to me – lightning not striking twice and that. I just need to finish so Bob can get on with the damp proofing. It's holding everything else up." I am grateful that Richard is such a practical man with little imagination.

But over a cup of tea in the kitchen I begin to wonder if I am right about the imagination bit when Richard changes the direction of the conversation.

"So Owen's back, then?"

"Yes."

"He OK?"

I nod. "Seems to be. He's treating it like he just went on holiday."

"I know – that's what the police told me. They dragged me back in yesterday, to ask if I wanted to change my statement."

"And did you?"

"I told them that if it wasn't Owen I saw then it must have been a ghost."

"What did they say?"

Richard turns his mug in his hands. "Something snide about breathalysers. But they did mention Owen told them he'd walked across the old bridge that morning and maybe that's what I saw. But I didn't; Alice, the more I think about it, the more sure I am – I saw someone jump – no question."

"It must have been the other Owen."

"But who is he? The ghost of the man Margaret told us about?"

"I…I don't know. I don't even know if I believe in ghosts. Anyway, aren't ghosts meant to be wispy things that float around moaning? This…other Owen…he always seems so…so…real."

"I know – it's driving me bonkers – I'll end up as nutty as Owen if I'm not careful," he laughs.

So that's what he thinks – that I'm hooked up with the village loony. There is a little voice in the back of my head telling me he's probably right.

"But what is there to know?" I ask him. "If they're not real, how on earth do we find out about them? And if they are real…or were real…where on earth would we start looking?"

Richard looks puzzled. "They?"

"Well, it's not just the other Owen – I saw him talking to a woman in grey once, and..." No – it seems too fanciful to say out loud.

Richard leans back and folds his arms. "Go on, Princess, spit it out."

I sigh. "Well, the crying we heard…I can't help thinking it's all tied up with the baby." I look down at my tea. "Richard – this is such a weird conversation to be having."

"I hate to say it – but there's always been weirdness around Owen."

"Look, I know you think he's a charmer, not just a herbalist..."

"Well he is. The weird stuff proves it."

"But it mightn't be him – it might be me that's causing it. Or you even – you've seen and heard the same things as I have."

"But has anything like this ever happened to you before?"

I shake my head. "No. After my father died I was desperate to see his ghost, but I never did. How about you?"

"Yes. And that was to do with Owen, too. But it was a long time ago, I have to say."

"How long?"

"Well, we were just kids – probably even before we started school – or maybe just after. Owen and I were very good mates when we were nippers – my mum and Owen's mum had been friends, you see."

"So were Owen's parents around then?"

"No. It was a shotgun wedding and his dad scarpered when he was just a baby – very embarrassing for his gran, but worse for his mum. She lost the plot completely apparently – I can't even remember her – she topped herself before Owen was out of nappies."

Richard's telling of the story is matter of fact but it grips me – just how abandoned must Owen have felt when he was old enough to know what happened? But I don't want to be sidetracked so I point Richard back in the direction of his original story.

"We were playing on the village green one afternoon and it was very hot. It was just Owen and me, and a little girl called Alice. After a while Owen's gran came out with a couple of homemade lollipops and when she gave them to us I asked if there was one for Alice too. She looked shocked for a moment, then gave me a hug and told me I was a special little boy.

"After she'd gone I asked Owen what all that was about and he just said it was probably because he was normally the only one who could see Alice. It was then I realised Alice wasn't there, but Owen said she'd gone home to Ravenswood Farm. Later I asked Mum if there was a girl called Alice living there and she said not. But I'd been playing with her for half the afternoon. I couldn't understand it."

"Did you ever see her again?"

"Only once – in the distance. I was in the car with my dad and she and Owen were walking along the road by the church."

"So you saw someone that only Owen could see?"

"Not just saw – I played with her, spoke to her – but she wasn't even real. She was a figment of Owen's imagination and he was so completely persuasive I bought into it too."

"So is that what you think we're seeing and hearing? Figments of Owen's imagination? That's just not possible."

"Of course it's possible – he's a charmer – he's got special powers. What on earth is it going to take for you to believe me?"

"That's absolute rubbish – no-one has the power to make other people see what isn't there."

"But Alice – charmers cure people by the laying on of hands. If they can convince them they're well just by doing that and stuffing a few harmless herbs down their necks, think how persuasive they can be in other ways."

I fold my arms. "You're only saying this because you don't like Owen, and that's all there is to it."

"I only wish it was that. Still, if you're so besotted you're not going to see reason then I'm clearly wasting my breath." Richard stands up and gathers his keys. "I'll finish the floor on Monday, OK?"

He is gone before I can say another word.

# Chapter Forty-Four

Richard's theory is so ridiculous I put it right out of my mind. The more I think about the other Owen, the more I wonder if he has been real somewhere along the line, and if that's the case then maybe there's a clue in Owen's gran's story. So I decide to broach the matter with Margaret.

We have been busy in the garden all morning; it's been growing like topsy while I've been working in the café and I find it hard to know where to start. So after Margaret has finished her chores in the greenhouse she takes me in hand and we both set to on the small patch in front of the house. It's soothing working with Margaret; letting her chat about the village wash over me while I chisel away at the dandelions in the lawn.

By lunchtime the whole place is looking much tidier. We wash our hands and make ham sandwiches and tea, which we take to the bench next to the pond. William follows us, looking excited about the sandwiches.

"So," asks Margaret, "how's Owen?"

I stop chewing to think about phrasing my answer. "This is going to sound silly, but I don't actually know. Apart from the fact he's making every excuse under the sun not to go to church, he's trying so hard to make everything super-normal I can't see what's underneath."

She nods. "That's the impression I get too."

"When he was missing, Christopher said he'd have a hard time coming to terms with what he'd done so maybe this is his way of coping with it. I'm just not sure it's terribly healthy."

"It isn't. But unfortunately it's Owen all over – he was just the same when his gran died. It's not that he didn't show any emotion at the time; he certainly did, except that before very long he was his bright and cheerful self, and his life seemed back to…well…normal."

"Except that he never went back to his career."

"No. I did think it odd at the time, but then I wondered if he'd only become a pharmacist because it's what his gran would have wanted so now he was free to do something else. He does seem to enjoy running the café."

"So you think he'll just bury all this and not talk about it again?"

"Very likely."

"But Margaret, I can't do that. I want to know what happened – and so does Richard. He says he knows what he saw by the river that morning and he needs to make sense of it."

"I have to say I've been puzzling over it too. One part of me says it has to be linked to that old story of Owen's gran's but then I start wondering if I remembered it that way just to fit the facts. I hadn't thought of it for so long and anyway, just because it's local folklore doesn't mean it actually happened."

"I wondered if that story was our link to the past as well. But it's so very hard; I don't even believe in ghosts."

"Well I do," says Margaret.

"You do?" I have to say I am surprised.

"If only because we can't know everything. Maybe 'ghosts' is the wrong word – maybe paranormal is a better term – outside normality, if you like."

It sounds sensible and I nod. A small bird drops down onto the edge of the pond and William barks, frightening it away. A car passes along the lane. I feel a deep flash of empathy for Owen wanting everything to be ordinary.

"I guess the first thing to do," Margaret continues, "is to find out whether these people do have any historical basis."

I feel much braver and less stupid knowing I'm not alone in my crazy ramblings. "But how on earth do we do that?"

Her answer only frustrates me. She taps the side of her nose. "I admit there isn't a lot to go on – but I've got a few ideas. You concentrate on looking after Owen and leave the past with me."

I feel as though I am sitting on my hands. I don't even have Owen to look after as she suggests – he keeps saying he's busy – and I keep telling myself I don't need him around here all the time, do I? It's not like he's moved in or anything.

Even so I am delighted when he's free on Friday night. It is August Bank Holiday already and I am determined to make the most of the last knockings of summer so I decide we'll have a barbecue. William's nose goes into overdrive due to a couple of lamb chops and some sausages and Owen turns up in good time to light the charcoal and open the bottle of wine he's brought.

It only takes one glass before the question that has been at the back of my mind hurtles forwards and out of my mouth.

"So, how are you feeling, Owen?"

"Fine. Why do you ask?" He is making quite a show of looking puzzled, but something else crosses his face first and I don't quite catch what it is.

"Well, you know, you weren't great before you disappeared..."

He interrupts me. "My *holiday,*" and he emphasises the word, "did me the world of good."

I want to shake him. "Owen," I remind him, "You're talking to me, Alice, not some customer in the café you hardly know."

The stunned expression on his face is completely false. "Well, what do you want me to say?"

"The truth."

"It is the truth. I'm absolutely fine. Aren't you pleased?"

He's seriously defensive now and although I'm getting angry some instinct tells me not to corner him. I guess I'm scared that I might say or do something that would send him racing off across the fields again.

"Of course I'm pleased." I make myself reach out to stroke his hand. After a few moments he turns his palm upwards and grips his fingers in mine, squeezing them together until one of his nails cuts into my flesh. I glance up at him, only to see an incredible amount of pain in his eyes. When I look back down I see blood oozing from my index finger and seeping under his nail.

# Chapter Forty-Five

I do not follow William into the garden but watch from the door as his fur darkens and starts to cling to him. He doesn't seem to mind the curtain of rain which restricts my view to the blurred outline of the trees by the beck. I lean on the doorjamb and spoon cereal into my mouth, chasing the final cornflake around the bowl. I have no idea why I am hurrying to finish my breakfast.

Even the house is getting me down. The new shower in the utility room has been plumbed in but the brickwork around the door is unfinished and grubby boxes of tiles invade my kitchen. Richard has been laying the new floor in the barn but I resolve to drag him straight back inside so I don't have to live with this mess a moment longer.

I dry William off in an old towel and give him a biscuit. His tail thuds damply against my legs. The sofa and a good book beckon but if Richard is going to be working inside then I can't skive off either. Anyway, it's time I started to turn the dining room into a hall.

I empty the dresser and Richard helps me to move it into the living room. Then I pile the chairs upside down on the table, take down the curtains and start washing the walls. I work my way from the kitchen door to the window. I scrub at the dinginess around the light switch, making my fingers raw.

Richard has put the radio on and sings along tunelessly. I am glad of the background noise but even the happiest songs do not lift me. I haven't seen Owen for almost a week and my mind wanders off down a familiar path.

He wants out and he's too kind to tell me – it isn't in him to be cruel. And maybe that's not such a bad thing after all. He's too screwed up for me to help him anyway. But on the other hand, perhaps we're both just suffering from the backlash of his disappearance. But how the hell can we move on when he won't tell me the truth about what happened? How can we get anywhere when he won't talk?

Harry Nilsson's 'Without You' comes on the radio and Richard's screeching reaches a new crescendo. I am amazed William doesn't start to howl as well.

I yell through to the kitchen, "Turn that bloody racket off."

The song continues but Richard's head appears around the door. "What's got into you?" he asks "Don't like my singing?"

"Piss off."

"Oo – don't take it out on me if you've had an argument with your boyfriend."

"If he's never here, how can I fall out with him?" I snap, and despite myself my lip starts to quiver.

"Hey, come on, stop that." He puts his arm around my shoulder and gives me a squeeze.

I lean into him for a moment and he is warm and solid and smells vaguely of tile adhesive. "Sorry." I take a deep breath and he squeezes my shoulder once more.

"Better?" he asks after a few moments.

I nod.

"OK. You go and wash your face and I'll put the kettle on."

When I come back Richard is leaning against the work surface nursing a mug of tea. He picks up another one and hands it to me.

"Thanks, Richard," I say, "I didn't mean to embarrass you."

He shrugs. "I just don't like to see you upset, that's all. Owen's an idiot anyway, if he's got someone else."

"I'm not sure it's that..." I start, but then I look at his face and it says it all.

"Purely circumstantial evidence," Richard continues. "And I wouldn't have mentioned it if you hadn't said you had problems. It's just that I've seen his car parked outside the same house in Scruton a few times recently and I've kind of put two and two together. Making about sixteen too many, probably."

"Do you know who lives there?" I ask.

"A local jeweller called Imogen Cutt. She works from home, sells her stuff from the house or on the internet."

The name sounds familiar but I can't place the woman.

"What's she like?" I ask him.

"D'you really want to know?"

"Yes."

"OK then. It's my mum's birthday tomorrow and I need to get her a present. She likes Imogen's jewellery – want to help me choose?"

My palms are sticky as we pull up outside a pair of neat Georgian cottages fronting the road at the edge of Scruton. In the window of the left hand one is a sign that reads 'Hand crafted jewellery by Imogen Cutt'. I stand behind Richard and trail my hand over the wet tips of a lavender bush as he rings the bell.

I can't immediately see the woman who opens the door. It is not until Richard steps aside to introduce me that I get the full impact of her waif-like frame and blonde, ephemeral beauty; she is like a little elf and my heart sinks because I know that she is exactly Owen's type. I feel clumsy and awkward next to her.

"This is Alice," says Richard. "I'm doing some work for her at the moment and she's very kindly offered to help me choose something for Mum's birthday."

Imogen laughs. "I thought you had a new girlfriend for a moment."

Richard shakes his head. "Chance would be a fine thing. Alice was snapped up by Owen the moment she moved into the village."

"Owen Maltby?" Imogen looks sufficiently puzzled for me to feel decidedly suspicious.

"Well, he's the only Owen around here as far as I know."

Richard looks at me fondly. "Smitten with her, he is, too. Hardly surprising though." And I so want the floor to swallow me up.

But Imogen saves me. "Oh shut up, Richard, you're embarrassing Alice now. And I've got just the thing for your mum – a necklace that will go with the earrings you bought her last year."

Mercifully our visit is a short one. The necklace is lovely – silver thread and amber beads – and once it is gift wrapped we take our leave.

"I didn't embarrass you, did I?" asks Richard as we climb into his van.

"Yes, you did as a matter of fact. Why did you say those things?"

"Because they're true. And because if she's got designs on Owen she ought to know he already has a girlfriend."

I sigh. He is only trying to help so I can't be cross. "She's very pretty," I venture.

"Can't hold a candle to you. Listen Alice, your problem is that you're sitting around waiting for Owen with nothing much else in your life. Why don't you come to Mum's party tomorrow night? It's just a bit of a bash up at The Black Horse, but you might meet a few people, take you out of yourself a bit."

"I can't gatecrash your mum's birthday."

"Of course you can. She won't mind. More the merrier, she always says."

I can't go to the party without at least buying Richard's mother a card. So I take myself off to Northallerton while Richard gets on with tiling the shower room.

It is only once I park my car and start to walk away from it that I realise I'm going to have to pass the café to get to the shops. It's a tough one; Owen hasn't called, but still I don't feel I can actually walk past without dropping in. But if I do, it might seem over keen – especially without a reason to visit. I hate feeling this way; all tangled up inside when everything should be straight forward – Owen's my boyfriend, goddamit. At the moment, anyway.

So I decide I'll just stick my nose around the door to ask if he or Adam need anything in town. Maybe he'll be too busy to chat.

But there is nobody waiting at the counter, only Owen wiping down the coffee machine.

He turns when he hears the bell and his face splits into an enormous and genuine grin. "Alice," he says as he comes forward to hug me. "What a lovely surprise." All of a sudden I am smiling up into those deep blue eyes and feeling totally happy.

"I just dropped by to see if you or Adam want anything in town."

He kisses the tip of my nose. "That is so sweet of you. I don't need anything but I'll just ask Ads."

As he disappears into the kitchen I catch sight of a neat pile of leaflets on the counter. They look vaguely familiar and in a sickening moment I see that they are Imogen's. Perhaps Richard is right after all, but I don't have time to think about it because Owen comes back.

"No – Adam's fine. Fancy a coffee before you go?"

"No thanks. Hectic day today – I'm off to Richard's mum's party at The Black Horse tonight and I've got loads of stuff to do first. See you." I throw my reply over my shoulder as I walk towards the door and I want to really make an exit, but as luck would have it two women with pushchairs are just coming in. I hold the door open for them and as they are thanking me I hear Owen call cheerily:

"Good morning, ladies. Two skinny cappuccinos, is it?"

For some reason I feel even angrier.

## Chapter Forty-Six

I am in two minds as to whether to have a large gin before Richard collects me, and in the end decide I can't face a room full of people I don't know without one. But there is another reason I need a drink. When I came home there was a note from Margaret and she's found out about some of the first inhabitants of New Cottage from the parish records. In 1729, not that long after the house was built, a cheesemaker called Alice Fulton married a Charles Allen of Ravenswood Farm. The next year they had a son, Joshua, before Charles died in 1742 and Alice in 1750.

So the cheesemaker was called Alice – just like Owen's imaginary friend. Just like me. No wonder I need a drink. Or two. But they do buoy me up and by the time I hear Richard's horn outside I am definitely in the mood for a party.

Richard's mum, Susan, is a striking woman with long dark hair and I can immediately see where Richard gets his looks from. She is wearing her birthday necklace which dangles over the generous bosom revealed by her low cut top. In complete contrast his father, John, is comfortable-looking rather than glamorous, probably a few years older than his wife and with plenty of laugh lines around his eyes.

It is much later in the evening when John seeks me out.

"Hello again," I say, glad of an excuse to turn away from the two old biddies who've been giving me a blow by blow account of the last few episodes of Coronation Street.

He laughs. "Hello again? We haven't met." I am totally confused and don't know what to say, but then he continues, "You think I'm John, don't you?"

"Aren't you?"

"I'm Cyril – his twin brother."

"You are alike," I say, like an idiot. They must have been hearing that for years. In an effort to sound at least a little more intelligent I continue, "Twins run in families, don't they – are there any more in yours?"

"Oh yes; my niece has a pair of girls and I've traced Wainwright twins back to 1862 at least."

"You mean you've researched it?"

"Yes – one branch of the family goes all the way back to Durham in 1698."

Now I am all ears. "How did you find that out?"

"Well, when we were little Granddad had a family bible and all the births, marriages and deaths were recorded in it, going back to 1862. It used to fascinate me and when I got older it became a bit of a hobby."

"But how did you fill in the gaps?"

"Parish records, census information – the internet helps, you know, there's loads of stuff on genealogy and forums so you can get in touch with people researching the same name. I've found Wainwrights in Australia, Chile – Japan, even, would you believe."

"I'm interested in the history of my house..." I start but he interrupts.

"What, when it was built and how it developed over time? There's a bloke at the Northallerton Historical Society could tell you all about that – he's an expert. Where do you live?"

"New Cottage in Great Fencote. But although it would be interesting to date the building – the barn especially – I'm more concerned about finding out about the people who lived there."

"You're so right – people are far more fascinating than bricks and mortar – but try telling Richard that. He's..." He puts his head on one side, looking at me. "You're not the lass where Richard found the baby's body, are you?"

I nod. "That's why I'm interested in the date of the barn. The archaeologist said the baby was definitely buried after it was built, and although I'm assuming it was at the same time as the house, it would be good to actually know."

"Well, I can certainly put you in touch with this bloke. But perhaps you'd be interested in joining the Historical Society? We're a bit short of young blood, to be honest."

I take the plunge. "I would like to join, yes."

He slaps me on the back. "Good girl. There's a meeting in a few weeks so I'll take you along."

I know there is absolutely no chance of Richard seeing me home and I don't fancy walking, so I step outside into the lobby to call a taxi. But when I take my phone out of my pocket there's a text from Owen: 'Let me know when you're leaving and I'll pick you up'. I bite my lip. I am still angry about Imogen but it is kind of him – perhaps an olive branch? Except he doesn't know I'm angry, and maybe he just texted to make sure I'm not going home with Richard.

I text back 'Thanks, but I can get a cab.' Before I can call one there is a reply saying he's on his way. I don't want him turning up at the pub so I set off into the drizzle.

I have only just passed the village shop when his ancient Peugeot chugs into sight and pulls up next to me. He leans across to open the door.

"I didn't think you'd start walking – just as well I spotted you. Hop in."

"I wanted some air."

"Had a few drinks then?" he teases.

"Just the normal amount for a party." But I know I sound huffy so I add, "Thanks for coming to collect me."

"Well I knew Richard wouldn't be gentleman enough to see you home."

I don't like his jibe – Richard has been very kind to me. "I wouldn't expect him to," I flash back.

"Well he asked you to go with him."

"He didn't ask me to 'go with him' – he asked me if I'd like to go. Two entirely different things."

"Not in my book."

"Oh – is that the same book that means it's OK for you to spend most of your evenings in Scruton without a second thought about me?"

He starts to say something but instead he puts the car into gear and executes a neat three point turn before setting off back to Great Fencote. We are outside my house in a matter of minutes.

"Thanks for the lift," I say as I start to get out.

"Alice?" Owen's voice is tentative.

"Yes?"

"You're angry with me, aren't you?"

I think about it, seriously, and then I nod.

"It would be foolish of me to ask why," he continues, "because I know. I've done nothing but make you unhappy recently and I'm sorry. If you want us to call it day, you only have to tell me."

It is a very cowardly way of dumping me and I'm not going to let him off the hook that easily. "Let me think about it," I tell him. "I'll call you." I plan to give him quite a taste of what it's like waiting for the phone.

# Chapter Forty-Seven

I set out the four match pots of paint I have purchased on the windowsill. Warm colours – they have to be for this room. I paint two wide stripes of each one on each wall; the first is too dark, the third too orange, the others are OK – I will have to wait until they dry to make a final decision. I stand at the window counting the minutes between the passing cars.

Ravenswood Farm is clearly visible at the other end of the green. I can't look at it without thinking about Alice. Not me, of course, but Alice Fulton who had this house built and married the farmer. And Owen's imaginary friend Alice too. None of it fits – none of it – but then in a weird way it kind of does. I wrap my arms tightly around me and turn back into the room.

I share Margaret's new information with Richard when we go to the pub in Bedale to watch a local band. His lack of interest surprises me; he'd said he wanted to get to the bottom of the mystery but now he seems more concerned with downing a few beers and having a laugh while we listen to a couple of ageing rockers belt out Quo numbers.

"I thought you wanted to know too." I shout at him across the thudding bass.

"Well you already know what I think – you just don't believe me."

"But now we know that Alice actually lived."

He smiles down at me. "Look – it's Friday night and I'm out on the town with a beautiful woman. Don't spoil it for me by having an argument, hey? Let's just enjoy ourselves."

And if he won't talk about it, what else can I do?

So we listen to the band and his arm finds its way around my waist once or twice but when I move away he gets the message. We chat about nothing all the way home but as we leave the outskirts of Scruton Richard swears.

"Bugger it! Sorry, Alice – we shouldn't have come this way."

"Why ever not?"

"Owen's car – outside Imogen's."

I hadn't noticed and I shrug. "It's no big deal."

When I get home William is surprised that instead of shooing him into the garden I slip his lead around his neck and set off up the village. It feels as though there might be an early frost and I wrap my fleece tighter around me as we walk briskly towards the church and Owen's house. I don't know why – to torture myself with the fact he's not there, I guess.

Or to find out that he is. At least, his car is; parked right at the far end of the lay-by, sixty yards or so beyond his gate. I look back but there are no lights on – he must have practically followed Richard and me home and then gone straight to bed. I let out a deep breath I didn't know I was holding; at least he isn't spending the night with her.

William starts whining – he must be cold too. I crouch down on the pavement and give him a hug. If there was a light on in Owen's house I'd knock on the door, but instead I fish out my phone to send Owen a text, quickly, before I change my mind. 'Please don't think I'm playing games or messing you around – it's just I really don't know what to do for the best x'.

I wait until my knees are stiff, but there is no reply. Whether it is because his phone is turned off, or because he's just not replying again, I don't know. I put my hand on the front wing of his car to haul myself up and the metal is so cold I flinch and almost lose my balance, stumbling against it and soaking my fleece with icy condensation.

"You're a mess, Alice," I whisper. Then William and I trudge home.

# Chapter Forty-Eight

Owen does reply to my text – even though I have to wait until half past ten the next morning for him to do so. 'Fancy going for a walk tomorrow?' he asks.

Without hesitation I reply 'That would be really nice'

'About 4? Lunch at Adam's Mum's'

'Fine'

'See you then'.

When Owen turns up on Sunday afternoon he has Kylie with him.

"I thought we could take the dogs to the trout pond," he explains.

Once William realises where we are going he starts to pull on his lead and I swap it to my other hand. It isn't many moments later I feel Owen's fingers searching for mine. I give them a squeeze and look sideways to see that he is smiling right to his eyes.

"That's better," he murmurs, and it is.

Once we are on the island we let the dogs off the lead and wander around picking blackberries, which Owen wraps in his handkerchief. We end up with a good handful, but that's all.

"Not enough for jam," says Owen. "What can we do with them?"

"I could make a blackberry and apple tart for supper – d'you fancy that?"

"It would be lovely – but could we make it one night in the week? I have to be somewhere else by 7.30."

Something inside me explodes, but it is a contained explosion. I pull William's lead out of my pocket and call him, and thankfully he comes straight away. Owen says nothing and as I stalk across the bridge he doesn't try to stop me.

I glance over my shoulder and give him a filthy look. "I suppose I should be grateful you've fitted me into your hectic schedule at all."

He catches up just as I reach the main road. "Alice – Alice – I'm sorry. It's not like that at all. I know you're angry but..."

"Of course I'm angry but I'm not going to have an argument walking down the street."

"No...No...of course not," he mutters, and falls into step just behind me.

We say nothing more until we reach the garden room and he closes the door deliberately behind him.

"I'm sorry, Owen," I tell him, "but I just can't live at the bottom of your priority list anymore."

"Alice," he pleads, "you, more than anyone, know how it is. With the café and that..."

It is like he's pushed the wrong button. I was determined to keep cool, but his words shove me right over the edge. "Of course I know what it's bloody like at the café. And I also know you make it worse for yourself and Adam because you won't ask for help. There are a million little things I could do to give you guys a break, but do you let me? No. Because you're so bloody stubborn you won't even accept a hand of kindness when it's offered – let alone ask."

"That's not true – it's..."

But I haven't finished. "It's your business – I can live with that – however stupid you're being about it. But you can't expect me to hang around waiting for when you have a spare half hour or so because you're too busy in the evenings as well."

"Alice, please, you are my priority. If only you knew..."

I fold my arms. "Well alright, tell me. If I'm your priority, what's so important that you have to disappear off somewhere tonight?"

He looks at his feet. "It's the healing."

"Healing? The charming, you mean."

His tone becomes icy. "I am not a charmer."

I think of his car parked outside Imogen's house. "Whatever you call yourself, it's pretty cloak and dagger, isn't it?"

"I don't know what you mean."

"The way you don't tell me anything – you just say you're too busy. If you told me, I..."

"I have told you."

"No you haven't – I want specifics. I want to know where you are."

"I can't tell you."

"Why not?"

"It's just the way it is, that's all..."

"You don't trust me; you can't talk to me about what's important to you – what sort of relationship is that?"

"Please, Alice – don't cry. I do trust you – probably more than I've ever trusted anyone, but..."

"Balls, Owen – total balls! You're making excuses not to see me and you're avoiding telling me the truth. Just like you comprehensively avoided telling me about when you ran away. Because that's what you did – you know it and I know it. I saw what happened – I was there, remember – but will you talk about it? Will you even start to help yourself get over it? No! You're just running away from it all over again – and now you're running away from me too."

Owen doesn't reply. His face is paler than pale. He stands motionless for a moment then shakes his head. Then he turns very slowly towards the door, pulls on Kylie's lead, and he is gone.

# Chapter Forty-Nine

I know I ought to let it be over. Imogen or no Imogen, every word I said is true, and if Owen can't accept it then I'm better off being apart from him. But it's one thing convincing my head; quite another convincing my heart. So I think up lots of things to keep me manically busy by day, and in the evenings renew my acquaintance with the bottle.

But not every evening; I finally commit to Jane's book club, join a weekly salsa-cise class at Northallerton Leisure Centre and even go to the Historical Society with Cyril Wainwright. I can't say I am that excited by the idea of a talk on All Saints Church, but it is actually pretty good. And chatting to other members I find out about the Northallerton Reference Library and its local history collection. I make a mental note to visit it at some point in the near future.

In fact I enjoy my evening so much I go back again, for a talk entitled 'Morality before the Victorians'. The speaker is very amusing, with all sorts of anecdotes about how life was rather less straight-laced before they stuck their noses in, but one slide stops my laughter in its tracks.

It is a black and white engraving of a crowd beating pots and pans gathering around a cowering man, with a young boy on a pole pointing accusingly at him, and it is almost the exact image of the dream I had about Owen the night after he disappeared. The speaker explains it is a folk punishment for sexually inappropriate behaviour, called a riding. It ties in exactly with Margaret's story of the man who threw himself off the bridge, but rather than set me back on his trail it freaks me out to the point I spend all night throwing up.

It is a wake-up call to forget the past and ground myself in the present. If I don't do that I'll never be able to get over Owen. The weird stuff has stopped happening now he isn't around, so perhaps Richard is right – maybe it was Owen causing it.

I got over twelve years of marriage quite quickly, so I can certainly get over a couple of months with Owen if I can stop myself dwelling on it. I know what I need to do; I have to set about finding a job and expanding my social circle.

In the short term I start shopping in Bedale and always walk William towards Kirkby Fleetham. I defy Owen by taking sleeping tablets whenever I need them. I invest in a decent coffee machine and make my own lattes in the morning. I trawl the internet for local motor dealers and hand deliver my CV to every single one.

But it's hard. In my darker moments I wonder if Richard was right and Owen has cast some sort of love spell over me.

One evening when drawing the curtains, I catch sight of his car going past. In my mind's eye I can see him flick at the indicator with his ring finger, pull into the lay-by and switch off the engine. He sits back in the seat for a moment before reaching behind him for his rucksack, then he makes his way slowly to his front door. As he puts his key in the lock he turns and glances in the direction of New Cottage.

Instead of the Sleep-Eazee I find myself making a camomile tea. I don't think my bed has ever felt so empty.

# Chapter Fifty

The parcel arrives towards the end of November. The postman hands it to me as I am scraping the ice off my car ready to go to work one Saturday morning. I struck lucky when a sports car dealership in Richmond needed a part time receptionist. I get to do afternoons and Saturdays because that's when the owner's wife would rather be at home with the kids, but it suits me just fine.

I sign for the envelope, recognise Neil's handwriting, and sling it on the back seat. And there it stays until part way through the evening when I remember it again, and, my curiosity piqued, I venture out into the cold to fetch it.

Inside is a scribbled note from Neil saying he and Angela had found some stuff relating to New Cottage when they were clearing out ready to move. I tell William who the parcel is from as I spread the papers over the kitchen table. I expect him to prick up his ears at the sound of Neil's name, but he doesn't. I envy him his short memory. I fondle his ears and he looks up at me lovingly. Thank goodness for William; some nights, coming back to an empty house would be more than I could bear.

It's clear the papers relate to the history of New Cottage and despite myself my stomach lurches with excitement. I stand up abruptly and walk over to the wine rack. Supplies are low, but there is a lone bottle of red in the bottom corner. I've been avoiding it because it was one that Owen bought me but needs must. I burrow in the kitchen drawer for the corkscrew and pour myself a large glass.

Some of the documents are handwritten on thick creamy parchment and my fingers start itching to pick them up. When I do I am disappointed to find myself wading through several leases and deeds from the late nineteenth and early twentieth century.

But right at the bottom of the pile is something more relevant. It's a legal agreement, dated October 1785, between Henry Allen of Thames Street London, cheesemonger and John Almond of Fencote, for the 'absolute purchase' of the property. I rush into the garden room to dig out the note Margaret left me; Alice had married Charles Allen about sixty years before and surely this was a descendant. A cheesemonger too. Clearly Alice's cheese had passed down through the family, even if her house had not.

Instead of phoning Margaret to share the news I decide to tell her about it after church. I go every Sunday; there's no chance of running into Owen – he hasn't been near the place since he did his disappearing trick. I guess he's too embarrassed but that's his problem not mine.

Owen is destined to be pushed to the forefront of my consciousness today, because during the prayers for the departed Christopher reads out the name Audrey Cutt. She has to be a relation of Imogen's and while we chat over coffee in the vicarage I discover it is her mother.

Without thinking, I blurt out, "Oh dear, Owen will be upset."

Margaret looks at me in surprise but Jane nods. "I expect you're right – he was very good to Audrey, after all."

Another lady I know only by sight agrees. "When I saw her last she was so full of praise for him; every night he's been around there, giving her inhalations – she said they eased her breathing much better than anything the doctor suggested."

I start to collect the dirty cups and plates and take them into kitchen.

Margaret follows me and leans against the worktop as I stack the dishwasher.

"That's the first time I've heard you mention Owen since you split up."

"Yes," I reply. "And look where it got me."

"Whatever do you mean?"

"Well, I almost made a complete fool of myself."

"I don't follow you."

"I'll tell you later," I mumble as Jane comes in with another load of plates.

I have no intention of doing so but Margaret is nothing if not persistent and I begin to wish I hadn't offered to show her the papers. As we walk back to New Cottage she starts again.

"You were going to tell me why you thought you'd made a fool of yourself back there."

"I didn't – I just almost did." I know I sound like a petulant child and I immediately apologise.

She pats my hand. "Look, I don't want to stick my nose in, but..."

I take a deep breath. "It's nothing really – it's just that I thought Owen was going out with Imogen, not helping her mother…Well, I still don't know for sure he isn't, of course."

"He isn't." Margaret is categorical.

"How do you know?"

"Because he's breaking his heart over you, that's how."

"Rubbish."

"It's not. He's..."

"Margaret," I tell her, "he could have put me right about Imogen when he had the chance – he could have told me where he was going, but he refused. He could have told me lots of things – but he wouldn't. He knows how to fix this – it's not in my hands." The last bit isn't strictly true, but it's good enough. "Let's just consider the subject closed," I finish rather lamely.

I am completely deflated by the conversation and strangely devoid of any enthusiasm for my discovery. I rather perfunctorily show Margaret the document selling New Cottage out of the Allen family and send her on her way. All I want to do is wallow in my misery over Owen.

# Chapter Fifty-One

For quite some time the hall – or dining room, as it was – has been almost finished, just waiting for the curtains. I found some lovely apricot velvet in the haberdashery in Northallerton, and luckily one of our customers at the garage is a seamstress so she made them and delivered them yesterday.

Even so, it is late in the afternoon and almost dark before I decide to pull myself together and put them up. I spread them out over the easy chair in the corner of the hall; they look beautiful against the rust coloured walls and they are exactly what the room needs to finally make it feel warm.

But first the old curtains have to come down. I shut William in the garden room so he won't caper around at a critical moment and then I climb onto a kitchen chair to start releasing the hooks. I have one curtain down and am starting on the second when I lean a bit too far, the chair slides, I make a grab for some fabric and it rips, leaving me tumbling to the floor.

My chest is agony as I fight for the breath knocked out of me by the cold slabs – I will never be able to fill my lungs again and I begin to panic. But someone is nearby and I stretch out my hand. It is ignored as they carry on their conversation.

"...late this year, the rennet will have soured."

"No, child, you did right to wait. Grief is more likely to turn rennet than the passing of the seasons."

"Then the cheese will taste bitter, all the same."

There is a pause and I become aware of a wooden paddling sound and its rhythm is strangely soothing. But it comes to an abrupt halt.

"Mother – how do you bear it?" The young woman's voice is anguished and it resonates inside me.

"Because I must. And you must, Alice – although Lord knows your losses are greater than mine."

"No…Thomas…a child…a grandchild…it's all the same."

"But the fruit of my womb was with me for twenty-seven years, not ripped away at the moment of birth. I have memories – and good ones, at that."

"I caused Thomas such pain."

"No, child. Not you; it was the circumstance you found yourselves in. You did what you believed was right."

There is a rustle of cloth behind me and a brush of rough fabric across my face. I look up to see an old woman with clear blue eyes, and for a moment our gaze seems to meet. I am still stretching out my arm, but with a brief shake of the head she says:

"The help you need will be forthcoming. Accept it and the line of the charmers will not end."

"You are right, Mother, I know that," the other Alice replies. But I have the strangest feeling that the old woman wasn't talking to her.

I hear a door shut, but tangled up with it is another sound – an urgent rapping on the window. I have enough breath in my body to sit up to look and Owen's face is pressed against the glass – he is mouthing something but I can't hear him through the double glazing so I gesture towards the unlocked kitchen door and he disappears.

I am trembling but I don't know whether it's due to the fall, or what I've just witnessed, or lying on the cold flagstones. But I am not on flagstones now; I put my hand down and run my fingers along the familiar smoothness of the polished floorboards.

The kitchen door opens and closes and moments later Owen drops to the floor beside me.

"Alice – are you alright? What happened?"

"I was putting up my new curtains and I fell off the chair – I winded myself, that's all. I'm OK, really."

He puts his hands gently on my shoulders. "But you're shaking."

"I know…it's just…I thought I..." I grind to a halt. I can't tell him what I saw – it might drive him away and that's the last thing I want.

"You thought what?"

"Nothing. I was just a bit disoriented for a moment, that's all."

"Did you hit your head?" His lovely blue eyes are full of concern.

"I'm not sure to be honest. But I don't think so."

He puts his hand on the top of my head and starts to feel my cranium. "Let me know if anything hurts," he says. He works his way around my skull and then along my temples. Yes – it hurts – but inside me, with the pain of loss. So I don't tell him.

Instead, when he finishes I say, "That all seems fine then."

He sits back on his heels. "Just let me know straight away if you get a headache, or blurred vision, or feel sick or faint."

"I will."

"Just make sure you do. Come on – let's get you off that floor."

Owen helps me up and leads me into the snug, his hand solicitously under my elbow. He sits me down on the sofa.

"Right," he tells me, "I'm going to make some tea."

I smile, "With about a ton of sugar in mine, I guess."

"You guess absolutely right," he laughs and disappears into the kitchen.

While I am waiting for him to come back I remember William and set him free from his garden room prison. Naturally, as soon as he sees Owen he starts to growl.

"William – behave," I tell him, and he slinks away with a great sham of reluctance to lie in his favourite place in front of the wood burner.

Owen passes me my tea and sits down next to me.

"So," I start, "don't take this the wrong way – I'm really pleased to see you – but why did you come?" Did the old woman somehow send for him? I have to know.

He looks briefly down at his mug and then back at me. "Margaret's spent half the afternoon chewing my ear off. She...she persuaded me I owe you at least an explanation, if not an apology."

"Maybe it was me who jumped to the wrong conclusion."

"About Imogen, yes. But I can see why you thought it and I should have told you more about what was going on. It's not just the confidentiality thing, it's well, I...I find it so difficult to talk about stuff."

It is the first time he has even admitted it. I reach out and put my hand over his. "I know."

He looks at me hopefully. "You do understand, then?"

"Owen, I try. But the trouble is, when I know there are things you aren't exactly telling the truth about it's very hard to trust you when you tell me nothing at all."

"W...what sort of things?"

But he knows – I am sure he does. "Like you saying you went on holiday when we both know you ran away."

There is a silence and for once I am not tempted to fill it. If he won't answer me then he can walk out of my life forever, but if he will...if he'll even just try to...I swallow hard.

His hand is trembling on his mug and he won't look at me.

"Owen," I say finally. "I saw you take off across the fields that morning. I saw..." But somehow I can't say what I saw. "I...I blamed myself. I...I should have been more supportive the night before."

"Alice, believe me, there was nothing more you could have done. I was at the end of my tether. Everything...everything...had got on top of me. I wasn't you or Adam or...it was me."

"So did you try to jump off the bridge?"

He pushes his hair back from his face in that oh so familiar gesture. "I can't remember getting to the bridge, honestly I can't. I don't know, I...it's all so muddled...if I could really remember it then I would tell you, I promise..." He trails off, biting his lip. His face is deathly white and there are beads of sweat on his forehead – I have pushed him far enough and at least he tried. I cast around for a way to take the pressure off him without completely changing the subject.

"Richard thought perhaps he'd seen the ghost of that man in your gran's story."

"Gran's story?"

Of course I am being horribly vague; she must have had loads of stories. "Margaret told us – the one where the philanderer who couldn't have the girl he wanted threw himself off the bridge."

Owen looks puzzled. "I don't remember that one."

Is he being evasive again? "Well, she must have had so many tales..."

"She did. I...I could tell you some of them sometime if you're interested?"

I try not to sound too eager but probably fail miserably. "I'd like that – how about you come to supper one night?"

I am rewarded with a genuine smile. "I'd love to Alice, really I would."

When Owen leaves I go back into the hall. There is a shortened floorboard near the radiator and it's a bit loose but I can't prize it open with my bare fingers. I fetch my carving knife from the kitchen to ease it up; it's not ideal but it does the trick. And underneath? Flagstones. Just like I knew there would be.

## Chapter Fifty-Two

I know Owen is at the door before he even knocks because William breaks into a furious volley of barking. Despite this, Owen bends down to fondle his ears but William bares his teeth and backs away.

Owen sighs, "I'm never going to win with that dog, am I?" He turns to me and smiles, "So how are you, Alice?" and the soft smoothness of his voice and the way he says my name twist something inside me. The way I feel about him hasn't changed at all.

I take the bottle of wine he's proffering. "Fine thanks. You?"

"Yes, good. I hope red's OK; I had a sudden panic walking down here that maybe you'd cooked fish and it wouldn't go."

"You're OK – it's lamb."

"Perhaps if I feed William some titbits under the table he'll stop growling at me."

"No, Owen – you mustn't – Richard does that and it drives me nuts."

There is an uncomfortable moment before Owen asks, "So how is Richard? I haven't seen him for ages."

"He comes here every day it's too wet for him to work outside and given the weather recently that's been quite a lot. He's almost finished the barn so I'm planning to decorate the bathroom on Sunday – at least that'll be one room over there done and dusted."

"Want some help? I'll only worry about you falling off chairs or something..."

"Oh, Owen, that's so sweet of you, but I couldn't ask – it's your only day off."

"You're not asking, I'm offering. Change is as good as a rest, isn't it?"

I feel myself smiling "Then I'd love it if you would. It's not much fun on your own. It needn't be an early start though; I won't steal your lie-in."

"Do I look as though I need it that much?"

I gaze at him long and hard. The hair around his temples is greyer and his laugh lines have been joined by a few deep furrows on across his forehead. His eyes may be bright but the rings under them are dark and deep. He looks as though he's lost weight, too.

"Yes, actually, you do." I mean it to sound like a joke, but instead the words come out softly and I am embarrassed I've let down my guard. "So how is the café?" I continue brightly, hoping he didn't notice.

"Busy – which is good. The bank's off my back for the moment so we must be doing alright. And Adam even had a week's holiday."

"How did you manage that?"

"The college approached us about taking on a young chef for work experience so it all fitted together pretty well."

"I'm glad Adam got a break."

"Yes, so am I. He has a new boyfriend – nice chap, paramedic from Middlesborough. They went off to Cyprus for a week and had a fantastic time."

"Really? I'm so pleased for him."

"It is good to see him happy. So – what have you been up to, Alice? I hear you've got a job."

"Just part time but that suits me at the moment. I like being back in the hustle and bustle of a car showroom, but I managed to put one of the salesmen's noses out of joint this week because I sold a car and I'm not meant to – I'm only the receptionist after all..." And I prattle on about work, and Owen talks about the café, and the evening passes very quickly.

It is just after ten o'clock when he leaves. He gives me the briefest of little hugs – like he used to when we were only friends, right at the very beginning.

"It's been lovely, Alice," he says, "I'll see you on Sunday morning" and he disappears down the path.

I stand in the doorway while William makes his last trip of the day to his favourite drainpipe. While my mind is happy with the way the evening went, my body is aching for Owen. The little hug has only served to kindle a flame and I am desperate to be touched by him in way I soon discover I can't even satisfy for myself.

# Chapter Fifty-Three

When I get home from work on Saturday Richard has left me a note: 'bathroom all done – go have a look'. So I don't bother taking off my coat and I wander over to the little side door of the barn and flick the light on.

As I step onto the smooth concrete floor the smell of damp plaster greets me and I notice the stud wall that divides the garage from the apartment has been skimmed. To my right a sink is plumbed into the wall and various electric wires hang out; Richard is waiting for me to choose the units to make up the kitchenette. I really do need to get a move on.

I am standing where the baby's body was found. I've heard nothing from the archaeologists and I wonder how long it will take. I'm curious, but by the same token I don't want to be landed with the tiny skeleton now Owen is back on the scene. Our little boat is rather too delicately poised to be rocked at the moment.

I look up at the end of the beam where it slots into the lime washed wall. Cyril's mate from the Historical Society came around to take a look and he was fairly certain that because of the shape of the beams, the house and the barn were built at the same time. He got excited about the one that runs across the centre of the hall ceiling then dragged me out to the barn to show me this one but I still don't really see what he meant. I guess you have to be an expert.

As well as the barn, he was very knowledgeable about which bits of the house were added when. Originally it was a two-up, two-down cottage with a ladder from what is now the snug (then the scullery – surprise, surprise) into my bedroom, which probably connected with a bigger room where the dressing room and landing are. Because it's north facing he said that the hall would have been the dairy but I didn't need him to tell me that either.

I climb the narrow stairway and cross the upper room to the bathroom. The terracotta and cream tiles give it some warmth and my pots of ochre emulsion stand ready for tomorrow. The lights are on dimmer switches and I turn them very low; the burnished copper taps glint invitingly and I am tempted to christen the Jacuzzi, but with no heating as yet it's a bit too cold. I'll have to bring a fan heater or two over tomorrow for when Owen and I are working. And maybe some towels and a bottle of wine for when we've finished. We did the friendship bit on Wednesday and that was OK; now it's time to bring some romance back into our lives.

I get up early on Sunday and prime the bare wood before going back into the house to shower and have some breakfast. I take William for a quick wander up the garden then lock him in the garden room; I don't want him running around getting paint on his fur – or growling at Owen for that matter. I tape a note to the door saying I'm in the barn.

It isn't long before Owen arrives. I hear his footsteps on the stairs just as I am replenishing my paint tray. I straighten up and poke my nose around the door.

"I'm in here," I call.

"Good morning, Alice," he says with his usual politeness. "Sorry if I'm a bit late."

"You're not late – I just started early."

"Saved something for me to do I hope?"

"Of course. If you're worried about me standing on ladders then you can do the ceiling."

It takes a good few hours to finish the job but eventually we're able to sit on the edge of the Jacuzzi and admire the results of our labours.

"It looks smashing, Alice, really it does," Owen tells me. "Really warm and inviting to have a long soak after a day walking on the Moors."

"What about a soak after a hard day's decorating? Fancy trying the Jacuzzi out?"

My heart is in my mouth as I say it, but Owen shakes his head. "The steam wouldn't do the wet paint any good, would it?"

He is being pragmatic and decidedly unromantic, but you can't fault his logic. I am desperate to close the physical space between us though so I pat the back of his hand. "Sensible as ever." I tell him.

He looks at me sideways. "No, not always – sometimes the exact opposite." He turns his hand over and intertwines his fingers with mine for a moment, before letting go and standing up. "Anyway, I'd better get on."

"Oh. I was going to cook you a meal to say thank you."

"Don't worry – I've got some leftover chicken casserole of Adam's that needs finishing up."

It's hard but I tell myself to be grown up about this and hide my disappointment. After all, he's just spent most of his Sunday helping me out. But I must have failed because Owen stops at the bathroom door.

"Come to think of it, there's quite a lot of chicken casserole – I'm sure it would stretch to two. There's a few things I need to do right now, but if you wanted to come over at about 7.30..." he trails off, looking as uncertain as I feel.

I put on a bright smile. "It won't have to stretch so far if I bring a pudding, will it?"

He grins back. "A veritable feast. See you later."

I am left remembering the touch of his fingers on mine and thinking perhaps there is hope; maybe he just wants to play things ultra slowly.

When I arrive at his house he does nothing to disabuse me of this thought. I have changed into a skirt and pretty cardigan which I leave rather too unbuttoned and as he helps me off with my coat he briefly places his hands on my shoulders and tells me I look lovely, but that is all. Not even a little hug, and certainly no kiss, although for a moment I sense the thought of one in his eyes.

But he is happy and chatty as he dishes up the casserole and we put my apple crumble in the oven to warm. It is almost as though we have gone back to our early days – or to square one, in my book – except now I am craving intimacy even more because I know what I'm missing. Owen opens a bottle of wine and I pray that a couple of glasses will embolden one of us to make the first move.

So when he says, "Alice, there's something I want to talk to you about," I feel my mouth go dry.

I lean towards him over the table and rest my chin on my hand. "Go on," I encourage.

"I think I'm about to get busy with my herbs again, in fact, I know I am. It might mean I don't have much spare time for a while and..." he trails off.

"I don't suppose you have the slightest idea how long..."

He shakes his head. "It's another case of emphysema, like Audrey Cutt – word gets around."

"It's because you're so good at helping people," I find myself saying and suddenly I feel very proud of him.

He looks down at his hands. "I use the gifts I have been given, that is all."

"Have you ever thought of making a career as a herbalist?"

"No. These are gifts, Alice. They are not to be used for profit."

I nod as though I understand. "Did your grandmother teach you?"

He hesitates. "Mainly, but some of it I feel I've always known. The gift is passed down, Alice, from generation to generation."

"So you will pass it down to your children?"

"Not any child, it would have to be a daughter. But it's academic. The buck stops here."

I am puzzled. "Why?"

He stands up to start clearing the plates "Because who's ever going to marry me?" he laughs.

"Now you're just fishing for compliments," I tease, and the moment passes.

Later I go to use the bathroom. It is the first time I have been upstairs and I am confronted by three doors on the landing. Owen told me the bathroom is at the back, but the front bedroom door is open and I can't resist a peep. It is clearly Adam's room, judging by the Leeds United scarf draped over the mirror and the large navy donkey jacket flung on the bed.

The door to the back bedroom is closed but my wine-fuelled curiosity gets the better of me. Downstairs I hear Owen usher Kylie outside so I very gently turn the handle.

But this isn't a young man's room; it is an old woman's. There is a pale yellow candlewick bedspread on the bed and from what I can make out from the shaft of light from the landing, yellow and white floral curtains. The furniture is dark oak, and on the bedside table is a black and white photograph in a plain silver frame. Peering around the corner at the dressing table I spot an ivory hand mirror and clothes brush, and a collection of china dogs. The only trace of Owen in the room is a vague smell of his aftershave. I close the door and go back downstairs. After a very short while I make my excuses and go home.

# Chapter Fifty-Four

The heady mixture of damp raincoats and perfume is too much for me and I escape up the escalator to the household department. The thudding behind my eye eases a little as I rise serenely above the fug and I take a deep breath as a display of white fluffy duvets appears in front of me.

My momentary calm is shattered when I turn a corner past the pillows and am confronted by piles of candlewick bedspreads. My head starts to thump again and I make straight for the coffee shop, but the cappuccino is bitter and the chocolate brownie too dry. Instead I open my bottle of water and pop two paracetamol from their plastic blisters. The water spills down my chin as I take them and I wipe it away before anyone sees.

I pick the froth off the top of my coffee with the tip of my teaspoon, thinking that I will hate candlewick bedspreads forever. I didn't even know you could still buy them; they belong to another age – the age of Owen's grandmother. I don't even know her name.

She has always been standing in the shadows behind him but I didn't realise how little he had let her go. Perhaps I shouldn't be surprised; ever since I've known him he has proved completely incapable of facing up to his feelings. That he should creep into his grandmother's bed rather than move on should not have taken the stuffing out of me the way it has.

And yet, after he picked me up off the floor the Sunday before last, he tried to talk. And I remember, when we were arguing all those months ago, he said he trusted me more than he trusted anyone else. I dismissed it at the time, but what if it's true? What if I can help him to turn his life around and it's just because I'm so bad at loving people that I'm thinking about running away.

Reality check: every bit of pap psychology I've ever read is telling me he's trouble. The guy needs professional help – he'd just never admit it. I worry he could even be dangerously unhinged but I have no evidence of that. Owen is kind and sweet and spends all his time helping people. Is he perhaps too good to be true? Or does his seriously dodgy self esteem depend on him doing stuff for other people? Seeing a sale basket emblazoned with the words 'damaged goods' does nothing to improve my state of mind.

All afternoon at work I battle with the headache and by the time I set out for home it has been joined by a distinctly sore throat. It's Friday night and I am due to go to The Black Horse for a few drinks but I can't face it and spend the evening curled up in the snug with William, feeling very sorry for myself.

Next morning I am no better; if anything, my throat is worse. I struggle into work but I'm sent home again within an hour and stumble gratefully into bed and fall fast asleep.

I am woken by my phone bleeping a text. I feel disoriented; I have no idea what time it is – except that it's daylight and for a moment I wonder why I was asleep. Then I stretch out to pick up my mobile and my aching head reminds me.

The text is from Owen: 'Fancy taking the dogs for a walk tomorrow afternoon?' Of course I would, but even getting out of bed is too much of a challenge at the moment. 'Would love to but not feeling too good' I text back.

Almost at once my phone rings and almost splits my skull in two. It's Owen.

"What's wrong, Alice?" he asks.

I try to sound cheerful, "Apart from my throat feeling like sandpaper and my head thumping fit to burst..."

"You're not at work, are you?"

"No. They sent me home. I'm tucked up in bed."

"Good. That's where you should stay until I get there. The weather's lousy so it's quiet at the moment – if it keeps that way I'll try to finish a bit early, but I can't promise."

"Owen – you couldn't pop into the chemist and get me some throat sweets, could you?"

"No. Because I'll bring you something better than that."

When I open the door to let Owen in he gives me a great big hug and I hope that's what he meant by something better than a throat sweet.

"You poor duck," he says, "you look absolutely rotten," and he leads me into the snug and sits me down on the sofa.

"Now, let's take a look at that throat. Open wide." He peers inside and tuts. "It's all red and inflamed. I bet you've got a temperature too." He puts the back of his hand on my forehead and nods.

"I've also got the headache from hell," I mumble. "Did you bring anything from the chemist?"

"I've brought one of my own tinctures. But first of all I think you need to gargle with some good old fashioned salt water to stop that infection taking hold."

I screw up my face. "It'll taste foul."

"It'll sting like mad too, but I'll only ask you to do it once – after that you can stick to echinacea."

"To what?"

"Trust me, Alice," he squeezes my hand, "I know what I'm doing."

The salt water is horrible but he is right – it takes the edge off the soreness and he puts a glass of water with some echinacea on the bedside table for me to sip every hour or so. Finally he gives me two little tablets for my headache and puts a cool flannel smelling of rosemary on my forehead.

He sits on the edge of the bed and takes my hand. "I'd like to come back later to see how you are – would that be OK?"

"Lovely."

I drift off to sleep with the thumping in my head fading and the scent of rosemary wafting into my nose.

# Chapter Fifty-Five

I come to with a start as a different type of pain pulses through my body. It builds from deep inside my abdomen and grips me, making me gasp for my breath. I cry out in agony and shock – yet at the same time the pain is oddly expected.

As is the old woman's soothing voice beside me. "Shush, child. It is good mother nature, that is all. It will pass soon enough."

She is right, it does fade, but I know it will come back. She moves across the room to an opening where there shouldn't be one, and pushes a curtain aside.

"Thomas," she calls quietly, "you must go to Ravenswood and tell them to prepare. Alice's time has almost come."

I hear footsteps on a wooden stair. "I cannot do that, Mother."

"Thomas – you must."

"I cannot. You will have to go."

"Don't be a fool – I cannot leave Alice at this time."

"I will stay with her."

"A man has no place in the birthing chamber – it is ill luck."

"I have the gifts, Mother. It is different with me."

I feel myself struggle on the bed, trying to pull myself away from that time. But then there are gentle hands on my shoulders as Thomas slides onto the pillows beside me. The shape of his body, his touch, his scent, are all so very familiar.

"Alice," he pleads, "do not let them take our baby."

"It cannot be undone now," I find myself murmuring.

"I beg you, Alice..."

"We would have nothing, Thomas, less than nothing."

"It matters not." His voice is sulky, like a child, but I open my eyes and see his gazing down into mine, filled with a pain which is very much a grown man's.

"Thomas, I..." But the pain is back. He grips my shoulders as I writhe and he murmurs soft words I cannot properly hear. When the contraction passes the warmth of his body against my back steadies me, and I drift into sleep, my breathing in a rhythm with his.

I know this peace can't last and I somehow manage to will myself away from that time. I can hear rain on the window and I can smell rosemary. The scent helps me to wake, and when I open my eyes the room is bathed in the steady glow of the bedside lamp and not the flickering of a candle. I feel sick with relief.

But it was only a dream. Or was it? Yes, it must be my fever making it seem especially real; after all, I know about Thomas and Alice the cheesemaker, so why would I not dream about them? Then I remember the flagstones under the floorboards in my hall; I knew nothing about those, but they were there all the same.

I haul myself up the bed and hug my knees. I need to go back to what I know from historical facts; I know that Alice existed and that she married Charles from Ravenswood Farm. I know they had a child called Joshua. I know that at some time – maybe while her family still owned New Cottage – a baby was buried in the barn. But I know nothing about a Thomas, or his mother, and I badly need to talk to Margaret about how to find out.

I pull on my dressing gown and set off down the stairs to find my phone, but as I reach the hall I hear a key in the back door and William starts to bark. Within moments Owen appears through the door and the dog slips past him, making a beeline for the kitchen.

"Oh, God – I haven't fed him. What time is it?"

"Almost ten o'clock – and what are you doing out of bed?"

"I...I wanted a drink," I falter. I can't tell him the real reason I came downstairs; it's too complicated.

"Come on then, let's sit you down in the kitchen and I'll make you one. Then you can tell me what to feed William; at least if I do it he might start to like me a bit better."

Owen is right. As soon as he opens the can of dog food William calls a truce. He even rather endearingly puts his paw on Owen's leg, the way he does to me when he thinks I've forgotten to give him his biscuit.

Without asking what I want, Owen makes two mugs of camomile tea and carefully drops some tincture into mine.

"It's OK, you won't taste it," he tells me as he puts the mug in front of me.

I sniff it cautiously. "What is it?"

"It's good for fever – and sore throats."

I am too tired to ask him to be more specific.

I look across the table. Owen's eyes are sunk into his head and the circles beneath them are almost bruises. Both his hands are clasped tightly around his mug, but I reach across and stroke his fingers.

"You do too much." It is a statement of fact.

He shrugs. "I have no choice."

"You do."

"No. Could I have left an old man gasping for his breath? Could I leave Adam to run the café on his own? Could I not come back to make sure you're OK?"

"I am OK."

He loosens his hand from the mug and puts the back of it on my forehead. "Apart from the high fever, that is."

"I'll be alright. My throat only feels like one person's sandpapering it now, and not an entire army."

"Oh, Alice," he smiles and shakes his head. "That still doesn't mean I'll not worry about you all night."

"Then stay."

I don't know what makes me say it and he looks shocked that I have. "Oh come on, Owen," I bluster, "I don't mean it in any sort of...you know...sexual...way. But if you're here then you won't have to worry about me so you'll sleep. And I won't have to worry about you worrying about me and so I'll sleep."

He gives my hand a little squeeze. "I'm sorry Alice, I can't."

"Why not?"

"I just can't."

"That's not a reason."

He drains his camomile and stands up. "No, it isn't, is it?" He is half way to the kitchen door when he stops. "I don't suppose your spare bed's made up?"

"No, it's not. It's OK Owen, if you're uncomfortable with it, then that's cool. But if you could just let William out then help me upstairs before you go – I really do feel rotten." I'm laying it on with a trowel, but it's for his own good.

He nods. "I'll take you up first."

He says nothing more as I lean on his arm all the way to the bedroom and he tucks me under my duvet. Then he disappears to let William out and I am scared he won't come back. But after a while he does, with a glass of echinacea water and the rosemary scented flannel. He places it gently on my forehead then to my surprise stretches out beside me.

"I'll just stay until you drop off," he explains, but in truth it is he who falls asleep first.

## Chapter Fifty-Six

It is not an exaggeration to say it is complete and utter bliss to wake with Owen beside me. Even though he is semi clothed and half in and half out of the duvet. At some point during the night he must have woken and peeled off his cords and jumper, but I can't remember – I have slept the sleep of the dead. Just like he's doing now.

But William isn't and I can hear him scratching and whining in the garden room. I creep out of bed as quietly as I can and go downstairs to let him out. The rain has stopped but it's a dank, chill morning and I can't see the Moors for the low cloud that envelopes them. That it is light means we have slept for a long time but when I check the clock I am amazed to find it's half past nine. I do feel better though; hardly any headache and no sore throat at all.

Just as I'm giving William his biscuit I hear Owen's footsteps on the stairs. Damn. I'd been going to take him a mug of tea in bed – and climb back in next to him. Clearly it's not what he wants and I feel confused and rejected. What the hell is going on here? I want to scream the words at him, but of course I don't.

"How are you this morning, Alice?" he asks, as though nothing has happened. Which, of course, it hasn't.

"Much better thanks," I mumble.

"You're sure?" He reaches out his hand and puts it on my forehead very tenderly. I suddenly soften towards him.

"Yes. I had a really good night's sleep and my throat's fine. Honestly. Come on, I'll make us a cup of tea. And maybe some toast? Are you hungry?"

He shakes his head. "No, as long as you're sure you're OK I have to be getting on. There's a mountain of paperwork I need to catch up on and today's my only chance."

It is hard to stop myself turning away from him. "That's fine – I understand." But I don't. Not really.

"Now just you keep taking that echinacea and I've left a few headache pills in the kitchen." And he is the concerned herbalist again, no more and no less, and I am so bitterly disappointed I don't even wave him down the path.

I mope all morning and instead of moping all afternoon I decide to go to see Margaret. I am increasingly certain that the man who jumped off the bridge was the father of Alice's baby and he was called Thomas, so logically (if there is any logic to this at all) he may well have been the philanderer in Owen's gran's story. Hopefully Margaret won't think I've put two and two together to make about nine.

Thankfully, she doesn't – or at least I don't think she does, anyway. We are sitting in her conservatory in the fading afternoon light so I can't see her face very clearly, but she doesn't sound overly perturbed when I tell her about the conversation I heard between Alice and Thomas' mother when I fell, and about the dream I had yesterday evening. In fact, she takes it all in her stride.

"So we're looking for a Thomas, then? One who died between...what did we say now? 1723 and 1729?"

"Yes, that's right. It would have to have been before Alice married because, well, you don't think the dream means that the baby was Alice and Thomas's, do you?"

She looks at me, head on one side. "You do, don't you? Even though Owen's gran's story implies that she turned Thomas down."

"I don't know, Margaret; one moment it all fits together in my head and the next it seems so improbable."

"Well, if we do find a Thomas who jumped off the bridge it would seem to give credence to the rest of your visions."

"Visions?" I shudder. I hadn't thought of them as visions. That makes them scary somehow, like I'm a clairvoyant. Except that clairvoyants see the future and I see the past. I sink my head into my hands.

"Margaret – I just want this to stop. Whatever it is."

"I suppose," she replies slowly, "that it's easier for me, just looking on. It's a little adventure – a bit of excitement. But you are in the middle of it, experiencing it. It must be pretty frightening."

"I think it would be more frightening if Richard hadn't seen and heard things too. And it helps hugely that you don't think I'm a complete and utter nutcase or that I'm making it up."

Margaret smiles. "Well you've always struck me as pretty grounded, Alice. Does Richard have any idea about why it might be happening?"

"He thinks it's Owen. He says weird stuff's always happened around him." And I tell her about the young Alice.

"So is Owen seeing these people too?"

"I haven't asked him."

"Do you think you should?"

"Oh, Margaret, I can't. For a start he looks so exhausted and worried all the time, and then I don't really know where I stand with him, although thanks to you we are at least friends."

"Thanks to me?"

"Well yes – he told me you'd been bending his ear all afternoon that Sunday so he'd decided to come around."

"Hardly. He just popped in for a quick cuppa and I told him you'd got the wrong end of the stick about Imogen. Still, I'm pleased it spurred him into action. He was miserable without you and you were miserable without him."

I look at her dumbly. I am still miserable without him. Or with him. I don't even know which. I change the subject.

"So how are we going to find Thomas?"

"I think the best place would be the County Records Office. It might be fun if we went together – how about one day next week?"

I agree without hesitation.

# Chapter Fifty-Seven

In Monday morning's post, among the Christmas cards, is a letter from the archaeologists. It's a bulky little package that I have to sign for, because it contains the key and the few scraps of ribbon they found around the baby's neck. The letter itself says that the skeleton is too young for them to be clear about its gender and the size probably meant it was the product of a late miscarriage rather than a pregnancy that went full term. They are also a bit woolly about the date – first third of the eighteenth century, but Lucy did warn me that carbon dating is not too reliable with so recent a find.

They are now awaiting my instructions about what to do with the skeleton because of my wish to give it Christian burial. Not my wish – Owen's. Somehow I can't bear to leave it in the archaeologists' office any longer so I arrange to collect the baby on my way to work.

When I get home I am at a loss about what to do with it. The tiny skeleton is neatly packaged in a cardboard storage carton with the date and place of find written on the outside. It is clinical, a little harsh, and it makes me feel uncomfortable. I put the box in one of the empty kitchen units in the barn, as close as I can to where the bones were found.

I still want to share this news with someone (not Owen), and the need to find out just who Thomas was now seems more urgent.

So I give Margaret a call and we decide to visit Northallerton Records Office next morning.

The original coroner's records have been put onto microfiche so Margaret takes 1720 to 1725 and the librarian sets me up at the machine next door with the next volume. She fusses and flaps, showing me how to insert the fiches and to move the focus of the machine around and I become increasingly impatient.

Finally she leaves me alone and I start to scan the words in front of me; tiny, old fashioned handwriting I find hard to read. I search the screen for any name which could be deciphered as Thomas.

We have been going for about half an hour when I find him. I am so surprised to see the name leap out of the copperplate I almost squeal with excitement – then I remember where I am.

"Margaret," I hiss, "I've found Thomas."

She jumps up and stands behind me, while I read the entry aloud.

"'In the matter of the death of Thomas Winter, charmer, of Great Fencote on 2nd inst. The court heard evidence of Giles Westland, incumbent of the parish of St Andrew's, and Charles Allen, farmer, that the deceased was of good character and sound mind. The coroner therefore orders the death of Thomas Winter to be recorded as by drowning and that his body be released to his mother for burial. Dated this seventh day of May, year of our Lord 1727.'"

I turn to look at Margaret. "It fits."

Her fingers touch my shoulder. "It's a bit scary, isn't it?"

"What? That Richard and I have seen things that have a basis in historical fact?"

"Yes."

"I don't know if that makes it more or less scary right now. Anyway, I'd better copy it down so I can show him." My hand is shaking as I do so, and once I have finished Margaret bundles me off to Caffé Bianco for a restorative coffee. But only after I make her promise not to tell Owen where we've been.

She agrees. "Perhaps now isn't the right time."

When we walk into the café Owen makes such a big fuss of us that Adam comes out of the kitchen. I haven't seen him for ages.

"Come out back with me a minute," he urges, "then I can tell you all about Dean while I get the mince pies out of the oven."

The kitchen is warm and spicy, and I prop myself on the edge of the table. "So – what's he like? Are you happy?" I ask, settling down for a long chat.

Adam puts the baking tray down. "He's wonderful, I'm fine – but it's Owen I really want to talk to you about. Any chance we can meet up for a quick drink tonight?"

"Not tonight – Historical Society."

"Do you have to go?"

"I do, rather. How about tomorrow?"

"Fine. Let's make it at the leisure centre then Owen will think I'm going to the gym."

I hesitate. "He…he doesn't seem himself, does he?"

Adam shakes his head. "You don't know the half of it, Alice – not the half of it."

## Chapter Fifty-Eight

The bar of the Durham Ox is packed with office party revellers. Cyril and I squeeze through the chatter and clink of glasses to a small table which has been ignored – probably because it is half hidden by an enormous Christmas tree. A piece of tinsel gets caught in my handbag.

It is clear Cyril has been bursting to tell me something all evening and as soon as we sit down he delves into the plastic bag he's been clutching and pulls out a bundle of paper. As he unfolds it I realise that it is one huge sheet, sellotaped together in a higgledy-piggledy fashion; it is his family tree.

I am itching to know what all this is about and Cyril takes a long time getting to the point, clearly loving having an audience and insisting on starting with Richard and his sisters and working backwards. He is a sweet old man and I try very hard not to be impatient as his finger meanders up the chart, regularly fuelled by pit stops for long draughts of Guinness.

With agonising slowness it moves past his father and back to Sidney and Henry, born together in 1890, then back to their father Herbert, who was also one of twins.

"Was he the chap who had the family bible?" I ask.

"Yes, that's him, but it's this next lot you'll be interested in, because although Herbert's father was from the Durham line, his wife Sarah was born in Great Fencote. They settled in Kirkby Fleetham, mind, but their marriage was in the Great Fencote register, and her birth."

It is her birth name that grabs my interest – Sarah Allen, born 18th September 1837. Allen. My eyes move quickly up the paper to see that her father was Joshua, born in 1812, so not Charles Allen's son Joshua, but clearly a family name. And his father was Thomas Allen – and his father too. And this is where the direct connection is made: Thomas Allen, born in 1754, was Joshua senior's youngest son. Alice's grandson. Richard is clearly descended from Alice Fulton and Charles Allen and despite the crush of people around us I go cold – especially when I remember that I called Richard Charles all those months ago after the village fair.

I steady myself by asking an inane question. "So one of Richard's ancestors was actually born in New Cottage?"

Cyril beams. "Exactly. Funny co-incidence if you ask me, with him doing so much work on the house, and finding the baby, of course," he adds.

But that thought is not where my mind scrambles off to. Is his relationship with the past the reason why Richard heard the crying and saw Thomas Winter? Is it perhaps Richard who holds the key to all this, after all? The thought has never occurred to me before. What if this is nothing to do with Owen?

## Chapter Fifty-Nine

It is almost quarter past eight on Wednesday night when Adam bursts into the leisure centre cafeteria. I came an hour or so ago for a swim and have just finished toying with the toasted sandwich that was meant to be my supper.

Adam apologises as he thumps into the chair next to me. "Owen had the car and he was late back."

I raise my eyebrows. "More healing?"

"It's pretty relentless at the moment. He's running himself into the ground."

"I know. I tried to talk to him about it but he said he had no choice."

"It's what he tells me but it's all getting out of hand, Alice, and I just wondered if there was anything you could do."

"I don't think so. He seems to be…I don't know…holding back from me?"

"Well he's not much of a talker when it comes to himself – never has been."

"I didn't mean like that. I meant…well, to be honest Adam, I don't even know whether we're in a relationship or not."

Adam leans forward. "But I thought you guys were back together."

"It's like…like we're just friends again. But…then sometimes he's really affectionate, but only for a moment…I can't make it out."

Adam sighs, "He's totally fucked up, Alice, if you want to know."

"Like he was last summer?"

"Worse. He even talks to himself."

I try to laugh. "Well, I do that sometimes."

"Sometimes is fine – we all do it a bit. But all the time? Any time he's in a room on his own he's constantly muttering. But then it's not strictly constant – sometimes he asks questions and waits for a reply, then carries on. It's like he's having a conversation with someone – it scares the living daylights out of me."

"What does he talk about?"

"I can't rightly hear the words. He's muttering, like I said, it's not clear..." he tails off.

I don't really know what to say. "It does sound odd."

"Dean says it sounds psychotic."

"What – talking to yourself?"

"No. Thinking someone's replying."

"You can't know..."

"Alice – he asks questions, then waits a while before speaking again. What does that sound like to you?"

I have to concede it doesn't sound good. "Has he ever been like this before?" I venture. "Perhaps when his gran died?"

"No. He'd cry a bit – you know – when it was just me and him around – but then that was understandable. There was one night he went a bit strange and he kept telling me over and over that he couldn't see her any more. But that was only a few weeks after the funeral, so I thought it was maybe delayed shock and he seemed right as rain the next day."

"He's never got over her though, has he? I mean…his bedroom..."

Adam's eyes widen in surprise. "You've seen it?"

"He doesn't know I have. I took a wrong turn looking for the bathroom. It freaked me out, to be honest."

"I thought he might change it, you know, when he started going with you. I thought things might get better. But instead it's just like he's losing it completely."

"Have you tried to talk to him? About the talking to someone, I mean, not his bedroom."

"I did sort of mention it once, but he said he didn't know what I meant." Adam picks up the pepper pot and starts to fiddle with it. "To be honest, Alice, I've been pretty involved with Dean and I haven't been there for him as much as I should. But it's hard – I'm torn in two."

"I'm sure Owen wants you to be happy – he's delighted about you and Dean, and that you had a holiday and everything."

"I know, but after all he's done for me I feel like I'm letting him down. Dean's very understanding but it's important for us to spend time together as well. And when I'm up in Middlesborough I just worry about Owen alone in the house, and whether he's OK, and if there's any more I could be doing."

"So that's where I come in, I take it?"

"I didn't think you'd mind. You see, I thought you and Owen were going out with each other again."

"Well we're not."

"I feel bad about that too. I should have knocked your heads together when you first fell out but I'd only just met Dean then and..."

"Adam – please – this isn't getting us anywhere." I yank the pepper pot out of his hand and slam it on the table. I take a deep breath. "I appreciate you have a life and you need to live it, but wallowing in blame isn't going to help anyone. Look, Owen's probably just really tired and stressed out. Perhaps you could close the café for a week or two in January and then he'd get a proper break."

"He'd never agree to that. Alice – I don't want to dump all this on you but won't you even talk to him?" There is a note of desperation in Adam's voice.

I sigh. "Adam – I'd move heaven and earth to help him – but what the hell am I supposed to say?"

He looks at me for a long time. "I don't know. But I'm so scared for him, Alice. I feel that by doing nothing we're letting him down."

The tears in Adam's big grey eyes remind me of how he was

when Owen disappeared – how we both were, in fact. I can't let that happen again so I put my hand over his enormous one. "OK, I'll ask him to supper on Saturday and take it from there."

Quite what I'm going to say to Owen is another matter.

## Chapter Sixty

I glance at the clock on the cooker; Owen will be here in ten minutes. I drain my gin and tonic and open the oven. The comforting scent of oregano and roasting tomatoes greets me and I pull out the casserole to stir in the pasta. I look at the clock again – eight minutes to go.

Normally I would be looking forward to seeing Owen but this time I feel sick with misgiving. All afternoon I have been waiting for a text from him, but this time hoping he would cancel. My fingers play with the lid of the gin but I stop myself and open a bottle of red instead.

The little green numbers read 19.32 when I hear the scrunch of footsteps on the drive. Owen's face is pinched and pale, and his eyes have a feverish spark in them I haven't seen before. Our fingers brush as I reach to take his coat and he jerks his hand away, although he tries to make a joke of it.

Owen does try to get over his edginess, although he fails miserably. When the timer on the cooker goes off he jumps out of his skin and he gulps at his wine as though he is using it to force his dinner down. All the same he asks me dutifully about my day and I try to entertain him by showing him the pictures on my phone of the enormous Christmas tree we put up in the car showroom. It isn't exactly scintillating and he finds it hard to look that interested. I am at a loss for much else to say.

So is Owen – his social ease has completely left him. I ask if he is OK and he protests that he's fine, so I just smile and top up his wine. And tell him I bumped into Adam at the leisure centre and isn't it great he's so happy with Dean. I feel guilty through and through because I am wondering if perhaps the awkwardness is me being chary with Owen after what Adam said. It's all so complicated that I want to cry.

Eventually I send him packing into the snug while I put the kettle on. I stack the dishwasher and give William a biscuit (or two) before loading up a tray with tea and mince pies. I glance at my watch – it's not even nine o'clock – and I wonder just how soon I can feign tiredness and send Owen home. And then what? A night tossing and turning, feeling guilty about not trying harder to find out what's wrong. As I pick up the tray I resolve to have another go at getting to the bottom of it.

I never get the chance. Owen is standing in the middle of the snug holding the letter from the archaeology service in his shaking hand.

"Why didn't you tell me?" he bursts out.

I put the tray down. "I was just going to."

"But the letter's dated well over a week ago."

"It arrived on Monday – Christmas post I guess."

"You came into the café on Tuesday. Why didn't you say?"

I look away from him. "I…I didn't think."

"How could you not think? This is so important."

He is getting angry but so am I.

"Well OK, I did think. But I didn't want you making the sort of scene you're making now in public, did I?"

"But if you'd told me straight away..." There is a pleading, manipulative note in his voice.

I step forward with a verbal olive branch. "I'm sorry. I didn't mean to upset you."

He turns away and his shoulders heave. "I'm not upset," he says, but his voice is harsh, rather than shaky, and I can see that his fists are clenched. All the warning signs are there – but I choose to ignore them.

"Anyway," I carry on as brightly as I can, "there's no need for you to worry because I've brought the remains back so we can arrange for a proper burial if you still want to."

He spins around. "You've brought him back? The baby's here?"

"It's not a 'he'," I reply. "The letter said they couldn't tell its gender."

Owen stalks across the rug and puts his hands on my shoulders. "Alice – where is the baby?" There is ice in his voice and his eyes are small and dark. I begin to feel just a little bit scared.

"It's alright. It's safe in the barn, close to where Richard found it." I badly need a justification for stuffing the box into an unused kitchen cupboard.

His grip relaxes a little. "Shall we take a look?" He asks as though he is suggesting a walk in the garden or a picnic.

If it will keep this strange, mercurial Owen even vaguely rational I will agree to anything. I smile at him as bravely as I can. "Yes, let's."

I pick up the key to the barn on our way through the garden room. I don't bother with a coat – this shouldn't take very long. But I shiver as we walk along the edge of the lawn; the frost is already beginning to form on the grass.

It is no warmer inside the barn and I lift the box carefully from the cupboard and place it on the work surface.

"Show me," Owen commands, and I take off the lid and pull away the top layer of packing, exposing the bones in their nest of bubblewrap. To my surprise he reaches into the box and strokes the little skull; then he begins to say Christopher's prayer.

When he has finished I interrupt before he can start the recitation again. "Shall we take it into the house?" I ask.

He shakes his head. "To the church, Alice, not the house."

"The church?"

"Yes." Owen's voice is quiet and firm. "He needs to rest somewhere sacred, not be stuffed into some kitchen cupboard." He almost spits the last words out.

"OK," I reason, "we can ask Christopher tomorrow."

"No, Alice – now. We'll take the baby to the church now."

"But won't it be locked?"

"I know where Christopher keeps the key."

"But shouldn't we..."

"Alice – for the love of God – just do as I ask."

Something in his voice makes me frightened not to. Owen replaces the packing reverently on top of the skeleton, closes the box, and tucks it awkwardly under one arm. I wonder why he doesn't use both hands but then he grabs my wrist. "Come on," he says. He won't even let me stop to lock up or fetch my coat, and all but drags me down the drive. I can hear William barking.

I may be frightened, but I convince myself it is for Owen, not for myself. He is on the thinnest of knife edges and there is no knowing which way he will fall. That he will fall is now certain, and a detached part of my mind is simply amazed that I didn't see the inevitability before. My teeth chatter as he pulls me up the village but I don't try to run away. I let him down before when he was right on the edge and I'm not going to do it again.

The church is in total darkness. Owen lets go of my hand and puts the box on the bench in the porch before reaching into a recess high in the wall. The key glistens in the frosty moonlight as he pulls it out and fits it into the door. It creaks as he pushes it open and it is such a familiar sound I feel as though I can breathe again.

Owen tries to grab my wrist once more but I dodge past him into the church. "You don't need to do that," I tell him, and busy myself turning on all the lights.

Although the Christmas tree has been put up ready for the children's crib service on Sunday, the church won't be fully decorated until Christmas Eve. The crib itself is tucked away in the vestry; I know because I helped Jane wash all the little wooden animals yesterday morning. Thinking about such a mundane task re-roots me in reality and I feel calmer as I follow Owen up the aisle. Perhaps, once the box is stowed to his satisfaction, I can persuade him to let me fetch Christopher to say some prayers.

"Where are you going to put the baby?" I ask. He doesn't answer me, but keeps walking, slowly, reverently, as though he is part of a funeral procession. At the altar rail he stops to lift the centre section, then moves into the sanctuary and places the box in front of the altar. He bows his head for a moment then backs away from it, like a man in a trance.

But if it is a trance it is broken by the sight of me as he turns at the rail. His face is full of hatred as he yells, "Kneel, Alice! Kneel and pray!"

I turn to run but he grabs the top of my arm to pull me back. I start to struggle but he wheels me around shouting, "Pray for the child, you she-wolf, pray for the child you would have cast away and for your own treacherous soul."

Once again I try to tug myself free but this time he pushes me to the floor, my shoulder catching on the altar rail and making me cry out.

"Pray!" he screams, "Pray for your life you filthy whore, because how you dare to live after all the suffering you caused I do not know" and he hauls me up and forces me against the rail until it is digging agonisingly into the bottom of my rib cage.

Never before in my life have I known pure terror, and my first instinct is indeed to pray. "Our Father..." I start, but then, miraculously, I hear Christopher's voice, loud and clear, asking what in heaven's name is going on.

The weight of Owen's body behind me vanishes and he runs up the aisle. Christopher blocks his way but Owen dodges into a pew to avoid him.

"Stop him!" I yell "Don't let him go – he'll hurt himself," but as Owen jumps over the seatback he stumbles and barrels into Christopher who holds him firmly with both arms. There is a moment of silence then Owen begins to sob.

I sink onto the communion step, trying to catch my breath. Owen's head is buried in Christopher's shoulder and he is crying fit to break his heart. And mine. And probably Christopher's too.

"Oh, God, Chris – what have I done?" he moans. "Alice – she's my world, my whole world...and look what I've done."

After a little while I stand up shakily and walk towards them. I want to touch Owen, to tell him it's alright, but I am so stunned that I come to a grinding halt.

Christopher looks up. "Are you OK?" he whispers over Owen's sobs.

I nod.

"Go to the vicarage," he continues. "Let Jane know what's happened. I'll bring Owen over when he's feeling calmer."

I stand and stare at him. I don't want to leave but I am beginning to shiver again.

"Go on," Christopher hisses, and I escape into the night.

I hurry across the road and up the vicarage path. I hesitate to ring the doorbell at this time of night, knowing the children will be in bed, so instead I push on the door and it opens.

"Chris – is that you?" Jane's voice floats down the hall.

"No, it's me – Alice."

She appears from the kitchen. "Oh, I thought it might be Christopher. He saw the lights on in the church and went over to investigate."

"He's over there now, with Owen. He told me to come and tell you."

"With Owen? That's alright then. I was worried it was vandals or something."

"It's…it's not alright, Jane. Owen's in an awful state. He's really lost it this time."

She takes my hand and leads me into the kitchen. I huddle next to the Aga while she makes tea and I tell her exactly what has just happened. All the time my mind is tumbling and racing, trying to make sense of it – but I can't.

Jane is pouring the water into the teapot when the front door opens again and we hear footsteps in the hall. I fall silent as they pass and the study door opens, and after a few moments, closes. Then Christopher appears in the kitchen.

"Is there enough in the pot for Owen and me?"

Jane nods and pulls another two mugs out of the cupboard.

"How is he?" I ask Christopher.

"Not much better really."

Suddenly my mind is made up. I can't go on with this endless uncertainty any more – I need to take action. There are things that need to be said and everything is so bad right now I cannot possibly make them any worse.

"Can I take him his tea?" I venture.

Christopher nods. "I think he'd like that." And I hear an echo of Owen's voice sobbing, saying to Christopher that I was his world.

"Give us five minutes," I tell him.

Balancing the mugs in one hand I push the study door open. Owen is curled as tightly as he can be into one corner of the sofa, his face hidden in a cushion on its squashy arm.

I put the tea down on the desk and touch his shoulder. "Owen? I want to talk to you."

He doesn't move but he mumbles "I'm sorry, Alice. I'm so sorry."

"I know you are. Listen, Owen, this is important, will you look at me?"

He rubs his face into the cushion, which I take as a shake of his head.

"Well OK, but you have to listen very carefully." There is no response so I blunder blindly on. "It's something I should have told you months ago – back in the summer even – but it never seemed the right moment. I don't know…it's lousy timing now and it shouldn't be like this but anyway..." I need a deep breath. This is hard, so very hard. Once the words are out there will be no turning back, not ever. But in the middle of his shifting world it is vital that he knows just exactly where he stands with me at least.

"Owen – I love you."

"No, Alice, you can't – you don't." His voice is muffled by the cushion.

"Well I do."

He does raise his head now, his eyes full of panic. "But you mustn't – I'm not who you think I am; I'm…I'm..."

"Shhh. You're ill, and you need help, that's all. I still love you. I won't let you down."

"But Alice – I'm beyond help. I'll always be this way – you can't love me – you must be strong and..."

"I have no choice in the matter, Owen. I do love you. OK, it's a nightmare at the moment, but we'll get through this together." I falter, suddenly feeling a bit unsure. "If you want me with you, that is."

His voice is almost steady as he begins to reply. "I want you more than you could ever know. But it's not right, it's not even real..." and once again, he dissolves into tears and buries his face in the cushion.

I sit down next to him and put my arm over his heaving back. "Cry it all out," I whisper. "Cry it all out, then get some rest, and then on Monday we'll get you some proper help."

"That sounds like a good plan." I hadn't noticed Christopher come into the room, but I am glad he is here. He sits down on the chair next to his desk.

"You don't understand," Owen sobs, "I'm beyond help."

"Everyone feels like that when they're in crisis," Christopher explains soothingly. "It's part of what a crisis is. But people do come through it, and you will too."

"No – no, I mean it. It's been going on too long – it'll never change now, not ever."

I feel too choked to speak. I thought I knew what heartbreak was before, but I was wrong.

Christopher looks at me. "Maybe we should phone his GP now, and not leave it until Monday?"

Owen looks up, startled. "No – you can't do that. They'll lock me up."

"Why would they do that?" Christopher probes gently.

"Because I don't know what's real."

"In what way?" Christopher asks, but Owen just starts to sob again. I pull him towards me and he doesn't resist. I circle him with my arms as he burrows his wet face into my jumper. And I am scared beyond words. Yet, at the same time, I don't know – I feel a kind of strength. I think perhaps it is emanating from Christopher but when I look at him he seems broken too.

"The help that you need will be forthcoming," I find myself saying. Christopher stares at me, goggle-eyed. I have the strange sensation of looking down on the three of us, as though from above, but at the same time I know I am still in my own body because I can feel Owen's shuddering warmth.

"You are close to the end of the pathway," I continue. "Bury Thomas's child and you will be giving peace across the generations. The line of the charmers will not end."

Christopher is now open mouthed and we look at each other in horror. "Alice," he whispers. "That wasn't like you speaking at all."

Suddenly Owen looks up. "You heard it too? Oh, God – tell me you heard it too."

We both nod.

"And I've seen them," I breathe.

Owen is shaking from head to toe. "Who have you seen? Alice, you must tell me."

"The…the old woman…and the young woman in grey – she's Alice, Alice Fulton, the cheesemaker, and Thomas; he looks so like you I thought he was you but..." I stop. "But you know that – because you've seen him too."

"I've seen Alice and I've seen Thomas," he whispers.

Christopher leans forwards. "So this is what you told me about, Alice, when Owen disappeared, that you'd both seen this… Thomas…only then you were calling him the other Owen."

"That's right. I didn't know anything about him then but I had to find out."

"But you've seen Alice too? And Mother Winter?" Owen's voice is desperate, pleading.

So he knows the old woman is Thomas' mother – I was right. But how I know, or how I've seen what I've seen, or felt what I've felt…the enormity of it is beginning to hit home but I shut it away. You could drive yourself mad with it if you didn't. Instead I just nod in answer to Owen's question.

Christopher is clearly fascinated. "So you've both seen these people, quite independently?"

Owen's voice is very quiet. "I've been seeing Alice since I was a child. My Gran knew – she went along with it – or she knew who she was anyway." I think about Richard playing with Alice too.

Christopher leans forwards. "What did you do together? What did you talk about?"

"We were kids, Chris, tiny kids. We just met on the green and played. When I went to school she sort of faded away – I was too young to remember, really. I had forgotten about her completely, but when Gran was ill, she came back. I…I used to sleep in a chair in Gran's room and one night Alice was there, sitting at my feet. She was someone I could talk to about it all, you know, about not being able to ease things for Gran better..." He grinds to a halt, close to tears again.

"Go on," Christopher urges him. "Finish the story."

"Just before Gran finally passed away Alice brought Mother Winter with her. It…it wasn't like with Alice…Alice, well, I'd really see and hear her – I can describe how she looks and her voice, but with Mother, at first, I just seemed to know things – about the herbs – things I hadn't thought of to help Gran. And they worked.

"After Gran died Alice stayed with me for a while, but then she went too, not long after the funeral. It was…well, never mind how it was…but I never saw her again. But Mother – she's here now, she's always here, she's at my shoulder..." Then he does break down and I gather him to me again. These people have haunted him, driven him to the brink of madness, and I suddenly feel very angry. I want to scream at them to leave him alone, but then I realise that they will – just as soon as the baby is properly buried.

"When we bury the child, she will have her peace." This time they are my words, and my voice. Even if I cannot be completely sure where the thought comes from.

"She's pushing me, Alice – she's inside my head. Like before – like when we first found him – it was as if I'd become someone else – and recently, more and more – I couldn't tell…if I was me, or..." He grinds to a halt.

"It's no wonder you thought you were going mad," says Christopher. "What you're describing sounds just like a psychotic episode."

"Exactly!" cries Owen. "That's what I thought it was." He

buries his head in his hands. "Only I still can't really be sure – am I just imagining Alice saying she's seen them too? Is that part of it? Or is she just saying it to humour me? I…I still can't tell what's real."

"They're not but I am. I even know their names for God's sake, I wouldn't know that if I was just humouring you. And it's not just me – Richard's seen them too."

"Richard?" Owen sounds surprised.

"Well it wasn't you he saw jump off the bridge, was it?"

"No, but..."

We look at each other, at a total loss. Even for clever folks like Christopher and Owen this is a lot to take in, but for me it is like my brain is going into overload. My teeth start to chatter, even though the room is stuffy and warm.

Owen puts a comforting arm around me. "Oh Alice," he says.

I try to pull myself together, for his sake more than anything. "I'll be alright. I'm just very tired I think."

"Me too." He takes a deep breath. "Come on, we'd better go."

Christopher is hesitant. "Are you sure you'll be OK? You can both stay in the spare room here if you like."

I stand up. "No, I have to go and see to William."

Owen stands too. "I'll walk you home."

The frost is thick on the ground and we don't have our coats. Instead we tuck ourselves up in each other's arms and walk briskly through the silent village, lost in our own thoughts. I don't speak until we are at my back door.

"Stay with me, Owen." It's not a question – it's a command.

He nods.

# Chapter Sixty-One

It isn't even light when William starts to whine. Owen is fast asleep next to me; he tossed and turned for ages and I am glad he's finally found some rest. I just curled up on my edge of the bed and stayed there. He didn't seem to want to touch me, not even a little cuddle.

As I reluctantly push myself off the pillow my shoulder buckles in pain and I am left sitting on the side of the bed clasping it and wondering why it hurts so much.

The moment I hear Owen ask if I'm OK, one of the most unreal parts of last night comes back to me and I remember him throwing me against the altar rail – although why my shoulder is only hurting now is beyond me. Adrenalin, probably. I'd better drum up some more of it from somewhere.

"I must have knocked my shoulder when I slipped in the church."

"When I pushed you, you mean," he replies.

"I was hoping you were so far out of things that you wouldn't remember."

"Oh, I remember alright," he says. "Come on, let me take a look."

His fingers are warm against my skin. "It's a really nasty bruise," he continues, "But at least it's coming out."

"There's some arnica in the bathroom cabinet."

Gently he pulls my pyjama top up. "I can do better than arnica. Tell you what; you have a nice warm shower. I'll go home and feed Kylie, and come back in about an hour with some ointment."

"OK." I swivel around on the bed to face him – he looks awful. "Owen, how are you feeling?"

He shrugs. "A bit numb, to be honest."

"That's not really surprising though, is it?"

"I don't suppose it is."

To be fair, I feel a bit numb myself.

Less than an hour later I hear Owen's key in the door and William rushes from the kitchen to the garden room, barking and snarling. Rather than trying to make peace Owen ignores him and eventually he stops and slinks away to his basket.

Owen's hair is still wet from his shower and he has shaved, although not made a very good fist of it. There is a cut on his chin and a good sized chunk of stubble he's missed on his neck. I notice that it is flecked with grey.

He puts his keys and a little plastic jar of ointment on the table in front of me.

"Compress first," he says and starts to fill the kettle with water. I nod.

Neither of us seems to know what to say and he busies himself preparing the herbs for the infusion while I gaze glumly at the table. As I stare I find myself looking at his keys, and in particular a small, worn, bronze one. I vaguely recognise it as the one that opens his herb chest, but there is something more – something else about it.

In a flash of comprehension I scramble out of my chair and into the snug. There, on the floor by the sofa, is the little plastic pocket the archaeologists sent, containing the key that was around the baby's neck. As I pick it up, Owen is behind me.

"Alice – what's wrong?"

I hand the pocket to him and I can see from his face he knows the key.

"Where did they find it?" His voice is hoarse.

I can hardly answer. "It was around the baby's neck. That's what the scraps of ribbon are."

"There's only ever been one key to the chest," he whispers.

"It looks the same," I venture.

"It is the same. It has to be."

"Shall we try it and see?"

He nods. "Come on."

Poultice and ointment forgotten, we pull on our coats and rush up the village to his house. In the dining room he hauls the chest out of the sideboard and puts it on the table. My hands are shaking too much to fit the key in the lock, so he takes it from me and tries it himself. Although it goes in smoothly, at first it refuses to turn.

"The lock's worn, but the key isn't." Owen takes it out and compares it closely with his own and I can see the edges of his are smoother.

He puts the key in again and eases it gently this way and that, and eventually we hear a click as the mechanism shifts. Slowly, he opens the lid of the box.

"Thomas," I whisper, "it was Thomas's key – he must have buried it with his baby."

"But how did I end up with the chest?" Owen muses, almost to himself.

"The same way you became a charmer – it was passed down through the generations."

He shakes his head firmly. "I'm not a charmer. I heal people with herbs, that's all." There is an uncomfortable silence and then he continues, "But if Thomas died, and his child died, how was the knowledge passed down?"

"Perhaps Mother Winter had other children?"

"Maybe Thomas did. If Gran's story was right and he was a bit of a ladies' man..."

Suddenly I remember the riding. "He…he was. I saw him being jeered by a crowd of villagers because of it. I found out later it was called a riding and..."

Owen cuts across me. "How do you mean, you saw him?"

I blush to my roots. "I don't really know. Margaret calls them visions, but I find that word too scary. Christopher said something about echoes from the past."

"Oh, Alice – why didn't you tell me?"

But that is just too much and I turn on him angrily. "Why didn't you tell me?"

"Because you would have thought I was stark, staring mad. It's what I believed myself."

"But I was so worried about you. I was eating myself up with it – it was...the worst thing in my life ever, I think."

Owen gazes at the floor. "I'm sorry, Alice." He sounds like a man defeated.

I turn away from him and look out of the window, but instead of the wintry garden I see a tiny white skull on the barn floor, illuminated by a shaft of evening sun. I close my eyes.

Eventually Owen puts his hands gently on my shoulders. "Do you know what I'm finding hardest to deal with? I've never believed in ghosts. I'm a scientist – logically, they can't exist. Last night I was lying awake and while there was a part of me that was full of relief that I wasn't going crazy I still wasn't able to accept this is something supernatural. I think I only slept because I was so exhausted by it all – and because you were there, of course."

I am close to tears but not entirely sorrowful ones; there is a new honesty in Owen's voice, a tentative openness.

"Perhaps that's why you thought it was all in your own head in the first place. When it first happened to me I did wonder that myself but as I spoke to other people I realised I was in the minority not believing in the paranormal. And anyway, what does paranormal mean? Just something that's outside of the ordinary, by definition it's something we don't understand. As a scientist you must accept there are things we haven't found out yet."

"I thought it was all inside my head; that I was completely psychotic. You sometimes read about these things..."

I wrap my arms around his waist. "But you're not – it isn't just you. We're in this together and if nothing else, I think we understand each other better because of it. And we know what we've got to do to make it stop."

"But how do we know, Alice? By what means?"

I start to shake my head but he continues, words tumbling out one after the other.

"Something's hounded me, Alice, something I've come to know as Mother Winter. From the moment I said I'd help you to kill our unborn child she was in my head telling me it was wrong. Then when Richard found the baby's skeleton it felt like my retribution; I had to atone for what I'd done – I just had to – there was no other way to describe it. And she said I had to have you – possess you – and it sounded like it was a perversion of my own mind, I wanted you so much. So I had to resist – oh, Alice – it's been so hard but I had to because it wasn't fair on you because I was going mad – and then she'd be on at me day and night…Alice, I can't take any more – I want my life back."

"And when we bury the baby, you will have. Then you can get on with your life – or our lives, if that's what you want."

He is looking at me as though trying to imprint my face on his brain. Finally he pulls me to him. "More than anything," he murmurs into my hair.

## Chapter Sixty-Two

We meet Christopher in the churchyard and already he has the funeral all worked out.

"As long as the weather holds so we can dig the grave we ought to be able to fit it in before Christmas. I thought we could put the baby in front of the east window, where the other children are buried," he says.

Owen shakes his head. "It's the wrong place."

"The wrong place?"

"Yes. It needs to be near the yew hedge by the kissing gate."

"Owen, I'm not sure..."

But Owen interrupts him. "Come on – I'll show you the spot."

Owen leads us around the back of the church. The grass is still damp from last night's frost and I wish I was wearing my wellies and some thick socks. There is a cinder path to the kissing gate and I hop onto it, but Owen makes a beeline for a spot on the edge of the empty space, just under the hedge.

He turns to Christopher. "Here."

"But Owen, I'm not sure this land is even consecrated."

"It's in the churchyard, why would it not be?"

"There's sometimes an area left for those who can't be buried under church law; non-believers, suicides, that sort of thing."

Owen looks puzzled. "You're sure it's here?"

"Well yes, I always understood it to be this empty patch of land."

"This plot is right on the edge of it though."

"Yes, I know, but..."

"It's the right place." I say it very quietly and they both turn to look at me. "The first Sunday I was here – I left part way through the service and I saw a woman kneeling at a grave just there, and it was freshly dug. It must have been the start of it all, only of course I didn't realise. I convinced myself it was a trick of the light.

"I wonder...perhaps it's where Thomas is buried? I know his death wasn't recorded as a suicide but that's what it was. Maybe there was some sort of compromise about where he was buried – the vicar spoke up for his good character, so maybe...but of course, we'll never know."

"Oh, but we might."

We both look at Christopher.

"There are plans of the churchyard that show where the burials are. The recording can be a bit sketchy and I'm not sure they go back that far, but you never know. Come on – they're in the vestry."

The vestry is rather too small for three people so I ask Christopher if he has the parish register for the very end of the seventeenth century and I take it through to the church while he and Owen start their search of the burial records.

The daylight is already beginning to fade so I flick one of the switches next to the vestry door. A pool of harsh electric light illuminates the area closest to the altar. The crib is now in its place but I ignore it and sit down in the front pew, setting the register on seat beside me. This is the place to find out if Thomas Winter had any brothers or sisters.

The book ends in 1703 and I work backwards. In 1701 I come across the death of a John Winter, aged forty-one years, so probably a relation but certainly not a sibling. The next Winter I find is Thomas's birth – the very last entry in 1699, on 31st December. A child born on the very turn of the century – was that perhaps part of the reason he was considered to be special?

I turn the pages over quickly; I doubt there would be a sibling in the same year. But there is an entry – in late May. The marriage of Sarah Beckford to John Winter. Sarah was just sixteen years of age, her husband thirty-nine. It looks as though Thomas was an only child.

I try to picture Mother Winter as an innocent teenager made pregnant by a much older man. But somehow the image doesn't fit. At that tender age did she already have her exceptional gifts? Was it the child she really wanted, to carry on the line? Is that what she wants now?

My gaze travels to the crib and I put the book to one side and wander over to it. The wooden shepherds and kings that Jane and I so carefully washed are settled in the straw, along with the little woolly sheep, placed there by excited chubby hands. Watched by their proud mothers. What must it be like, to be a mother? I am thirty-five and I don't know. But I want to know, and the ache inside me is real in a way it hasn't been since I found out about Neil and Angela's baby.

I try to sweep it away but I can't. I have to turn from the crib, and as I do so, something catches my eye. Half way down the church, just in front of the font, a woman wearing a grey dress is kneeling in prayer. I am transfixed – it is Alice. Her head is bowed and she is completely unaware of my presence. If indeed I am present for her – do the echoes through time travel both ways?

"He's here – he's underneath the altar," I breathe.

She raises her head, and as I lift my arm to point to where her baby is resting, the vestry door clicks open behind me.

"We've found the boundary – the plot is just on the consecrated side, but as far as knowing who's buried..." Owen tails off. He has obviously seen Alice too.

"Tell her, Owen, tell her where her baby is," I whisper.

I don't know if he hears me but he sets off across the church. I watch, spellbound, as he walks up to her. She turns towards him and her sad face is illuminated by a smile – she knows him, that is clear – but does she see Owen, or Thomas? He stops at the end of her pew and I can see his face in profile, full of tenderness.

Christopher is behind me. "Who's he talking to?" he hisses.

"Alice."

"You can see her?"

"Yes."

"That's incredible," he breathes. "For me, there's no-one there."

His words bring home the awful unreality of the situation. I feel myself go hot, then icy cold, and the muscles in my legs begin to tremble as though I have no control over them. I don't. I need to sit down but I cannot move, and when I try to I feel myself falling.

Christopher stops me hitting the floor but I am panicking now, gasping for breath. This cannot be happening; not to me. Then all of a sudden Owen's arms are tight around me.

"Make them go away," I sob, "please, make it all stop."

He buries his face in my hair, saying my name over and over again. Or is it my name? Or is it hers? But his voice and his arms calm me, and he takes me home and puts me to bed. And later, for the first time in almost forever, we make love.

## Chapter Sixty-Three

I wake from my doze when Owen strokes my cheek. The pool of light from the bedside lamp illuminates the top half of his face but his lips are in shadow as he reaches forward and they touch on mine with the gentlest of kisses.

"I'm going to have to leave you for a little while," he whispers, "I promised I'd pick Adam up at the station."

"Are you going to tell him what's happened?"

"I don't think so. I'll just drop him off and come straight back here, if that's alright."

I prop myself up on my elbow. "Of course it's alright for you to come back – once you've told him."

"Alice, not tonight. I..."

"Yes, tonight. He's worrying himself sick over you. He's heard you talking to Mother and he's seen how stressed you are. He thinks you're going mad and he's terrified for you."

"He told you all that?"

I nod. "At the leisure centre on Wednesday."

"And you still wanted to see me?"

I nod again.

"Alice, you are the most amazing person. I don't deserve you."

"Well you've got me – I love you, remember? Now, are you going to do as I ask?"

He looks away. "I'm such a coward. Will you...will you tell Adam with me? I just feel stronger when you're around. I know that sounds pathetic, but I can't help it."

I wrap him in my arms. "It's not pathetic and it's not surprising you need some sort of support after what you've been through. Tell you what, you collect Adam from the station and I'll have a shower then wait back at your place. I might even bring a bottle of wine."

Owen looks at me gravely. "I think that could be very helpful."

So I sit and wait in Owen's kitchen, William stretched out along the radiator next to me and Kylie curled in her basket. Their breathing is the only sound, apart from the tick of the clock in the hall, but the silence is soothing. I have already opened the wine and helped myself to a glass.

I wander into the living room and study the china animals on the mantelpiece. Black cats with long elegant necks guard either end, seemingly uninterested in the blue tit, robin and field mouse between them. Whoever arranged them didn't consider the natural order of things. Unless they had a highly developed sense of irony, that is.

I know nothing about Owen's grandmother, not even her name. Yet she is all around me, shouting from the antimacassars, the ticking clock, the Lladro geese, to be discovered. I go back into the hall and pick a walking stick out of the stand. The knotted wood has been polished to a high gloss and it is very long. She was clearly a taller woman than me.

There is one place in the house where I can find out more about her than any other. I glance at the clock – Adam's train is due in about now so I have very little time. As I consider it I receive a text from Owen saying the train has been delayed by twenty minutes. I bound up the stairs.

Even with the light on the room is full of shadows. The wardrobe crowds in on me and in defiance I open its doors first. To my surprise it is full of Owen's clothes; white shirts to the left, blue and striped ones to the right, separated by a row of chinos and a suit carrier. Beneath them are neat piles of polo shirts, jumpers and jeans. Boxer shorts and socks are squeezed into a corner.

This isn't what I came to see. I perch on the bed and pick up the photograph on the night table. It is Owen's graduation captured in black and white. He looks so young it makes my heart ache; almost still a schoolboy in his gown and hood.

Standing next to him is a woman in a pale tailored suit. Like Owen, she is slim and neat, but she is a few inches taller than him which would make her almost six foot. I check the shoes – dark courts – not much of a heel. They look as though they match her handbag.

I don't know what I expected, but it wasn't this; she was a charmer, a healer, with an encyclopaedic knowledge of herbs and their folklore – here she is dressed as a suburban grandmother. I peer for clues in her face but it is largely hidden by the brim of her hat.

My fingers spread out on the candlewick beside me, tracing the ridges and valleys. A slam echoes through the house and I jump up before I realise it is next door, but I am on my feet now and I prowl along the dressing table while I pluck up the courage to open a drawer.

Again, a typical grandmother; a bar of Yardley's English Lavender soap nestles on top of a pile of underwear. Stately bras and substantial polyester knickers; pale pink, pale blue, peach. Peeking out from beneath an underskirt is the corner of a red felt covered jewellery box.

The fabric is worn at the corners and around the clasp. I ease my fingernail under the half moon of gold and it tears at my skin a little, but I ignore it and push the lid open. In front of me is a silver St Christopher on a thick chain and a solitaire diamond ring. But my attention is caught by the envelope stuffed into the lid. It is addressed to Owen in a bold, confident hand.

The seal is intact and this presents me with a conundrum. I am still staring at it when I hear a car pull up outside so I ram both box and letter back into the drawer and fly downstairs to reunite myself with the wine glass I left on the hallstand. I just make it.

Adam fills the hallway. "Alice!" he cries, "This is a nice surprise."

"And even better there's a bottle of wine in the kitchen."

He puts his head on one side. "Are we celebrating?"

Owen's voice comes from somewhere behind him. "No – we're explaining."

I pour us each a glass of wine and we settle around the kitchen table. Adam looks expectantly at Owen but he lowers his eyes and shakes his head.

"Let Alice start," he tells him. "I'll join in when...well, when I can."

"OK, Adam, let's cut to the chase. You can stop worrying that Owen's losing his marbles because that's not what's happening. Remember back in the summer, when Owen disappeared, Richard and I told you that we'd seen what we thought was the ghost of a young man? Well Owen hasn't been talking to himself – he's been talking to his mother."

"Owen's mother or the ghost's?"

"The ghost's. I know it sounds pretty incredible..."

Owen cuts across me. "It doesn't just sound incredible, it is. Ads, I'm still having major problems getting my head around this so you'll have to bear with me, but I'm just clinging to the fact that as Alice has seen what I've seen it means it is, well, in some way, real.

"For months I've had this...this presence...in my head. A woman from the early eighteenth century who wanted her grandson to be given a proper Christian burial. She was a healer too, Adam. She first came when Gran was very ill and she told me the right things to do to ease her passing. Things I wouldn't have known; combinations of herbs which must have been lost through the years. But they worked.

"I've been thinking about it today – I didn't question what was happening then because I was so desperate and I suppose afterwards I blocked the whole thing out." He lowers his eyes again. "You know, Adam, more than anyone, that I haven't coped."

Adam pulls his chair closer to Owen and puts his arm around his shoulder. "I know. I thought it was all catching up with you; back in the summer and again now. Add the stress of the café, the healing and everything..."

"And me." I can hardly speak. "And the stress of an on-off relationship with me."

Adam looks up from comforting Owen. "No, that hasn't helped either but it isn't entirely your fault."

"It's not Alice's fault at all." Owen leaps to my defence. "I've been impossible to love, and yet she's still loved me. I've done everything wrong and yet time and again she's been there for me. It's a miracle, really. I think without her I probably would be going under right now."

"You're still pretty close to the edge. You need time to get your head together then confront what's happened to you, not pretend it hasn't like you usually do."

Owen pulls away from him. "What do you mean, confront?"

"That drug counselling you made me go to all those years back – they made you look at the reasons you wanted to take stuff. For me it was an escape from things that hurt. You escape by ignoring them, Owen, but now they've caught up with you and you have to deal with them."

Owen runs his hand over the top of his head. "Ads, I'm too tired for this right now." His eyes are sunk right back into their sockets and there are deep bruises beneath them.

"OK," I say, "then let's go to bed."

He begins to put on his coat but I shake my head. "No, we'll stay here tonight."

"We can't! We..."

"It's alright Owen – I know about your bedroom. I've seen it."

He sinks back onto the kitchen chair, one arm still in his anorak. "You two..." he almost whispers it. "You two – you've got me all ways up."

## Chapter Sixty-Four

Owen sits on the edge of the bed. He waves a limp hand around the room.

"So you didn't run away when you saw all this?"

I sit down next to him. "It was the closest I came. It was the evening after we'd painted the bathroom. But you were so kind to me when I was ill – and I could see how much you were struggling…no, I couldn't run away."

He reaches for my hand. "It will seem odd, sleeping in Gran's bed with someone."

"Well she must have done it at some stage," I laugh.

Owen shakes his head. "I think not."

"Whatever do you mean? She was your grandmother." I stop in my tracks. "She was, wasn't she?"

"Yes. Yes of course she was. But she never married. My father was the product of a wartime affair with a Canadian army officer; he was a physicist in civilian life – she always said it was where I got my scientific brain from."

I think of the woman in the photograph and the big knickers in the bedroom drawer. "Owen, I've been snooping," I confess. "I was just so desperate to get to know her and when Adam's train was delayed it seemed the perfect opportunity. I looked at the photo but it told me nothing so I opened a drawer – a drawer I don't think you've been into since she died."

He drops my hand. "Like I said – you and Adam – you've got me all ways up. Cornered. Trapped." He stands. "Look – you sleep here and I'll go on the sofa."

"Owen – no – I shouldn't have done it but I'm not sorry I did. You see I found an envelope addressed to you – I expect she thought you'd find it after she died."

"So did you open that too?" His voice is heavy with sarcasm.

"Of course I didn't – but you should. In the top left hand drawer of the dressing table is a red jewellery box – it's inside the lid." I stand too. "You're angry with me, and rightly so. I'll sleep on the sofa – you stay here."

Of course I do not sleep. I hunch on the edge of the armchair, inwardly kicking myself for handling this all so badly. The china menagerie on the mantelshelf stares down at me malevolently and I can't say I blame them; I have probably destroyed every shred of trust Owen had in me. But he has to read that letter. I wonder if he will.

My fingers are stiff and knotted together. The voices from Margaret's muted TV have kept me company through the wall, but after a brief flare of music there is silence. I glance at the clock on my phone – it isn't even midnight and the date reminds me it's the longest night.

It crosses my mind to collect William from the kitchen and go home. The house is so quiet that Owen must have gone to bed and it is very cold. I cast around for something to wrap myself up in and then I remember the chenille cover on the dining room table. It will do.

I turn off the light but I know the haughty china cats are still staring at me and I am beginning to despise them. I burrow into the sofa, years of embedded dust and fluff irritating my nose. I stifle a sneeze and I lie there, listening to the silence.

A door closes quietly upstairs and I hold my breath for a moment, hoping for a creak on the stair. A car goes past outside, slowly and cautiously on the icy road. There is a hand on my shoulder and I jump out of my skin.

"Alice?" It is Owen, his voice close to my ear. I twist around to find he is crouched next to me. "I read the letter," he says.

I struggle to release my hand from the chenille, and when I do I stroke his cheek, smoothness and stubble on the ends of my fingers. "I'm glad."

"You're cold," he replies. "Budge up."

Our feet hang off the end of the sofa as we wrap our bodies together, my face burrowed into his chest, his breath warm in my hair. There is something unfamiliar about the feel of him and it takes me a moment to realise there is a chain around his neck. I nudge it with my nose.

Owen accepts the question. "My grandfather's St Christopher. You must have seen it in the box. Gran wanted me to wear it always."

"Is that what the letter said?"

"Yes." He pauses, "And plenty about grief, and regret, and love. She regretted Grandfather giving her the St Christopher because if he'd kept it he might have come back safe, but I don't think she regretted anything else."

"Then she was a remarkable woman."

"She also knew me very well. Like you and Adam know me; better than I know myself."

"What makes you say that?"

"One day, Alice, I'll let you read the letter but I'm not ready to share it just yet; it's too true and it exposes too many of my faults. Some of the things Ads said tonight…about confronting..."

"You don't have to do it alone, Owen."

"I know – and I can't do it alone either. But I have to find the place to start myself."

I hug him tighter to me. "You've read the letter. I think you already have."

## Chapter Sixty-Five

The frost stays away in the run up to Christmas so the gravedigger has no trouble doing his work. It is a small hole, but deep. He stops when he comes across another coffin. Margaret wants him to scratch around to see if there is a name on it but Owen says there would be no point. And for us there isn't; we know it contains the remains of Thomas Winter.

So on Christmas Eve afternoon we finally lay Alice and Thomas's baby to rest. We have a very short service inside. I expected Owen to take an active part, but he does not, and Christopher reads the lesson himself – the one about Jesus suffering little children to come to him – and then we troop across the churchyard for the committal.

Christopher leads the little procession, followed by Owen who is carrying the box with the baby's remains. Adam, Margaret and I are close behind and Richard trails after us. I don't know how he knew about the funeral but of course he has every right to be here. He found the baby, after all. And he saw Thomas. And he is descended from Alice Fulton.

It proves too awkward for Owen to lower the box into the grave on his own and it is Richard who comes forward to help him. As they both straighten I see them look at each other with something that approaches understanding. Then Owen steps back beside me and looking across the grave I notice Richard has mud on his suit trousers.

I cannot take my eyes off that mud as Christopher begins the committal. I need something to focus on; I am too scared to look around me in case I see Mother, or Alice, or even Thomas, watching proceedings. But whether or not I can see them I feel their presence. I glance at Owen, but he is staring into the middle distance. Who, or what, he sees, I cannot tell.

Richard takes his leave of us in the churchyard and Owen all but sleepwalks back to New Cottage. His skin has an unhealthy grey tinge to it. Christopher helps him out of his coat and guides him to the sofa in the snug. He speaks to him for a few moments then comes into the kitchen to fetch a cup of tea. By the time he takes it back, Owen is fast asleep.

The rest of us stay quietly in the kitchen.

"He's exhausted," Christopher explains. "He told me it was as though he's just healed half a dozen people."

I bow my head. "I wish I understood more about this healing."

Adam nods. "Me too. It's an amazing gift, but it takes too much out of him – I wish he would give it a break sometimes."

"I don't think he has a choice," Margaret chips in. "In that way it's a gift and a curse."

"Everyone has choices," Adam mutters.

"I don't think Owen does" Christopher says. "It's like a vocation to him, a calling. It's part of who he is."

After a little while Christopher and Adam leave but Margaret lingers in the garden room. She delves into her handbag and pulls out the charm wand.

"I know you gave it to me," she says, "but I think it needs to come home. I...I'd just feel happier if it did."

I nod. "The time does feel right."

"Perhaps it should never have left here."

"No – I think it needed to for...for things to happen. But that's all finished now." I give her a hug and a peck on the cheek. "Happy Christmas, Margaret."

She envelopes me with real warmth. "You too, Alice."

Owen is still fast asleep and I fetch a blanket from the airing cupboard to cover him. He doesn't even stir. I draw the curtains across the patio door and dim the lights to their lowest level, bathing the room in an orange glow. Then, very quietly, I close the door and retreat into the hall. I let William out of the garden room; he and I are going to decorate the Christmas tree.

It is something I've been looking forward to doing with Owen but I find I am quite content doing it on my own. It's not an enormous tree – about four feet high – and it is sitting in front of the hall window where everyone passing the house can enjoy it. First the lights go on, then the tinsel, and finally the baubles; all new this year, and all red and gold. I left the old Christmas stuff with Neil.

I step back to admire my handiwork then wander into the kitchen to pour myself the smallest of glasses of wine and take it back to the easy chair in the hall. William snuggles against the radiator, but in truth it isn't cold in this room any more – in fact it feels rather warm and cheerful with the tree lights sparkling and reflecting off the glass. Next Christmas there will be a child; of that I have no doubt. I can almost feel her starting to grow inside me.

I close my eyes and picture Owen's face, sound asleep in the next room. The long lashes covering those extraordinary eyes, the lines etched deeply under them, the fair hair tinged with grey. He may have aged physically these last few months but there is more than a little that is childlike about him, in both his looks and in his nature. From his simple kindness to his complete inability to deal with the tough things in life, like his grandmother's death. Although now I have every confidence that he will be able to.

It's always been in him. Taking on someone like Adam and turning their whole life around was a courageous thing to do. So is curing the sick and giving comfort to the dying, without a thought about the cost to yourself. No, there is plenty enough man in Owen to learn and to grow. He will make a fine father. And a fine husband.

He showed me the diamond ring in his grandmother's box and he told me that one day it will be mine. But not yet. He says he needs to get his head straight first, that he needs to be worthy of loving me. I laughed and told him the boot was on the other foot but he would have none of it. Stubborn he is for sure; but he will be worth the wait.

I take my wine glass back to the kitchen and rinse it out. The charm wand is where I left it, next to the kettle. I hold it up to the light and try to count the seeds but find it is impossible. I give it a little polish with the tea towel then tuck it on the ledge above the front door. No-one will see it, but I will know it's there. Then I settle down with my book.

I hear the church bell start to toll for Midnight Mass. I take a peep at Owen in the snug – he is still fast asleep. William slips past me and to my absolute amazement jumps up and curls himself on Owen's feet.

I fetch my duvet and tuck myself under it on the other sofa. I don't want Owen to wake alone. By whatever strange bonds we are already tied together, for better and for worse, just as surely as if the ring was on my finger and Christopher had said the words over us. After all, William's instinct is unerring.